Silhouette®

nocturne™

D0030114

USA TODAY **Bestselling Author**

LINDSAY McKENNA

UNFORGIVEN

Silhouette®

Where love comes alive™

ISBN-13:978-0-373-61748-7
ISBN-10: 0-373-61748-8

50525

 EAN

Praise for

LINDSAY McKENNA

"Gunfire, emotions, suspense,
tension, and sexuality abound in this
fast-paced, absorbing novel."
—*Affaire de Coeur* on *Wild Woman*

"...classic Lindsay McKenna,
with jeopardy, love, sorrow, hope
and enough reality to make readers shiver."
—*Romantic Times BOOKclub* on *The Heart Beneath*

"Another masterpiece."
—*Affaire de Coeur* on *Enemy Mine*

"Ms. McKenna brings readers along for a
fabulous odyssey in which complex characters
experience the danger, passion
and beauty of the mystical jungle."
—*Romantic Times BOOKclub* on *Man of Passion*

"Talented Lindsay McKenna delivers
excitement and romance in equal measure
in *Protecting His Own*, where her storytelling skill
paints a picture that draws readers
directly into the adventure."
—*Romantic Times BOOKclub*

LINDSAY McKENNA

is part Eastern Cherokee and has walked the path of her ancestors through her father's training. Her "other" name is Ai Gvhdi Waya, Walks With Wolves. At age nine, Lindsay's father began to teach her the "medicine" ways, or skills brought down through their family lineage. For nine years, Lindsay remained in training. There was never a name given to what was handed down through her Wolf Clan family lines, but, nowadays, it is generally called shamanism.

Having grown up in a Native American environment, Lindsay is close to Mother Earth and all her relations. She has taught interested people about the Natural World around the globe on how to reconnect spiritually with the Earth. She is now infusing her books with her many years of experiences and metaphysical knowledge in hopes that readers will discover a newfound awe for the magic that is around us in our everyday reality. Paranormal was known as metaphysics in Lindsay's family. She considers herself a metaphysician and her intent is to bring compassion and "heart" through her storytelling, for she believes the greatest healer of them all is love.

LINDSAY McKENNA

UNFORGIVEN

Silhouette Books

n⚫cturne

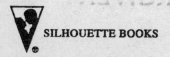

SILHOUETTE BOOKS

ISBN-13: 978-0-373-61748-7
ISBN-10:   0-373-61748-8

UNFORGIVEN

Dear Reader,

I know that *paranormal* is the buzzword today for
this kind of story. But in my world, as a shaman
coming from a family of shamans via my Eastern
Cherokee roots, the term is simply *metaphysics*. That
said, I want to introduce you to *Unforgiven,* the first
book of my new miniseries WARRIORS FOR THE
LIGHT, where you will meet Reno and Calen as they
begin a new dynasty (much like how the Trayherns
began MORGAN'S MERCENARIES). Like all
metaphysicians, these two have paranormal skills
and talents. Their mission is going to underline the
chaos that has our world by the throat today. Reno
and Calen see how things can be different—in a
positive, healing way—for Mother Earth and "all her
relations," which includes you and me, as well.

In these books, I intend to share with you actual
metaphysical "tools" that I was taught and grew up
with. Of course, they are all positive and help us
become better in all ways. As you get patterns for
quilting, crocheting or knitting from some authors,
WARRIORS FOR THE LIGHT will also give you
new patterns to try on and wear—only these are the
healing tools used by metaphysicians like myself. The
Vesica Piscis is the first of these tools and I have used
it in meditation for most of my life. I would like to
think that this incredible, ageless symbol can give
you gifts as it has given me.

So, sit back, enjoy a great story. Who knows, you just
might find new ways to connect with the everyday
magic that is around us—and have fun doing it.

Lindsay McKenna

To all those who yearn to experience the magic of our everyday reality. May the Vesica Piscis symbol be a doorway filled with a cornucopia of gifts for each person who uses it.

And to Tara Gavin,
Editorial Director of Silhouette Nocturne, who gave me a chance to fulfill my heart's vision, and to Patience Smith, Associate Senior Editor of Silhouette Intimate Moments, who has certainly gone "above and beyond the call of duty." My deepest thanks to both of you and your faith in me.

Chapter 1

One shot...one kill. The sixteen-pound sledgehammer came down with such fierce power that the granite boulder shattered instantly. A spray of glittering mica exploded into the air and sparkled momentarily around the man who wielded the tool as if it were a weapon. Sweat ran in rivulets down Reno Manchahi's drawn face. Naked from the waist up, feeling the hot July sun beating down on his back, he hefted the sledgehammer skyward once more. Muscles in his forearms leaped and biceps bulged. Even his breath was focused on the boulder. In his mind's eye, he pictured Army General Robert Hampton's fleshy, arrogant, fifty-year-old features on the rock's surface. Air exploded from between his thinned lips as he brought the avenging hammer downward. The boulder pulverized beneath his funneled hatred. One shot...one kill...

Nostrils flaring, Reno inhaled the dank, humid heat and drew it deep into his lungs. The only way he felt alive was to picture Hampton on every rock he destroyed. Revenge allowed Reno to endure his imprisonment at a U.S. Navy brig near San Diego, California. Droplets of sweat were flung in all directions as the crack of his sledgehammer claimed a third boulder victim.

Mouth taut, Reno moved to the next one. The other prisoners in the stone yard gave him a wide berth, since they instinctively felt his simmering hatred, the revenge that was palpable in his cinnamon-colored eyes.

And they whispered that he was different.

Reno enjoyed being a loner for good reason. He came from a medicine family of shape-shifters. The genes and training he'd inherited allowed him to transform from human to jaguar at will. But even this secret power had not protected him—or his family. What life did he have left? His wife, Ilona, and his three-year-old daughter, Sarah, were dead. Murdered by Army General Hampton in their former home on the USMC base in Camp Pendleton, California. The lusting son of a bitch had stalked Reno's Hungarian-born wife while Reno was deployed to Afghanistan to hunt down the Taliban.

Bitterness thrummed through him as he savagely pushed the toe of his scarred leather boot against smaller stones that were in his way. A massive black-and-white striated boulder stood in front of him. The prisoners, all military, knew he'd want the big ones. They were happy to give them to Manchahi. They wanted him to take his rage out on the rocks—not on them.

The sun poured down upon Manchahi's bare chest, grown dark red over time. From his straight black hair grazing his shoulders, his copper skin, broad face and high cheekbones, everyone knew he was Indian. When he'd first arrived at the brig and they'd discovered he was part Apache, some of the prisoners had taunted him and called him Geronimo.

Only once did they provoke him. During the fight that ensued, something strange had happened. Leaning down after he'd won the scuffle, Reno snarled into each of their bloodied faces that if they were going to call him anything, it should be *gan,* the Apache word for "devil."

His assailants had been shocked at the wounds on their faces—deep claw marks. Reno recalled doubling his fists as they'd attacked him en masse. In that split second, he had felt as if he'd gone into an altered state of consciousness. Because he had feared for his life, his jaguar guide had started to come over his physical body to protect him. A deep, growling sound had emitted from his throat as he defended himself in the three-against-one fracas. For an instant, strange changes occurred to his body—so fast, he thought he might have imagined them. His hands had morphed into the forelegs and paws, claws extended, of his jaguar guide. The slashes left on the three men's faces after the fight told Reno he'd begun to shape-shift. A fist caused bruises and swelling, not four deep parallel marks.

Stunned and anxious, he had buried his secret knowledge of what he was, promising the beaten prisoners that the next time he heard the name *Geronimo,* he'd smash in their front teeth and break their noses. If his spirit guide completely enclosed his physical form, they'd be staring into the yellow eyes of a jaguar. He had to keep that to himself and hope never to shape-shift again while in prison. If a guard ever saw a jaguar, he'd shoot to kill. Reno's best defense was to make all the prisoners so damn scared of him that they'd never consider attacking him.

Though he wanted to melt into the background, whispers about him circulated throughout the prison. Some said they'd heard the snarl of a big cat coming from his cell late at night. Reno just scoffed.

Yet he often saw two large, yellow eyes with huge black pupils staring at him in the darkness. And those eyes... Reno never divulged his odd dreams to anyone. His jaguar guide would talk to him in dreams, soothe him and try to help him during his incarceration.

No one called him anything after that first day. Just "the loner." *Alone.* Yeah, he was alone, all right. At age twenty-eight, in a way he never had envisioned. His heart clenched with anguish. Three years after the murder of his wife and child, Reno still couldn't avoid the red-hot agony that slashed savagely through his wounded heart every time he pictured Ilona with Sarah in her arms.

Hampton, a U.S. Army general, had adroitly covered his tracks, Reno had to admit. As he hefted the hammer, his muscles flexing, he pictured Hampton's face once again on the rock. *Revenge. Yeah. You're damn straight it's revenge.* His rage mounted as he remembered how the general had secretly lusted after Reno's beautiful, carefree wife. Hampton had watched Ilona's movements daily. And on that fateful night in December, shortly before Christmas, he had broken into their quarters. He'd raped and then killed Ilona to ensure her silence. And Reno's daughter, in the next room, was found strangled to death in her bed.

The steel hammer swept downward with hellish ferocity. As the granite groaned in protest, Reno shut his eyes for just a moment. More sweat dripped off his nose and chin. Mouth tightening, he opened his eyes, grunted and swung the sledge upward, then brought it down with such feeling that the boulder shattered, splitting into three huge, jagged pieces.

Oh, Great Spirit, why did you let Ilona and Sarah die? Reno still couldn't understand. All he could do was feel helpless rage. The general was smart like a coyote. He'd thought of almost everything. What Hampton hadn't counted on was Ilona's reaction to the assault. She'd fought back with the fury of a cougar, which Reno saw from looking at the photos taken of her in death. The Shore Patrol and Naval Criminal Investigative Service had performed DNA testing, and the results identified the general as her assailant. But before Hampton could be arraigned for the crime, the DNA results disappeared from the forensics lab, never to be located again.

Both Ilona and Sarah had been cremated before Reno had arrived home. He'd never got to hold them, to say goodbye or give either of them a final farewell kiss. Now he was truly a prisoner, in so many ways. Denied justice, denied his family, denied the wide-open spaces he loved. Only the pale blue sky above offered some escape from his depressing confinement.

Straightening, Reno wiped his furrowed, wet brow and looked around the rectangular yard enclosed by a twenty-foot-tall brick wall. Suddenly, his attention was caught by the sharp cry of a red-tailed hawk. Squinting, he looked up at the bird flying over the brig yard. Reno could make out its rust-colored tail. As a kid growing up on the Apache reservation in Arizona, he'd learned that all animals appearing before him could be messengers.

For a brief moment, he was lifted out of his grief and rage. The bird was less than three hundred feet above him. The prison yard was large, holding thirty prisoners and tons of rocks. The clanging of hammers striking granite didn't drown out the piercing shriek of the raptor.

Reno called mentally to the winged one. *Brother, what message do you bring me?* The Great Spirit knew how much he looked forward to getting out of his small, confining cell every day for three hours, even for this brutal manual labor. Reno's sanity hinged on being out here in the elements.

Allowing the sledgehammer to drop to his side, he concentrated on the hawk, which wheeled in tightening circles above him.

Freedom! the hawk cried in return.

Reno shook his head, his black hair brushing against his shoulders. *Freedom? No way, Brother. No way.* Figuring he was imagining the hawk's shrill message, he turned away. Back to his rocks. Back to picturing Hampton's smug face.

Freedom!

Reno heard and felt the piercing voice as if it were inside his head. Following the red-tail's flight, he allowed himself to hope for one second. Was he imagining this? Had to be, since the general had orchestrated a twenty-year prison sentence for him.

And yet Reno had spent his whole childhood out in the mountains on the reservation, learning to talk to animals. He could commune with the deer, the coyote, the hawk and the reptile nations, such were his abilities as a shape-shifter. Even golden eagles flying over his people's land would speak with him.

If Reno were set free, he would finally have his vengeance. Unleashed, he'd be more than dangerous. It was no accident that his last name, Manchahi, meant "wolf" in the Apache language. Reno always found his assigned quarry and shot him. Sniper teams disappeared into the steep, jagged Tora Bora mountains, seeking out Taliban leaders. One shot...one kill. That was a sniper's maxim. With forty-two kills under his belt, Reno was considered the best sniper in the U.S. military. Of course, his gift of shape-shifting into a jaguar gave him an advantage in picking up the scent of his enemy.

Freedom!

Shaking his head, Reno telepathically sent a message to the red-tail. *Ho, Brother! While I honor your coming to me, there is no way I'm going to get free.*

Freedom was impossible, and Reno knew it. He began work on the next boulder and tried to ignore the pleading call of the hawk stubbornly circling overhead. Reno had seventeen years left before he could hunt General Hampton down and kill him.

"Manchahi!" a young U.S. Navy brig guard near the door called.

Now what? Reno turned, the sledgehammer gripped in his hand. "What?" he snarled.

"Get in here! You have a visitor!"

Wiping the sweat off his face, he scowled at the eighteen-year-old guard standing with a second sentry in the shade of the doorway. The kid was new, and Reno could see he was afraid of him and his fierce reputation.

"You're wrong." The only visitors he'd wanted were his wife and child. They were dead. Gone, but never forgotten. His mother had died of a heart attack when she'd heard that his family had been ruthlessly slaughtered. His father, a Mexican Yaqui Indian, had had a massive stroke shortly after they'd found Reno guilty of assault on the general's aide-de-camp and attempted murder of the general himself. Reno had been two days into his twenty-year sentence when word came to him that his father had died. Reno knew he'd really died of heartbreak over his son's unfair sentencing.

Now, Reno had no one. An only child, he had few relatives. They lived on the Arizona reservation, and there was no way they were going to drive out to see him. His cousins didn't talk much on the telephone, nor write many letters. Reno never expected his relatives to get in contact. His only friend was his spirit guide, the jaguar, who was with him always.

Settling his gaze on the short, blond guard near the door, Reno barked, "Well, who the hell is it?" Couldn't be his lawyer. The bastard had more than likely been bought off by General Hampton.

"You'll find out. Get in here and get washed up. We're under orders to take you to the visitors' room as soon as possible."

Cursing softly, Reno threw down the sledgehammer. This guard was Navy bait, thinking he had authority. The only military Reno respected was the Marine Corps. His father had been a Marine. When Reno had gone through boot camp at Parris Island, then advanced infantry training at Camp Lejeune in North Carolina, the Corps had discovered his superior hunting skills. After he'd graduated, they'd sent him to sniper school. One shot...one kill. Reno wasn't a company player, and being a sniper was the ideal assignment for a hermit, out in the rough, natural world that he loved so much.

Quickly backing through the door, the sentry bumped into his partner, who was also retreating as Reno entered the dimly lit, air-conditioned hall.

Even the brig guards were wary of him, especially after they'd found four deep, long claw marks scored in the concrete wall near his bunk. His spirit guardian had shape-shifted over him one night, and Reno had tested the jaguar's strength by clawing a hole in the wall. When the guards discovered the gashes, he'd lied and said he'd chiseled them into the concrete. Prisoners weren't allowed sharp implements, so the guards had torn his cell apart, looking for the tool that had done it. They found nothing. Reno had decided that even shape-shifting wasn't going to break him out of this place, so he'd stopped the experiment.

The guards had said he wasn't human. That those marks were superhuman, not something a prisoner could etch into the wall. Reno just shrugged and pretended to be bored by their wild accusations and speculation. If the incident made the prisoners and guards leave him alone, so much the better.

Reno strode down the immaculate white-tiled passageway, following the usual drill, the guards trailing behind. In the shower area, Reno removed his dusty leather boots, shrugged out of his prison trousers and stood naked beneath the cooling streams of water. He washed away the odor of his sweat, the dust of the yard and the grayish, pulverized flecks of rock that had stuck to his skin. Scrubbing his hair with the coarse soap, Reno felt a brief moment of freedom in this simple act.

How many times had he imagined he was standing beneath a waterfall deep in the forest, and not in a prison shower room? Memories of his wild, free childhood had served to keep him sane within the prison bars that held his body. Those memories freed his spirit and allowed him to maintain his focus on the next seventeen years...and beyond. Ducking his head under the shower spray, Reno relished the feel of water splashing over him. If only briefly, the act made him feel alive, instead of dead inside.

Without warning, the powerful vision he'd had last night slammed back into his memory. In his dream, he'd been standing on a rock outcrop where he used to go as a kid to daydream the hours away. It was his favorite haunt, a place where sky met earth in a magical way.

Back there in his dream, Reno saw a black-haired woman with the most incredible and alluring green eyes materialize before him, about ten feet away. He'd been mesmerized by the mystical event.

Even more confusing was his strong reaction to her. His heart had welled up with such a fierce and unexpected wave of emotion that it caught Reno completely off guard. That kind of powerful response was reserved only for the woman he loved, which was Ilona.

The dream woman was dressed like an Incan priestess ready for ceremony. Her gown was long and white, the material innocently outlining her young, lithe form. Across her proud shoulders she wore the gold-and-black skin of a jaguar. Colorful parrot feathers adorned her straight black hair like a crown. Sensing she was from South America by the golden color of her skin, her high cheekbones and those slightly tilted green eyes, Reno watched as she lifted and extended her hand toward him.

"I need your help. Please, come to me. Come now...."

He stood there, perplexed by her request. His heart and body were responding to her as if he knew her well. He didn't, of course, but Reno could feel his pulse pounding through his veins like a drumbeat.

"Come where?" he demanded.

Reno saw her full mouth draw into a soft, patient smile. Turning, she pointed toward the south. "There. I will meet you there shortly. I am in danger. I need your help and protection...."

Reno recalled jerking awake shortly after that. He'd been drenched in sweat, his heart hammering. That had been one hell of a dream! As he'd sat on his bunk in the murky grayness of his cell, something had told him it was no dream. That it was real. His mother had had the ability to receive visions, and Reno was sure that this was one.

Shortly afterward, he'd fallen asleep, unable to comprehend the meaning of the mysterious woman's request. She was beautiful. Her eyes reminded him of a cat's— widely spaced, large and filled with a mystical radiance. At one time, jaguars had roamed the Southwest. Was there a connection there? She wore the skin of one.

Reno didn't know. Visions were never explicit. One had to figure out what they meant piece by piece, over time.

Shutting off the shower, he turned and splashed across the tile floor. Now, he wondered if the vision of the green-eyed woman and the hawk showing up were synchronistic events telling him that his life was about to change. Grimacing, Reno didn't see how. Grabbing a gray cotton towel, he began to dry his body. The guards appeared impatient, shuffling their feet in the passageway.

"Who's waiting for me?" Reno demanded, throwing the towel into an awaiting bin. He took his gray trousers and shoved his legs into them. He never wore Skivvies or boxer shorts, preferring to live as freely as he could, in loose clothing. If he could get away with wearing trousers and nothing else, he would have. But that was a no-go situation. He grabbed a gray T-shirt and pulled it over his head. As he tugged it down over his chest, he glared again at the guards.

The kid's mouth was tight with impatience. "Let's go, Manchahi."

Reno sat down on a wooden bench outside the

shower area and put on a pair of clean socks and his
scarred leather boots. Finished, he stood up, towering
over the guards. "I'm ready now."

"This way," the blonde ordered, pointing toward the
visitors' area.

His first visitor in three years. Who could it be? Reno
knew the routine. Halting, he held out his wrists so the
guards could put cuffs around them. Next came the leg
irons, and then the chain around his waist, because he
was considered dangerous. Reno stood there, smiling to
himself. He recalled the red-tailed hawk that had
screamed the word *freedom* at him. Was his visitor going
to offer him that? Reno laughed inwardly. A realist, he
knew life didn't hand out easy pardons. No way in hell
the military would ever let him out.

"Enter," the second guard told him, stepping away.

Reno moved into the large visitors' center, which
held white plastic tables and chairs. The space was
empty of people save for one man standing in a corner.
Reno's sixth sense instantly took over. Because he was
a shape-shifter, his awareness was highly honed, more
so than that of normal human beings.

His visitor, in his late thirties, was impeccably
dressed in a dark blue pinstripe suit. He looked like a
GQ model, sporting a white silk shirt, conservative tie
and polished black shoes. His light brown hair was
coifed and Reno could smell hair product from across
the room. Flaring his nostrils like the wolf he was
named after, he caught several other odors around the

stranger. Cigar smoke and a hint of alcohol. The man was about six feet tall and built more like a runner than a weight lifter. He had pale gray eyes, the kind that made Reno immediately suspicious of him.

As his gaze stripped the visitor, Reno became confident he didn't know this person other than by instinct. On the table in front of the man was a file folder. Reno knew this much about his visitor: he was an agent of some kind. FBI? No. Probably a spook from the CIA. Reno had worked with enough of their kind in Afghanistan. This dude had that arrogant look that said he was better than everyone else, a typical spook demeanor.

The chains rattled and clinked as Reno sauntered forward with an ease that belied the tension he held deep within.

"Sit down, Mr. Manchahi."

"I'll stand. Who the hell are you?" His voice was a low growl, like thunder rolling across the bluffs of the reservation on a blisteringly hot Arizona day.

"You'll find out soon enough. Now, sit down."

Reno debated his next move. The man wasn't afraid of him, which intrigued him. Curiosity won out. He pulled up a plastic chair, the legs scraping in protest against the concrete floor, and settled into it. Resting his cuffed hands on the table, he watched as Pale Eyes sat down. Reno's mother had taught him to read faces. And all human faces reminded him of a mammal, bird, snake or insect. With his long chin and shifty gaze, Pale Eyes reminded him of a coyote.

"I'm CIA Agent Brad James."

"So?"

He sat back, hands clasped on the table. "I'm here to offer you freedom."

Freedom. Reno kept his face neutral. Like any good Indian, he knew how to keep his emotions completely out of a conversation so no one could read him. He recalled the hawk, and its promise of freedom.

Scrutinizing the agent, he said, "I'm listening."

"Good." James smiled. "Because we need your services and talents down in Ecuador."

Surprise riffled through him, but Reno said nothing. He stared hard at the agent, who obviously had a weekly manicure, judging by his soft white hands and blunt, buffed nails. "Go on."

Leaning forward, James said, "I operate out of Quito. The U.S. government has had a plea from the Ecuadorian government for our assistance. There is an emerald mine, the Santa Maria, that is being plagued by a man on horseback. He murders guards and has been responsible for over three million dollars' worth of emeralds going missing. They call him El Espanto, the Ghost." James opened the file, picked up a color photo and dropped it in front of Reno. "Here's the mine." He threw another photo on top of the first one. "And these are the owners. They're known as the Guild. This terrorist rides a black horse. The mine's located on a mountain, and this ghost does his hunting of guards after dark."

Reno studied the third photo, which showed a wide green river flowing through a jungle, circling the base of a large mountain. The terrain was partly stripped of trees, where bulldozers had left scars across the steep slopes.

"So this El Espanto is robbing the rich and going after hired guards who are protecting mine property?" Reno sat back in his chair.

"That's right. In a nutshell."

"And you want me to...?"

James leaned forward and lowered his voice. "We want you to find this son of a bitch and kill him. We want him out of the way. He's caused havoc for two years now, and we've—I mean, *they've* lost a lot of guards in the process. We need someone who is an excellent tracker and sniper." Sitting up, James jabbed his finger toward Reno. "And that's you."

"Why me?"

"I have the ability to find out who is best for a situation like this. That's all you need to know."

"And if I do this gig for you?" Reno didn't like James at all.

After adjusting his tie, the agent flipped through the file, then pushed several papers toward him. "First of all, you find this ghost and kill him and bring proof of his death to the Ecuadorian authorities. The U.S. government will then be willing to forgive your debt to society, in a manner of speaking. You'll receive Ecuadorian citizenship after you have killed this man, but the States will be off-limits to you. Your American citizenship will be permanently revoked. Instead, you will become a citizen of Ecuador."

Reno's heart banged hard in his chest and his eyes narrowed on the CIA agent. James was looking far too confident, smug even. This was a city slicker who didn't like to dirty his hands in the real world. "In other words, I get my freedom if I track down and kill this hombre?"

"That's right. Your sentence will be commuted. You can live the rest of your life in South America. If you ever try to come back to the States for any reason, however, you will be picked up and thrown back into this brig, where you will die. No one will know you're here and no one will care." Opening his hands, James continued his hard sell. "It's a great opportunity for you, Manchahi. If I were you, I'd take it. Or you can sit here and rot another seventeen years. It's up to you...."

Freedom. The hawk had not lied to him. And his vision of the woman calling for him to go south was being validated as well. Reno looked through the photos again. It seemed like a simple, straightforward operation. Nothing that he couldn't handle with ease.

"What's the time limit on finding this ghost?" he demanded.

Shrugging, James said, "The owners want him caught as soon as possible."

"How long has he given the slip to the mine personnel and anyone else they've already hired?"

"Two years."

"So, this is not as easy an operation as it looks on

the surface." Reno stared flatly into the man's pale
eyes. "I want to know the rest of the story before I
agree to anything."

James stared back without saying a word, and Reno
realized he wasn't going to answer. Finally the agent
pointed down at one paper. "This is a need-to-know-
only mission, so forget about getting the whole story.
You see that? It's signed by the CIA, authorizing your
release. Read it. It promises you freedom if you find
this guy within a year of going down there. Given your
illustrious reputation of being the world's most deadly
sniper and tracker, I would think a year would be plenty
of time to hunt down this son of a bitch."

A lot didn't make sense to Reno as he studied the
paper and the signature. Agent James produced an
Ecuadorian passport and pushed it toward him. Opening it, Reno saw his photo already affixed.

"You will go down there under your real name. This
passport is valid. The owners of the mine want you to
assume a cover. While you were in the Marine Corps,
you were a certified paramedic. Correct?"

"I still am," Reno said. "I've kept up my certifica-
tion even in here."

James nodded. "Good. The Guild is putting the fin-
ishing touches on a small medical dispensary off
the mining property, down near the river where the
esmeraldos live." James grimaced. "This killer is likely
one of the *esmeraldos,* so this will be good cover for
you to insinuate yourself with them and find out who

it is. You are going to go in as a spy and pose as a paramedic running this charity clinic. You speak fluent Spanish because your father was Mexican."

"He was Yaqui Indian." Anger flooded Reno at the man's condescending tone.

James shrugged. "Whatever. You speak Spanish. You look Latino. The *esmeraldos* will come flocking to your free clinic because they desperately need health care. You will make friends among them. You will ask about this ghost. They should tell you what they know, sooner or later. Armed with that information, you will be hunting this bastard at night. You will be given the weapons you want, no questions asked. Basically, you are a free man down there. But…" James's voice lowered in warning "…if you try to escape without doing this job, I can promise you there are people who will put a round through your head."

"If I give my word to take this assignment, I will do it." The urge to sink his fist into the soft, citified agent's arrogant features was very real. Reno didn't like to be threatened.

"You need to know the rules of the game before going in. You will report only to Guild members about your progress. The head of Santa Maria security will also know who you really are, and you will work directly with him, most of the time. He'll see that you get whatever it is you need in the way of weapons and ammunition."

"I find this hard to believe," Reno said. "The U.S. government has got its nose in an emerald mine down in Ecuador? That's not your usual security risk or worry."

James's mouth thinned. "Why this is being done is none of your business, Manchahi. Your job is to track down and kill this person."

It never entered Reno's mind that he wouldn't be successful in this mission. *Freedom*. He would be free. Once again he could be out in nature, walking among the trees, fishing in a river, feeling the brutal ferocity of a thunderstorm whipping around him and rain slashing against his skin. He could breathe in the fresh air of the land, not the stale cigarette smoke trapped in this poorly ventilated brig.

James passed him a pen. "Sign this and you'll walk out of here with me." He produced two airline tickets. "You and I have a flight tonight from San Diego to Ecuador."

After signing the papers, Reno pushed them back toward the agent. "Sounds too good to be true."

"Better than staying in here," James murmured, gathering up all the photos and papers and sliding them back into the file. As he stood, the agent added softly, "But don't ever think that you're coming back here to even the score with General Hampton. Your life as you knew it has been erased. Your name, your social security number and anything about you is being destroyed as we speak. You are a man without a country. The only way you can have a second chance at life is going to Ecuador and hunting down El

Espanto. Until you succeed, you will be watched and monitored. You're still a prisoner, but your cell is a little different."

It was better than nothing. And Reno wasn't done going after Hampton, either. As he rose, he flashed a wolfish smile. "I'll find this ghost. He's dead already and just doesn't know it yet." Reno would shape-shift, pick up the scent and track him down.

"That's what I wanted to hear." James gestured for the guard to come forward. "Take the chains off this man. Get him the set of clothing I brought with me." James looked at Reno. "You'll take two suitcases, plus a paramedic bag—everything you need to start your new life undercover. After you've settled in at your clinic, call me at this number and check in." He handed Reno a card. "I'm your handler on this mission."

Nodding, Reno stood while the guard uncuffed him. As the chains fell away, he wanted to cry. *Freedom.* He was going to earn his freedom; the hawk had been right. What lay in his future? South America. The woman that appeared in his vision last night had been right, too.

What had the Great Spirit set him up for? Reno recalled his mother's wise words when he'd come down from the mountain after his last vision quest, before going off to the Marine Corps at age eighteen. She'd said, "Son, your vision is one of turbulence, transformation and violence. Be careful. Stay alert. Listen to your heart, for it will never lead you wrong. Have faith in all our relations. They will show you the way."

As the last of the shackles fell away Reno allowed himself, for the first time since his wife and child had died, to feel a flash of emotion. Joy surged through him, tempered by an instinctive wariness. What was the *truth* behind this mission? Reno knew as he watched the CIA agent waiting by the exit door that James wasn't telling him everything, not by a long shot. Reno would have to understand the situation before he went after El Espanto and put him in the crosshairs of his rifle. *One shot…one kill…*

Chapter 2

"**P**ablo!" Pilar shouted, dropping to her hands and knees and sticking her head into the tunnel. "I hear horses coming our way!" It was 2:00 a.m., the jungle below alive with the songs of insects and a nearby owl's warning hoot. The dank dampness of earth filled her nostrils. Thick brush hid their illegal activity on the slope of the Santa Maria emerald mine. They had cut through the barbed wire and entered the property to try and find an emerald pocket that would lift them out of their terrible poverty. It was a risk worth taking.

Breathing chaotically, Pilar peered anxiously into the darkened tunnel that had been dug the last three nights by her husband, Pablo; their eight-year-old son,

Manuel; and ten-year-old daughter, Francesca. The chirp of crickets, the bleep of frogs were muted by the heavy blanket of humidity.

Her black hair dusted with red dirt, Francesca scrambled toward Pilar on her hands and knees. She half dragged and half carried a bucket of freshly dug soil. Dim light from the kerosene lantern near the entrance made her daughter's pale face look like a death mask worn at the Day of the Dead celebration each October 31.

Pilar grabbed the bucket and tossed its contents aside. When Francesca held out her hands out for it, Pilar cried impatiently, "No! No! Crawl back in there as fast as you can! Get your father! Tell him I hear horses! The mine guards are near! They're looking for us! Tell him we must leave! *Now!*"

"Yes, Mama! I'll hurry!" The girl quickly turned around in the narrow space and scrambled away, disappearing back into the hot, airless gloom of the tunnel.

Looking warily over her shoulder, her heart thundering in her chest, Pilar heard the soft snort of a horse once again. The terror she felt couldn't be tempered by the fragrance of orchids scenting the night air. Sentries for the emerald mine always rode in pairs. They were armed with weapons that could fire endless bullets at unarmed *esmeraldos*. The guards would ask no questions. If the family was found, they would be cold-bloodedly murdered.

Fear sizzled through Pilar. She crawled into the

hole, but her hips got stuck near the entrance. It was only wide enough for her narrowly built husband to maneuver in. Pilar wanted to shriek out his name, but didn't dare. Any noise might alert the mine sentries. She panted, breathing in the scent of kerosene permeated with the sour stench of sweat.

Tonight was a jaguar moon—completely dark. It was said that at this time of the month the jaguar roamed, ten times more powerful than normal. A Quero Indian by birth, carrying the blood of the Incas in her veins, Pilar prayed to the Jaguar Mother to protect them from the sentries.

Stars above the forest twinkled like a spilled glass of milk flowing across the ebony vault tonight. To anyone except the *esmeraldos,* a sky like that was a beautiful sight to behold. But without the covering of thick fog that usually stole through the jungle, her family was even more at risk. A clear night made it much easier for the mercenary soldiers to spot intruders.

The jaguar moon phase always made Pilar jumpy. It was said, in the tradition of her tribe, that during this time the *Tupay,* or evil ones, roamed the land. Unchecked, the heavy energies spread freely because there was no light from the moon to chase them away. Only the great Jaguar Mother, who prowled the darkness to protect good-hearted human beings, was capable of combating this dark energy. The sentries were evil personified, in Pilar's view.

She listened for sounds coming from the tunnel.

Eyes watering from the oily, pungent lamp, she tried to hold her breath. They'd been digging nonstop from midnight until the gray light of dawn for three nights in a row. Pablo had estimated the tunnel was a good thirty feet long by now. Manuel, their brave young son, was deepest in the tunnel, doing the majority of the digging. He was whipcord lean, and his small form could maneuver in the tight, nearly airless space with his shovel. It was hard, slow work. Pilar had remained outside, ferrying bottles of water to them, small bits of food wrapped in cloth to keep up their waning strength, and hauling out the endless wooden buckets filled with heavy red clay.

Another snort. Oh, Jaguar Mother! Whimpering with fear, Pilar tried to wriggle farther into the tunnel, but her wide hips were jammed. No matter how much she strained, she couldn't advance. As she squinted, her breath coming in gasps, she detected a sliver of light around the curve of the tunnel. Manuel had their other precious kerosene lamp with him, in order to see where he was digging. They all hoped he would stumble across a pocket of emeralds, an amazing array of dark green crystals jutting up like the buildings of Quito, just waiting to be taken.

She heard Francesca's high-pitched voice begging her father to get out quickly; that the death riders were coming.

Finally!

Pilar wriggled out of the tunnel. Drawing in a deep

breath of fresh, humid air, she stood and nervously
dusted off her threadbare cotton shift. They were surrounded by heavy brush here, but were high up on the
dormant volcano. Pablo had chosen this area on the
steep slope. Few tried to tunnel at this elevation; it was
too long a run to reach the safety of the jungle below.
Most *esmeraldos* chose to dig tunnels near the fence.
That way, they would have a chance to flee off mine
property and escape if they heard patrolling sentries
riding their way.

It was excitedly whispered there were rich pockets
of emeralds for the taking on the lofty slopes, gifts from
the *apu,* or mountain spirit. Pilar had always had a bad
feeling about her husband's desperate plan to leave
their village in the Andes of Peru and come to Ecuador
in search of riches. Their children were starving now,
nothing more than skin and bones as a result of a dream
that had not come true. Pilar often cried herself to
sleep, because her children went to bed pinched with
hunger, their stomachs growling from not eating all
day. At least back in their village they could grow some
potatoes and beans, and had the support of others who
suffered as they did.

Pilar had said nothing in disagreement to Pablo
about his risky venture. They had to take a chance! But
now, as she quickly gathered up their meager supplies
into a large cloth bag, she again questioned Pablo's
daring plan. All their remaining food, their tools and the
plastic water bottles scavenged from where the sentries

carelessly tossed them into the brush, were contained within the sack—nearly all her family possessed.

The mine guards were mostly foreign mercenaries, ex-soldiers who had been flown in from around the world. Soldiers for hire, some of whom who were known to hate brown-skinned Indians, they were under orders to shoot to kill. The guards never had a problem following orders from the heartless men who owned the emerald mine. The sentries were paid handsomely for their willingness to commit such butchery. Some of Pilar's friends from the camp below, on the Esmeraldas River, had died up here. Oh, Jaguar Mother! Too many, too many had died!

Spinning around on her callused feet, Pilar heard the snort of a horse yet again. The guards were much closer! They were coming this way! Pilar hurried to the mouth of the tunnel and crawled inside once more.

"Francesca!" she rasped, choking on the odor of kerosene. "Come out of there! *Now!*"

Tears stung Pilar's eyes at the terrifying thought of her family being murdered. Her heart fluttered in panic as she backed out of the tunnel and struggled to her feet. Dirt, soft and damp, clung to her knees and palms.

Francesca crawled rapidly out of the earthen hole, the second bucket in her small hands. It was a heavy wooden pail, and she dropped it at the base of the growing pile of red soil as she stood.

"Leave it!" Pilar whispered frantically to her daughter. She sank to her knees, the sack of meager possessions pressed protectively to her ample bosom. Peering into the tunnel, she hissed her husband's name. No time was left! Was Pablo so crazed with emerald fever that he didn't think they were in danger? Did he think she was making this up?

The guards were so close! Pilar could hear the horses' hooves plodding the mountainside. If it rained, the clay turned into gooey slime and the sucking sounds of a horse's approach could be heard from farther away. It gave everyone time to flee so they wouldn't be shot to death. But it hadn't rained in days and the clay had hardened. Pilar had not heard the pair of sentries until one of the horses had whinnied, alerting her.

Gripping Francesca's thin shoulder, she pulled her daughter around. She looked into the girl's small, pale face and whispered in a terrified voice, "Run. Get *out* of here. Run for the fence, Francesca! You know the way!"

"But Mama—"

"Get out of here or you'll be *killed!*"

The girl hesitated fractionally.

Pilar flew at her daughter in panic. The horses were only fifty yards down the slope from where they stood. "Get out of here! *Now!*" She pushed her so hard the girl almost tumbled to the ground. Biting back a sob, Pilar knew they were going to be caught. She heard Pablo scrambling out of the tunnel now, but it was too late. Too late! Their daughter, however, had a sliver of a chance to reach safety.

"Run! I love you! Never forget that! Go!" Pilar waved frantically in Francesca's direction. This might be the last time she'd see her child. Burning her daughter's face into her memory, she watched her scamper down the slope, quickly disappearing among the spindly trees.

The scent of vanilla wafted into Pilar's nostrils. She loved the fragrance of orchids, but not on this night. The only odor filling the air shortly would be the stench of their spilled blood.

Choking back a sob, Pilar turned. To her right, she saw the shadowy outlines of two riders. The guards. They now knew where the tunnel was, and were heading directly toward it. *Oh, Jaguar Mother, have mercy on our souls. All we wanted was enough money to put food into the mouths of our babies. Have mercy upon us, protect us.* Praying fervently, Pilar gripped the old medicine bag around her neck that contained a bit of black-and-gold jaguar fur.

Pablo scrambled out of the tunnel on his hands and knees. He was covered in dirt from head to toe and gulped noisily for breath. Fresh, damp air assailed him. Dizzy from the poor ventilation in the tunnel, he was barely able to stand. He wiped his sweaty face as he rose unsteadily to his feet. The action only smeared the red mud.

He saw his wife looking anxiously down the slope. The mine guards!

His eyes were still adjusting to the starlit darkness after the feeble kerosene light in the tunnel. But he could hear horses snort. The clip-clop of their hooves echoed, so close that Pablo gasped in alarm. Heart pounding, he leaned down and grabbed for Manuel, who was slower crawling out. Pablo couldn't fault his son. The boy had been breathing in the fumes of the kerosene lamp. There was so little air that deep in their tunnel.

Gripping Manuel's sweaty, naked shoulders, Pablo helped him to stand. The boy's knees instantly buckled beneath him. Covered with mud, he was rasping for breath. This was what always happened after hours of digging, one of the many hazards they faced nightly. If the lack of air didn't suffocate them, then the fear of the tunnel collapsing and crushing them would. Pablo hated the world at that moment. His boy had dug relentlessly for three nights in a row, lengthening the shaft, searching for the elusive pocket of emeralds they hoped they would discover through sheer luck alone.

Gently gathering his son into his arms, Pablo felt his own knees shake with weakness. He wasn't very strong at the moment, either. After a night's labor, he would languish for hours, barely able to move. "Pilar! Run! Take Manuel here…."

Pilar turned on her heel and rushed to her husband. *It is too late!* She bit back the words she wanted to scream at him. The sentries were riding toward them, urging their mounts into a trot up the steep slope. The shriek of a nearby monkey seemed to echo the scream lodged in her throat.

"We must run!" she begged him, her voice cracking with fear.

Pablo shook his head and whispered unsteadily, "It's too late, *querida*. I'm sorry. I'm too weak, I can't." A bitterness coated the inside of his mouth. Pablo felt his wife, who was barely five feet tall, well rounded and so soft, throw her arms around his lean waist and crush herself against him and their son. Manuel began to cry, his arms slipping around Pablo's shoulders, his wet face pressed against his sweaty neck.

The sentries were in clear view now, visible through the swaying fronds. They dug their heels into their horses' flanks and started galloping toward them. His family was going to die. Here. Now. *Oh, Jaguar Mother, have mercy on our souls. I love my wife so much, and my son and my beautiful daughter. Have mercy upon them. Take me instead and allow them to live. Please, I pray in your name....*

Pilar turned and forced herself to look up at the guards. They proudly shaved their heads to show how different they were from the *esmeraldos* they disdained. They would also be able to spot one another more easily on their rounds. They wore bandoleers of ammunition across their chests, as well as bulletproof vests.

Trepidation choked Pilar as she saw the men scowl down at them. The larger sentry smiled. But it wasn't a smile that reached his dark, glittering eyes, rather, one of a predator finding its quarry. The mercenaries rode small Spanish horses that labored beneath their weight and bulk.

"Well, well, what do we have here, Garold?"

The larger sentry shrugged. "Looks like we caught them red-handed, Moriz." He pulled up his AK-47 rifle and slammed a round into the chamber.

The sound froze Pilar. She felt her son tremble violently. Manuel's sobs were loud and continuous, but the jungle was hushed, as if holding its breath. "Please," she cried piteously, "do not kill us! Let us go! We promise never to do this again! Please have mercy!"

The sentry called Moriz revealed his long canine teeth as he glanced at his partner. "Hear that? They want mercy. After they ignored the No Trespassing sign and cut through the fence. It looks like you've been here at least three nights in a row, *esmeraldos*. Seems like a clear violation to me, Garold. Does it to you?"

The first man nodded and aimed his weapon. "No question."

The other sentry shook his head. "Say your final prayers, my friends. Because you're going straight to hell." And he took aim.

Pilar's eyes widened. She clung to her husband, her son crushed between them. To her horror and dismay, she saw pleasure on the sentries' faces as they lifted their weapons.

For a split second, an odd sensation overwhelmed her escalating terror. It was as if lightning had struck, yet there were no clouds in the sky. What was happening? Pilar gasped as an unseen energy slammed into her like a tidal wave. The sensation took over her body. Somehow, she noticed the guards hesitate for just a fraction of a moment, confused and questioning looks on their faces. They'd felt it also. But what *was* it?

Suddenly, the harsh bark of rifle sounded, firing once, twice. The noise punctured the heavy dampness, creating muted echoes.

The biggest sentry slammed backward off his horse. The animal leaped sideways, frightened. The second guard, Moriz, was struck in the head, torn from his mount and landed with a thud on the ground. The animal reared, whinnied and spun around, galloping off in pursuit of the first one.

Stunned, Pilar saw a rider emerge out of the darkness. He rode a black horse that breathed fire from its nostrils. Though her fear mounted even more, Pilar followed the advance of the tall figure on horseback. He had no face that she could see. Where there should have been eyes were two glowing green circles. Was it *Tupay*—evil personified? Or was this their savior? The jungle suddenly came to life. Monkeys screeched raucously to one another after the harsh sounds of gunfire.

Gasping, her knees weakening, Pilar abruptly realized who it was. In a hoarse whisper to Pablo, she said, "Oh, great Jaguar Mother! It is El Espanto!" Yes! They had often heard from other *esmeraldos* who dared to dig on the slopes that this protector on a mighty black horse roamed the area, saving them from sure death by the hands of the guards. Those who had seen El Espanto said he had the eyes of a jaguar and was as silent as one.

Pilar plopped down upon the earth, her legs giving out beneath her. She sucked in the orchid-scented air as relief flooded her. Her family had just been saved from the evil guards!

The ghostly horseman halted his prancing mount ten feet away from where the three remained huddled. In his right hand was the rifle he'd used to kill the sentries. Pilar dared to look up once more at their rescuer. The restless horse was blanketed in a dark material with only his slender legs visible below. There was some kind of jacket around the torso of the rider. It reminded her of the bulletproof vests that the mine guards wore.

"You must leave this place and never return," the ghostly figure declared in a husky, booming voice. "Go home!" The horse impatiently pawed the earth.

In shock, Pilar recognized her daughter sitting on the back of the animal. The horse tossed its head, its silky mane flowing halfway down its massive chest.

"Francesca!" Pilar wailed, holding out her arms. Francesca was safe! *Oh, thank you, Jaguar Mother!* El Espanto had found her and brought her back to them. The animated horse suddenly halted. It became a living, breathing statue before them. Pilar watched with baited breath as the rider turned, picked up her daughter and lifted her off the horse. The animal didn't flex a muscle as Francesca was gently lowered to the ground. Her bare feet touched the earth and she stood uncertainly before her family.

With a cry of relief, Pilar scrambled forward awkwardly and opened her arms. The sobbing child flew up the hill and into her welcoming embrace. Pilar held Francesca tightly and pressed many small kisses to her mussed and dirty hair.

"Get off this mountain!" the figure on horseback told them in a low, warning tone. He lifted his gloved finger and pointed back down the slope toward the mining property fence. "Go back to the country you came from. Now!"

Wiping tears from her eyes, Pilar gripped her daughter protectively against her body. She saw the man's green jaguar eyes. Truly, he was sent by the Jaguar Mother! "Y-yes…" she whispered. Turning, she held out her hand to her husband, who was obviously dumbstruck by all that had happened.

"The sound of my shots will bring more guards. You have little time, my friends. Get out of here—now!"

"Yes, yes," Pablo said, holding his frightened son tightly in his arms. "We must go now. Thank you. We would surely have died. You saved our lives, El Espanto. Bless you…bless you!"

"Bless the Jaguar Mother of us all, friends. For it is she who roams at the dark of the moon. It is her time of power. Now, vamoose!"

Pilar pulled her excited and enthralled daughter alongside her. The girl continued to stare openmouthed at El Espanto, her eyes huge with awe. As Pilar picked up the cloth bag holding their meager belongings, she saw their rescuer reach into his belt.

"Here," he called, leaning toward her and placing a leather purse in her hand, "take this. Use it to get out of here and improve your lives elsewhere."

Stymied, Pilar heard the clink of money as she gripped the bag. It was so heavy! She could feel thick coins inside. "What *is* this, *patrón?*"

El Espanto moved his black Arabian to allow them safe passage down the mountain. "Enough money for you and your family to start a new life in a village where you can feed your children and yourselves, *señora.* Now, go! Time is not on our side."

As she stared up in wonder at her savior, Pilar also noted the beauty of the small-eared Arabian. It was no bigger than the Spanish horses ridden by the guards, and yet the animal's chest was deeper and broader, telling her it could run like the wind. It's coat was sleek and shining in the starlight. El Espanto must have ridden him hard and long because white bits of foam flecked the animal's deeply arched neck. The horse's nostrils flared, jets of white steam shooting violently out of them. Its eyes, too, were green and glowing. Surely, the animal was just as magical as its master.

To Pilar, the two mystical figures seemed to waver like the undulating heat on a hot day over the jungle. Though it was night, both horse and rider seemed like a mirage. Magic! Pilar had no doubt. Jaguar magic! The most powerful kind on earth.

Gripping the purse of coins, Pilar whispered in a tremulous voice, "Thank you, *patrón!* Thank you with all our hearts! We ask blessings from the Jaguar Mother for you."

The rider lifted his dark hand. "Leave quickly!"

Scurrying down the slope, their children between them, she and Pablo fled into the darkness, stumbling as they went. Pilar didn't want to leave El Espanto. She'd heard so many wonderful stories about him since they'd arrive here, hoping for a better chance at a decent life.

The owl that had warned her earlier called out to her again. Hesitating, Pilar turned and looked back up the slope. She saw El Espanto dismount and quickly stride over to the lifeless guards. The darkly clothed figure leaned down and divested them of their rifles, radio and ammunition, then turned and whistled. The black Arabian trotted forward. Tossing its small, fine head, the horse halted where El Espanto stood waiting. Taking the weapons with him, he remounted the animal, which stood again like a statue.

Pilar watched, fascinated by the mysterious rider who had saved them. He slid the leather sling of his own rifle over his head and settled the weapon against his back. After one last look around, he wordlessly communicated with his spirited mount. No lifting of the reins, no verbal command or kick of the heels against the horse's flanks... Knowing, the horse snorted violently, jets of steam flowing out of its wide nostrils as it leaped forward, galloping quickly up across the slope.

How could they run so fast on a night like this? The jaguar moon offered no light. And yet they raced across the brushy mountainside like ebony ghosts, assured of where they were going. Incredible! There were so many holes, rocks and exposed roots that surely, Pilar thought, the animal would stumble and throw its daring rider.

Perhaps they flew across the escarpment and didn't actually touch the earth at all? She watched breathlessly as the tall figure rode in fluid oneness with the horse. And then the darkness swallowed them and they disappeared into the night.

"Come on!" Pablo entreated, tugging Pilar's arm.

She burned into her mind and heart this last picture of El Espanto. Then, turning on her bare feet, she hurried down the slope at her husband's side.

"Mama, El Espanto rescued me!" Francesca cried. "Oh, Mama! I was afraid at first, but then he turned and told me his name! His green eyes glowed! I think he's a jaguar, not a man!"

"What did he say to you?" Pilar asked, panting as they jogged down the slope. The foliage was wet with dew and dampened her feet and ankles.

"He said, 'Hold on, little one.' He was so gentle with me, Mama. He knew I was scared. He told me all would be well. And his horse. Oh, it had green eyes that glowed, too! I could see the white smoke shooting out of his nose! Mama! It was magical! We flew up that rocky slope, and when I saw El Espanto pull the rifle off his back, I knew he was going to save you."

"Incredible!" Pablo whispered, his voice rough with adrenaline. Wide, thick leaves swatted at him as he pushed through them. They'd reached the lower slope, where the brush was thicker and hid them more easily. "What happened next, Francesca? What else do you remember?" A branch slapped him in the face.

Francesca sighed and trotted unsteadily between her parents. She gripped Manuel's dirty hand. "We rode upward. On the wings of the wind, Papa. The horse is small, but so mighty! And it just seemed to know where El Espanto wanted it to go.

"When we drew near, I saw the guards. I saw them lift their weapons. Oh! I was so afraid for you that I couldn't find my voice!" Francesca held up her hands to protect her face as they dived into a tangle of plants and palms. "El Espanto took his rifle and put bullets into it. When he fired, the noise hurt my ears. But the horse *never moved*, Papa! Not a muscle! I was so amazed!" She gulped and nearly tripped over an unseen tree root. Her mother's hand caught her before she could stumble.

"And then I saw the two guards fall off their horses. That's how I knew you were saved!" They left the thick patch of jungle and hurried across the chewed up earth.

Pilar gave her daughter a wobbly smile as they approached the fence—six rows of concertina wire. Her husband pulled out a rusty pair of wire cutters from his back pocket. Entering another thicket of palms, she protected her face from the stiff, sharp fronds. Pablo would cut through the barbed wire and they'd be safe. Safe! She gently stroked Francesca's hair as they came to a halt. "You have had an experience of a lifetime, child. No one has ever ridden with El Espanto! That is a first!"

"We aren't telling anyone, either," Pablo warned, shoving fronds out of the way. He began to cut the barrier, one wire at a time. His hands were shaking so badly that he had to fight with the rusted tool to chew through each of the strands. The scent of the nearby river surrounded them, a rich ripe odor. Dragging the welcome smell into his lungs, Pablo tried to stop his hands from trembling. Glancing at his wife in the darkness, he rasped, "We are leaving the camp tonight. We'll get past the village of Piedra Preciosa before dawn. El Espanto told us to go, so we're going. We will never speak to anyone of our experience. Ever. If they knew he gave us money, well, certain *esmeraldos* would rob us, for sure. We cannot risk that." Pablo cut the last strand of fencing. The concertina wire whipped back into a tight curl against the wooden post, leaving an open path for them to escape. Ahead were more palms and leafy brush.

"Come," he ordered his family. "El Espanto has given us not only our lives back, but a new life, as well. We're going home, to our village in Peru. We will not disappoint him. We will pray to the Jaguar Mother for him daily, wherever we go. His name will be on our lips until our last breath. Come, let us leave this green hell...."

Chapter 3

The black Arabian mare grunted and skidded sideways through a puddle of thick, slippery red clay and wet grass on the mountain slope. Magdalena Calen Hernandez steadied her mount by shifting her weight. The night was cool and humid; the stars twinkled innocently above. The rhythmic snort of her mare, Storm, soothed her tautly strung nerves. The rifle she carried slapped against her back with a bruising familiarity. Her Kevlar vest took the brunt of the thumping as she rode hard and fast.

They weren't out of danger yet. Keeping the mask in place, she brought the spirited Arabian to a halt roughly a mile away from where the guards had confronted the *esmeraldo* family. Her vision was extraordinary. The genes her parents had passed on to her were those of the mighty jaguar, and she could pierce the darkness without the aid of special night-vision goggles. Calen used the goggles only when she rode on these danger-ous midnight forays. The green, glowing eyes kept the mystical legend of El Espanto alive and well.

Her horse was another matter. Calen had fashioned a special hood for Storm so that the animal, too, looked through night-vision optics. This enabled her mount to avoid holes and obstacles that she'd surely fall into or hit without them. To anyone looking at her, the horse, too, would seem to have green, glowing eyes.

Standing up in the stirrups, her knees and calves pressed against her mare's barrel, Calen slowly scanned the area, absorbing its scents and noises. The smell of vanilla was strong, coming from nearby orchids growing in a tree. Unconsciously, Calen inhaled.

She knew this mountain as intimately as she knew her own body. Calen had been born on these slopes and had run free as a child before the barbed wire fences had been erected by the Guild. Gazing around, her eyes narrowing, she searched for more guard units on horseback. Their nightly movements followed no strict protocol. At any moment, she could run into them. And it would be a kill-or-be-killed situation—again.

Breathing hard, Calen felt the Kevlar chaffing and burning her skin. It was a necessary garment she wore over her black, one-piece spandex outfit. She gently pressed her calf against the mare's side. In response, the Arabian instantly lifted her front legs, shifted her weight and wheeled rapidly to the left. Sitting back slightly on the English saddle was a cue for Storm to halt. Calen never had to tug on the reins. The mare was so well trained that she would stop on a dime with a subtle shift of Calen's weight. Storm arched her neck, her thick black mane flowing forward, momentarily covering her wide, dished face.

Calen could discern the shadowy outline of tree trunks among the bushes that cluttered the slope where they stood. Foliage was spotty at this altitude, and Calen continued to scan for the figures of foreign mercenaries on horseback. Lifting her nose to the air, she sniffed. Many times, the guards smoked cigarettes, and she could hone in on them through odor alone. As a jaguar shape-shifter, she found her senses were heightened.

Nothing. Only the intense, nutmeg and clove fragrance of orchids and the wet, woody odor of jungle decay scented the heavy air.

Nothing yet...

Calen turned Storm in a northerly direction, halted and studied the uneven terrain above her. The dead guards hadn't had a chance to radio back that they were in trouble. Still, Calen knew that the sentries checked in with one another over the radio every half hour. When the squad didn't answer, the hunt would be on. Hopefully, by that time, the *esmeraldos* would be beyond the barbed wire fence and running for freedom.

Wiping her mouth, Calen realized how thirsty she was. But she couldn't stop to drink here even though she had bottled water in the bag behind the cantle of the saddle. Leaning down, she spread her gloved fingers against her mare's sleek, wet neck. Instantly, Storm preened and arched affectionately into her hand. Calen loved Arabians; they were more human than animal, and by far the most intelligent of all horse breeds.

"Where are they?" she whispered to Storm. If she shape-shifted she could hear a mile away. In human form, she was exceedingly limited, and relied instead on her alert horse.

The Arabian's small, pointed ears flicked restlessly back and forth. Something in Calen's gut, which had never lead her wrong, told her there were more guards north of her present position. That meant a unit could be above them. Through her special night-vision goggles, the world appeared in different shades of green to Calen. It was fairly easy to discern movement.

The Arabian tensed, then neighed softly, a warning that she'd heard approaching horses. Patting the mare's neck, Calen eased upward. She pulled the baseball cap down a little lower on her brow. Her horse was black, she was dressed in black. The guards would never see her coming, although she knew the animals they rode would certainly be aware of them.

Time to go to work. Easing the rifle from her back, Calen held it in her right hand, the butt resting against her thigh. She squeezed Storm with her calves, and the mare leaped forward, galloping nimbly across the rough terrain. It had not rained for several days, so the earth was a lot less slippery than normal. The stalwart mare sailed over exposed roots and dodged small boulders. She knew her job; she'd been doing this two or three nights a week for the last two years. Horses had an amazing memory; they remembered each tree, boulder, bush and root. If they had to traverse an area more than once, they would recall every detail and save themselves from sure injury.

The hoofbeats of the Arabian were muted, the clay soft and absorbent as her small hooves plunged into it. Calen knew the Spanish horses the foreign mercs rode would certainly hear their approach, but not the guards. They didn't react to slight sounds and seemed completely insensitive to their alert mounts. That was just as well.

Skidding to a halt beneath the wide, drooping branches of a tree, Calen saw the well-worn guard path just in front of them. She smelled the distinct odor of cigarette smoke. Now downwind from the sentries, she could tell by the pungency of the drifting smoke just how close they were.

Often, it was impossible to spot them until they were within thirty or forty feet of where Calen was hiding. Foliage density and distribution varied greatly across the mountainside and depended upon altitude. There were a number of bare spots due to ongoing bulldozer activity to sink other mine shafts. Only the main track around the base of the volcano was easily seen. All of the paths up here on the slopes led back into the jungle below.

Calen's heart pounded in her chest, the adrenaline making her tense and jumpy. If the mercs spotted her, they'd fire their automatic weapons and spray bullets all over the place. But if she could surprise them first, well, it was to her advantage. Gripping the Arabian with her thighs, she felt Storm quiver. That meant the guards were very close!

The first thing Calen heard was the Russian language drifting through the humid night. The mercs couldn't be more than a hundred feet away. Taking in a slow, deep breath, Calen let her superacute hearing pick up static on a radio. A deep-voiced guard spoke again. He was calling Pavel Borisov, the head of mine security. Sweat trickled down her temples beneath the cloth mask she wore over her head. Calen hated wearing it, but to protect her identity, she had to. As much as she wanted to jerk it off and feel the cooling jungle air against her sweaty face, she couldn't risk it.

The snort of horses sounded. They were close! Compressing her lips, Calen waited. She sat tall and straight in the saddle, silently raising the rifle in her hands. As she eased a dart into the chamber, she heard the same guard curse. Her Russian was getting better recently. Calen needed to know what they were saying, so she'd taken different language courses in Quito.

"Damn! Garold isn't returning our call."

The other sentry laughed. "Oh, he and Moriz are

probably taking a pee or a dump somewhere out in the bushes, is all."

"Maybe," the guard muttered.

"Give 'em ten minutes. Riding a horse for eight friggin' hours is enough to give anyone bowel and bladder problems. They're fine."

Calen watched as the pair of guards ambled past the thick foliage, the small horses laboring beneath their weight. Like many others, these two seemed to be ex-paramilitary men from the old Soviet Union. Carlos Cruz, the Guild director, had lured them over to Ecuador with the promise of many more rubles than they were making in the service of their own countries.

Mouth tightening, Calen saw one of the horses turn and look directly at the tree where she and Storm were hiding. A horse's sense of smell was acute. Would its rider glance back? Calen raised the rifle to her shoulder, just in case. No, he didn't. He was too busy fumbling with the radio to notice anything. It would be his downfall.

Calen waited until they had passed the tree. She adjusted the night-vision goggles and felt Storm tense with anticipation. One more minute…and then the guards would be on an exposed part of the trail. Her breath exploded from her mouth. Calen squeezed her calves. In an instant, the mare leaped out onto the track, no more than ten feet behind the unsuspecting guards.

Both Spanish horses bolted. The guards cursed, nearly unseated. They jerked the reins to control their startled mounts. Too late!

"Stop where you are, hombres," Calen told them in a purposefully low, husky tone. Her mare planted her feet solidly on the trail so no one could get past her. Standing in the stirrups, Calen knew the Arabian would remain motionless. She watched as the guards whirled their shaken, jumpy horses toward her. Their eyes bulged; their mouths fell open. They were staring down the barrel of her rifle. Satisfaction thrummed through Calen.

"Drop your weapons now or you're dead," she told them in Russian. The taller guard glared angrily at her. The other one, younger and shorter, instantly threw his AK-47 to the ground. His horse was skittish. It took everything he had to make the mount halt and stand uneasily in front of Calen.

"Hombre? You want to die like your two friends just did? If so, hold on to your AK-47 for three more seconds…." Calen trained the rifle directly at the guard's sweaty brow. The mercs didn't know she carried darts and not bullets in her weapon, and she wasn't about to tell them.

"You son of a bitch!" he growled. After throwing his rifle down, he jerked hard on the reins of his nervous animal.

Calen grinned beneath her mask. "Dismount! Now!" The guards grudgingly did as ordered.

"Throw the reins over your horse's head and slap it on the rump."

Again, they did as she instructed. The horses, eager to take flight, dug into the clay, sending clods of dirt flying as they galloped recklessly down the darkened slope. Calen's gaze never left the guards. The larger one wanted to jump her, she knew. She sensed it.

"Sit down and take your boots off, hombres."

"Why you—"

"Now. Or do I put a bullet into your head? Your call."

Cursing, the larger guard sat down and began to unlace his military boots.

Calen sat there, the rifle resting easily against her shoulder. The bead she had on the two was solid. Her Arabian's flanks heaved in and out, but Storm didn't move. For the horse to move at all meant that Calen might miss the mark if one of the guards tried to leap at her.

"Now, tie the laces of your boots together."

Sulking, the larger guard obeyed her huskily spoken instructions. The smaller sentry did it with badly shaking hands. He kept looking up at Calen, fear in his eyes.

"The radio. Toss it next to your boots."

The larger guard pulled the device off his belt and dropped it on top of his boots.

"Get up. Start walking that way." Calen pointed in the direction of the other two guards. "Go a mile. You will find your friends."

They rose. The larger merc hesitated.

"Do you want to join your brothers, hombre? Just thinking about trying to leap at me will earn you a place in hell beside them."

Her snarled words made them whirl around in horror, then walk away from her. They both started out across the rocky, root strewn path in their sock feet. Calen waited until they had gone a good hundred yards and disappeared into the bush-lined slope before she dismounted. Quickly scooping up their boots, she placed them in one of the saddlebags. She gathered up the AK-47s, emptied them of rounds and tied them behind her saddle. After jamming the radio into one of the zippered pockets on the right thigh of her outfit, she swiftly remounted. The next thing Calen did was remove the goggles. Glad to be rid of them, she stuffed them into the other saddlebag.

The Arabian pawed the earth, ready to run.

"Okay," Calen whispered, sliding the sling of the rifle across her back once more, "let's go home, Storm."

The black mare turned around, rear hooves digging deeply into the earth. Moments later, Calen was riding the wind itself as the animal thundered along the slope. It was a terrible night's work. Two guards were dead, and Calen couldn't forgive herself. The sentries allowed to live would carry their humiliating story back to the others. Patrón Cruz had had more than one-third of his surviving mercs quit in the last three months because so many had encountered bad experiences with El Espanto or with the rogue jaguar that roamed the mountain. Little did they realize it was Calen in one form or another. The guards she attacked in jaguar form were never killed, just swiped at with a good set of claw marks, or fangs sunk into their flesh to tell their story. Either way, the foreign mercs left. Which was what Calen wanted.

Galloping quickly down the slope on a little-known trail created by the jaguars that roamed the area, she and Storm raced through the darkness. Jets of steam shot out of the black mare's nostrils with each long, ground-eating stride she took. Calen rode with Storm, the rhythmic movements reminding her of the tidal flux and flow of the ocean, of life itself.

They descended swiftly to the trail at the base of the volcano. She then guided the horse along a seldom-used path bracketed with walls of foliage. The jungle was comprised of woody vines, three different heights of trees and very little underbrush. Over thousands of years, wild pigs and jaguars had created narrow trails into this nearly impenetrable area. Calen had chosen the little-used trail because it would take them straight to the cave. There, she would divest herself of her El Espanto costume and resume her other masquerade, as Ecuador's richest female oil baron.

Depending upon the night and circumstances, Calen would rarely use the same path twice. This trail was the only one that led directly to the cave entrance. Calen knew it was safe enough to utilize tonight. She'd taken out two of the four of guards riding the perimeter. The other merc teams would be on the far side of the mountain. Halting for a moment, she removed her baseball cap and then the black sack from around her head. The fresh air felt wonderful against her overheated flesh. She dragged in grateful breaths of the cooling air. With a squeeze of Calen's calves, the Arabian took off at a gallop.

Calen's legs, honed from over a decade of riding, clung easily to the barrel of her galloping Arabian. Storm's flying dark mane stung her face from time to time as she hunched forward, riding as one with the horse. Because of her extraordinary vision, Calen could see every root sticking up in the path, every branch that leaned out to swat her as they thundered by. She did not need a mask to see into the night, only to hide her true identity.

By three-thirty, they'd arrived at a wide river. It was barely ankle deep and had a pebbled bottom. Easing Storm into the water, Calen knew that, even if someone tried to follow them, the hoofprints would end here. They traveled about a mile downstream before coming to a wall of thick brush. At this point, a small tributary flowed into the river from beneath the foliage. It was the only clue as to where the cave was located.

To a tourist or hiker, no cave was in evidence, concealed as it was by the dense jungle. Calen halted the Arabian in the water and dismounted in front of the green wall. The horse heaved with exertion, white sweat trickling down her neck. Patting Storm gently, Calen drew the reins over the animal's head. Walking in front of the horse, she eased through the leaves along the streambed.

This mountain had once been an active volcano, creating the emeralds within its pegmatite veins. Unknown to most people, a series of caves had also formed from geological activity. Even locals no longer knew of their existence. Few entered this particular section of jungle because it was known to be the jaguars' lair. Locals stayed off the trails, spooked by myths of humans turning into jaguars and stealing children from the villages.

A ten-foot opening in the rock, which led into a lava tube and then on into a huge cave, was hidden by a hill overgrown with jungle. To curious hikers, it seemed to be one of the many small hills dotted around the base of the towering mountain above.

Brush slapped smartly against Calen's face and body as she pushed through it, hand held out in front of her to protect her eyes. She knew the way back to the cave by heart and sloshed steadily up the shallow stream. Her eyes were so accustomed to the starry darkness that she could see the opening ahead. Her Arabian mare knew the route just as well as she did. Easing past the last of the vegetation, Calen moved into the narrow tunnel. The trickling stream continued through it, less than three inches deep. The smooth, grayish black basalt tube had been created by a heavy magma flow millions of years earlier. Storm had to bow her head so her ears wouldn't scrape the roof, but Calen, at five feet ten inches tall, could walk upright without any problem.

Fifty feet farther, she reached into her front vest pocket and reset the entrance's electronic alarm box. The fifteen-second reset feature would allow them to pass, and the alarm would return to active mode.

The tunnel twisted like a snake, rising slightly. Making the last turn, Calen could see faint light ahead. They were almost home, and some of her adrenaline rush began to subside. She wiped her damp forehead with the back of her darkly clothed arm. It felt so good to relax! A cooling breeze from the cave hit Calen's overheated body, and she could feel the perspiration drying on her skin as they walked quickly toward the feeble light.

The final curve of the tunnel led them into a huge, U-shaped room. A lone battery-powered lantern revealed the jagged black-and-gray basalt vault overhead. Nearby was a small pipe corral and a set of horse ties. Her manager, Godfredo Santos, gave her a brief, tight smile of welcome when he saw her emerge from the tunnel. The Peruvian had been an indispensable friend. When Calen was ten years old and adopted by Maria Eleria Hernandez, he'd run her adopted mother's ranch south of Quito. A wiry man with large, sparkling brown eyes, Godfredo was in his late forties now. He came from Quero Indian stock and had silver flecks at the temples of his short, neatly cut hair. Calen could see that he was worried tonight.

When she was out riding, he kept track of her via a radio headset she wore over her ear and close to her mouth, so they could communicate if necessary. The two-way radio was a safety net; if Calen ever got injured on one of her forays, Godfredo would be there to rescue her. But she had never needed to call for help, thank goodness. Any call to him could potentially give away their position, should Cruz be smart enough to have the radio equipment to track them. Calen never wanted to take that chance.

She nodded to her friend as she drew near. "Nothing went right tonight." She handed over the damp leather reins to him and glumly pulled open the Velcro closings on her Kevlar vest. She hated the thing because it continually bruised her skin, rubbing her rib cage raw.

Godfredo gave her a cold bottle of water. "Not a good night," he murmured in agreement. He looked her over critically. "The scanner is going loco now. They've discovered the two dead guards. Are you sure you're all right?" His gaze was intense and anxious.

After drinking deeply from the bottle, Calen wiped her mouth with the back of her hand. She nodded. "Physically, I'm fine. Emotionally, my gut feels like a nest of angry snakes." Calen grimaced. "I don't like to kill, Godfredo. I'm torn up about what I had to do out there tonight. It's easier being a jaguar. I can just wound those guards and scare the living daylights out of them, instead."

"Sometimes, Calen, things go wrong. I know you didn't want to kill those guards."

"Everything happened too fast for me to exchange the bullet in my rifle for a dart," she muttered wearily. Her manager was one of only two people who knew her secret of being a shape-shifter. Her stomach churned with nausea. Calen didn't set out to take lives, only to protect the *esmeraldos* from being murdered. But what choice did she have tonight? Absolutely none.

Calen suddenly realized she was going to vomit. Hurrying to an empty pail nearby, she knelt down, grabbed it and retched violently. This wasn't the first time she'd thrown up over having to kill a person. Sitting up a while later, after racking dry heaves, she accepted the glass of water Godfredo handed her. Calen croaked her thanks and washed her mouth out. Her hands were shaking. Her gut was trembling with an inner earthquake as she got to her feet. Wiping her watering eyes, she dragged in a deep, unsteady breath.

"I'll be okay," she rasped to her manager. "It's a reaction to killing."

"Only an honest person would have your reaction, Dama Calen." Godfredo held out his hand. "Come and help me unsaddle Storm. Get your mind off it," he urged.

Wearily, Calen reached out, squeezed the man's work-worn hand and then released it. "Keeping busy stops me from thinking too much," she agreed unsteadily.

Godfredo nodded and hurried to remove Storm's bridle, replacing it with a soft nylon halter. He led the horse into the ties, where she stood quietly. Collecting the AK-47s, Godfredo transferred them to an open trunk. Next, he removed the English saddle and bags and placed them on a wooden stand. The quilted sheet was next. The fabric covered the horse to protect her chest, shoulders and hind quarters from stray bullets when the sentries fired at Calen. Kevlar panels had been inserted into the material that Storm wore on these risky rides. The fabric was soaked with sweat as Calen helped remove it.

"Good girl!" Godfredo praised the mare, gently patting her neck. "You've more than earned your ration of oats on this night." He snapped the ties into place on both sides of her halter.

Taking care of the horse calmed some of Calen's intense emotional reactions at being forced to kill instead of drug the guards. Godfredo had several buckets of warm water and sponges waiting nearby. She would first inspect her mare's legs to make sure she had incurred no cuts, bruises or swelling due to the run across the mountain. A horse with a bad leg was no horse at all. In the past, her mare had often received nicks and cuts as they dashed madly across the night-scape to protect *esmeraldos* from the brutal sentries.

Moving her hands with practiced ease down each of Storm's slender legs, Calen murmured, "She's fine, Godfredo…." She grabbed a sponge from a bucket and began to clean the mare. The pungent smell of Absorbine, a liniment that would brace Storm's legs and soothe her muscles after such a hard, brutal run, filled the space. The medicinal rub helped prevent any stiffness or soreness.

"Yes, she looks good," Godfredo agreed as he moved his hand across the Arabian's withers to ensure that the saddle had not caused a sore spot. He looked at Calen from beneath the belly of the horse. "So what happened out there?"

"The guards found a family and had their AK-47s trained on them before I arrived," she said tiredly. "I'd picked up the little girl, who had escaped. The guards wear Kevlar vests and it's tough to wound them in that kind of situation. Normally, I can go for a shoulder or leg shot with a drug dart, but tonight, I wasn't given that chance. There was nothing I could do, God-fredo…. Someone was going to die—either the guards or the family." Calen sighed and stood. Giving her Arabian a pat of thanks, she glanced across the animal's back at her foreman. Calen saw him shrug eloquently and give her a sympathetic look.

"It is two less, Dama. They have agreed to murder *esmeraldos* found on Santa Maria property. They could have chosen to let those people go. But they didn't even consider that as an option, so they paid the price." He saw the anguish in her light green eyes. "You did what you had to." Knowing that Calen never set out to kill guards, merely wound them, Godfredo suspected this incident would bother her for months to come. Calen had nightmares almost once a week, anyway. What she did out there was dangerous and stressful. Godfredo wondered how much longer she could stand the pressures of her double life.

Grimly, Calen whispered, "Yeah, I know. But the guards had mothers and fathers, too. Did they have brothers? Sisters? What were their hopes? Their dreams?" She took the sponge and squeezed warm water against the Arabian's neck, the foam running over Storm's broad chest and down her legs.

"Don't go there," Godfredo warned her. Moving to get another bucket to wash the mare's opposite side, he said, "They signed their own death warrant by agreeing to work for the Guild. It's not right to murder people who are trying to keep from starving to death. You know that and so do I."

Calen nodded and sluiced more liniment and water across the Arabian's broad, short back. "I know. The other two guards I caught tonight turned out to be routine." She managed a weak grin. "Did you hear me make them take off their boots and give them to me? I got their radio, too." Calen's tactics had been meant to shame the guards. If it came to a gun battle, she shot to drug, not kill them. In two years, only four guards had been killed by her. Four too many, in her opinion.

"The second meeting went as we planned," Godfredo agreed. "They will have sore feet and humiliated egos tonight instead of being dead."

Calen stood back and unzipped her pocket, producing the Guild radio. Holding it up to Godfredo, she said, "This will come in handy. It contains their present radio code."

Godfredo chuckled as he sloshed the sponge around in the pail of water. "Until they change the code—which they rarely do—we can use it to know their movements. That will make it easier for you to intercept and surprise them." He began to scrub foam and sweat from Storm's muzzle.

"What's wrong with them? That security chief, Borisov, is stupid, if you ask me. If I'm a guard and tell him that El Espanto has stolen my radio, don't you think he'd change codes instantly? But he doesn't. Dumb…"

"Borisov is an ex-KGB chief and he's arrogant. He thinks he can find El Espanto, and that makes Cruz think he's smart. Borisov is the fourth security chief in two years. We need someone like him who thinks he can outwit us." Godfredo laughed indulgently. "I'm surprised Cruz hasn't fired him yet, but Borisov keeps promising him that he'll find El Espanto."

With a strained chuckle, Calen agreed. The adrenaline was leaving her bloodstream now and she felt shaky and weak. She finished washing Storm. Godfredo would take the gallant mare to her box stall and give her a well-earned mixture of warm bran and oats, drizzled with molasses—a fit reward for her performance tonight.

Going over to the tack trunk, Calen put the stolen radio down. She hung up the irritating but necessary Kevlar vest on a hook drilled into the rough basalt wall. As Godfredo fed Storm, Calen moved behind a curtain and shimmied out of her black spandex outfit. Tossing the sweat-soaked articles aside, she climbed into jeans and a yellow T-shirt. Sitting on a three-legged stool, she replaced her drenched socks with a dry pair, and put on sensible, brown leather shoes. She ran her hands through her matted, wet hair, then rolled the smelly suit into a tight ball and dropped it into a nearby plastic bag. Time to leave.

"I'm going to the villa now," she called to Godfredo, who was shutting Storm's stall.

"Go ahead," he said, lifting his hand. "I'll be back just as soon as I get done here. See you tomorrow morning about 10:00 a.m. A good night's work, Dama Calen. Try to get some sleep, eh?"

"I'll try." She turned and hurried down another lava tube. This tunnel was much narrower, higher and dry. A horse could not get through this one. Calen's eyes adjusted immediately to the murkiness. Godfredo had to carry a flashlight to traverse this tube, which led back to her villa, but she did not. Cat eyes. That was what her real mother, Gina Alverez, a Quero healer, had said to her when she was six years old. "Daughter, you have the mark of the Warriors for the Light on the back of your neck." She'd gestured toward Calen's nape, where the chocolate-colored vesica piscis birthmark was located on her golden skin. It consisted of two rings overlapping in the middle. Hearing that the symbol was ancient and that only certain people with a metaphysical skill carried it made Calen feel different. Like an oddball.

"It is said that the person who wears this mark has a mission on this earth. Your destiny will begin when you're twenty-eight years old. Your life will become a journey of self-discovery, and you will know how to help the world," her mother had told her.

As Calen hurried through the nearly airless tunnel, her elbow occasionally brushing against the cool basalt walls, she swallowed hard. At ten years old, she had watched her family being murdered by mine guards on this very mountain. She'd once been an *esmeraldo* herself. Afterward, the only survivor of that nightmarish experience, Calen had found her way to an Ibarra Catholic orphanage, where Father Pio took her in. Less than three months later, she'd been chosen by Maria Eleria Hernandez, who could not conceive and wanted a daughter. Adopted, Calen was suddenly thrown into the sphere of the wealthy, and had gone to live in Quito.

Oh, how Calen wished her birth mother had not been murdered! Gina Alverez had been trained to bring out Calen's mystical talents. She had never had time to share all she knew with her daughter because of her unexpected death. Now, Calen wished mightily to have known more about her family's ancient Incan bloodlines and the sacred heritage that her mother had been teaching her. Calen understood she was vastly different from other human beings. That had been proved in many ways over the years; her unusual eyesight was just one of many skills she possessed. And the fact that in times of great danger, she automatically shape-shifted from human to a jaguar form to protect herself. Once the danger was over, she morphed back again. That was her metaphysical skill, her mother had told her; their family descended from the jaguar branch of shape-shifters. Starting from age three, Calen had been coached by her mother how to control and use this magical process.

Absently, Calen touched the back of her damp neck as she moved up the tunnel, which was becoming steeper. The mark of the vesica piscis. One of the last things she recalled her mother telling her was that when she turned twenty-eight, the gift of the very ancient symbol would be revealed to her. She would turn twenty-eight in less than a week. What would that mean? Calen didn't know.

Most of the time, she didn't think about her mother's promise that her life would change forever. Calen wasn't sure it was meant as a curse or a blessing. As a child growing up, she'd been trained daily so she could receive the mystical, sacred knowledge that would help her save a world riddled with chaos and imbalance. Her life, right now, was filled to the brim with responsibilities, plus trying to maintain her cover so no one would ever know she was El Espanto.

Her eyes filled with tears as she thought of her biological mother. Calen quickly dashed them away, surprised at her emotional response to those haunting memories. Maybe she was more sensitive than normal because she'd killed tonight. Calen had no one to talk to about the stress of leading a double life. How she wished for a friend she could trust with such knowledge. But Calen had no one except for her trusted manager, who was also Quero and knew of shapeshifters, although he was not one himself.

Up ahead, Calen could see a thin glow of light. Godfredo's wife, Eliana Santos, had left the door ajar for her. Moving swiftly, Calen reached the end of the tunnel. She pushed the massive mahogany door open and saw a large rose-colored candle burning on her dark wooden desk. Quietly slipping through the doorway, she walked through her large, airy office to the row of windows facing the dormant volcano that towered in shadow above them.

She then padded softly down the hall. In the laundry room, Calen threw the dirty uniform into the washer and started the cycle. First thing tomorrow morning, Eliana, the head housekeeper, would take it out and dry it. None of the maids who worked in the villa would ever see it. No, her secret was safe with Godfredo and Eliana. They fiercely protected her identity against the men who wanted her dead. There was a million-dollar reward for El Espanto, and Calen knew they would never turn her in.

Exhaustion washed over her, replacing the powerful energy she had felt before. She longed for a hot bath. The master bedroom was located on the second floor. The handwoven rust-umber-and-cream-colored Peruvian carpet muted any sound of her walking through the peaceful home. At last she reached the stairs and took the mahogany steps two at a time. Feeling gutted emotionally, Calen reveled in how physically fit she felt, despite her roiling feelings.

She opened the door to her room and breathed a sigh

of relief. Home. She was home. And safe. Once more, El Espanto had done his job and no one had found out who the ghost really was. Not yet...

Chapter 4

A sharp, powerful shift of energy whirled around Reno Manchahi. It was as if he stood too close to where a bolt of lightning had just struck, and he instantly went on guard. Reno wasn't sure what the hell the warning meant. He'd never experienced this specific sensation before, though similar psychic triggers had often saved his life when he was a sniper. His partner said he was more animal than human because of his extrasensory awareness. His partner had been more right than he could ever guess.

Reno was rummaging around in the hovel that Senor Cruz, the director of the Santa Maria mine, called a medical clinic, when the psychic turbulence snagged his attention. Fighting jet lag and lack of sleep, he'd arrived in Ibarra, Ecuador, less than three hours ago. Cruz wanted him in his undercover spy mode and didn't care if Reno had slept or eaten. There was a rusted gurney in the center of the main room, its rubber wheels misshapen by humidity, unrelenting heat and jungle rot. The wooden table stood on wobbly legs that had seen better times.

The morning was young; it was 0700. Outside the clinic, which did not have a sign announcing it was a medical station, at least twenty highly curious children of varying ages had crept cautiously up to the porch to stare at him. They were *esmeraldo* children dressed in threadbare apparel that certainly would not protect them from the cool winter temperatures. Every one of them was adorable. In one way or another, they all reminded Reno of his Sarah. His heart ached with the memory of his beautiful, slain daughter.

Lifting his head, Reno heard the snort of an approaching horse. The gawking children all turned in unison toward the sound. Cries erupted from them. "Dama Calen! Dama Calen!"

Reno watched as the tide of brown bodies, like leaves blown in the wind, tumbled off the porch. What was going on? Again, that same electric sensation made him feel giddy and euphoric. Not one to disregard such intuition, he placed his hands on his narrow hips.

Was it a warning? Danger? No. Maybe…

Reno wasn't sure. He'd never felt anything quite like

it and could not accurately interpret the sensation. Before, a jittery feeling always meant danger. But this time it made him feel happy, for no discernible reason. Scowling, Reno walked around the rectangular table and headed out the door, his boots thunking hollowly across the rough, plywood floor. He closed the sagging screen door, which screeched in protest, and saw the children running as fast as their spindly legs could carry them down the deeply rutted, red clay road. Squinting against the sun, which had just crested the eastern slope of the dormant volcano, he spotted a rider coming toward him.

A female rider. Who was she? Reno settled his tan felt cowboy hat on his head and drew the brim down a little to shade his eyes. He had excellent eyesight. It was one of the many talents required of a sniper. But Reno had exceptional vision because he was a jaguar shape-shifter.

He made out a woman on a big chestnut horse of good breeding. A tingle began in his chest and spread rapidly outward, with warmth accompanying it. What was *that* all about? Stymied, his mouth quirking, he focused on the horse. Its rider rode effortlessly, and he could tell that she had been born to a saddle. An unsettled feeling crept over him. Eyes narrowed speculatively on the woman, Reno felt as if he already knew her. *But how? No, that's impossible.* Yet the sense of joy and excitement at her approach bubbled up through him like a fast-running stream in springtime. Reno had absolutely no explanation for his reaction. None.

His gaze irresistibly traveled back to the black-haired woman with the ponytail. Something nibbled at Reno's memory. What the hell was it? And who was she? The children had said "Dama Calen." Usually, *patrón* or *patrona* was used in acknowledgment of someone powerful and rich. *Dama,* however, was a respectful Spanish word that meant "lady." It was usually reserved for a queen or someone of noble rank. Reno also knew that it was an affectionate expression used by people for someone they considered to be above them, someone they truly adored and loved.

As the rider drew closer, Reno's wariness melted and his curiosity took over. The woman, probably in her late twenties, was beautiful in an arresting way. He could see she had golden skin. Reno's heart picked up in beat, something unfamiliar to him as he ruthlessly studied the figure on the big-boned chestnut gelding.

Her face was oval, with high cheekbones. *Indian.* She had to be Indian, Reno guessed. And very rich, from the looks of it. In the cool, humid morning air, she wore thin black gloves, highly polished black leather riding boots and yellow riding breeches that hugged and cleanly defined her long legs. She was tall and willowy, appearing boneless as she moved in sync with her mount. This was someone who'd ridden daily for years.

Reno liked her regal form. She was of medium bone and had a curvy body that was taut and firm. Beneath her long-sleeved cotton blouse and red vest, he could see a hint of full breasts. Her waist wasn't tiny, and her hips flared as a woman's should, not like those sticks society called models. In many ways, her body type reminded Reno painfully of his wife, Ilona.

Instantly retreating from that connection, he settled his hands back on his hips and enjoyed the arrival of his unexpected guest. The children surrounded the woman, waving their arms, their hands held toward her in a pleading gesture. He saw her smile and call a warm greeting in Spanish. She halted and opened one of the saddlebags on the horse. Then, with a brilliant smile, she began tossing out wrapped candies to the milling children. Reno was amazed how fearless the little barefoot waifs were around the large hooves of the horse. The animal seemed to sense the children were vulnerable and didn't move a muscle.

Shifting his focus back to the woman, Reno fought an unfamiliar urge. A powerful magnetic force had been set off between them. The jolting charge was mesmerizing as well as unsettling to Reno, and yet filled him with hope. *Hope?* Mocking himself over that idealistic word, Reno remembered his life held no hope. Not since the death of his family. All he ate, tasted and dreamed about was revenge for their deaths. Looking at the woman, who was now less than a block away, Reno began to discern the details of her face. The breeze was picking up slightly. When she lifted her hand, Reno was reminded of a ballerina making a graceful gesture. With gloved fingers, she settled the black hard hat she wore a little more firmly on her head.

Frowning, he noted a difference in skin color near the back of her neck. What was he seeing? Snipers investigated everything and never overlooked details. It was part of an ingrained habit, because the one element he missed would be the one that could get him killed.

Her blouse opened just enough so that Reno could see a hint of collarbones beneath her golden flesh. But something wasn't right. What was it? He narrowed his eyes on the side of her neck near her hairline. *Discoloration*. Had she been burned? Reno's eyes constricted more. As she rode closer, he saw a vague outline of what appeared to be a circular shape. When he realized it had to be a birthmark and not a tattoo or scar, he felt even more fascinated. He wondered what the mark looked like, but couldn't see it from this distance or angle.

As his gaze ranged upward, Reno realized she had a stubbornly set chin. Her face might be oval, wide and attractive, but that chin told him she was a rugged individual. All his life, Reno had been able to read faces. Enjoying the respite from his disappointing medical facility, he honed in on her smiling mouth. She had full lips, incredibly soft looking. The corners of her lips tipped slightly upward, hinting she probably had a good sense of humor.

Reno watched intently when one little girl, about age six, begged for a ride. The woman laughed with delight, leaned over and drew the long-haired child onto her lap. Dama Calen gently guided the urchin's

bare legs across the English saddle and settled her protectively against her willowy form. The little girl
looked up with such adoration that Reno felt his heart
clench in his chest. That was undisguised love sparkling in her eyes—love for the smiling woman.

At least Dama Calen, who seemed financially well-
off, had a heart. It was more than Reno could say for
the members of the Guild he'd met thus far. They were
all cold-hearted bastards with only monetary gain in
mind. Certainly human compassion wasn't high on
their list. Reno was beginning to realize that finding
one emerald could make a life-changing difference to
any of the *esmeraldos*. Until then, the poor toiled relentlessly in the muddy waters just below the clinic,
sifting through the sand and examining every pebble
in search of that hope. The *esmeraldos* were the poor
from the slum areas in every major Ecuadorian city.
They could not get a job working at the mine. Instead,
they camped like unwelcome squatters below the mine,
at the river, hoping to find one emerald that would
change their lives. To the Guild, they were little more
than pests to be kept off the mining property.

Reno simply couldn't stop staring at the woman. That
was bad manners, he knew, but dammit, he couldn't help
himself. What an exotic-looking face! Somehow, he
knew her. Ruthlessly combing his memory, Reno still
couldn't recall where or how. He saw her smile disappear as she looked up and spotted him for the first time.
Reno felt bad about her reaction toward him. The child

riding in her arms was grinning like a beam of sunlight, thrilled to be up on the chestnut with her.

Why had the woman stopped smiling? Oh, Reno knew he was an ugly-looking bastard at best. He was no lady's man, that was for sure. His face was rough-hewn, as if it had been cut out of the coarse black basalt of the Arizona canyons where he grew up. His flesh had been toughened by extreme weather, the demands of being a sniper for so many years. Maybe that's why she had such a poor initial reaction to him. A prominent scar ran down the left side of his jaw. All these things could make a woman respond negatively.

Swallowing his disappointment, Reno stuffed his personal emotions away. As the rider drew closer, he saw that she had given out the last of the candy from her saddlebags. The children called their thanks and raced one another back to the river camp. Probably to share their gifts with their parents or their siblings, he supposed.

As she came closer Reno got a better look at the woman. She had pale green eyes with huge black pupils and a black ring encircled her irisés. The color of her eyes was highly unusual. It reminded him of young grass shoots just coming up after a hard winter. Grass always had a fresh, light green color when it first sprouted. Only later did it darken to a standard bluish green. Her lashes were thick, emphasizing those large, wide-set eyes. She was damned intelligent looking; Reno could sense that as well as see it. This was no prima donna rich woman. She was nothing like the

Guild members he'd seen in action earlier. Her lips became firm and somewhat grim as she met and held his inquiring gaze.

Suddenly, Reno recoiled. Bolted to the spot, he realized why she seemed so familiar to him. The vision! She was the woman in his precog! Reeling from that memory, Reno felt coldcocked for a moment. Oh, she wasn't wearing a white gown or a crown of colorful macaw feathers now, but that didn't matter. She looked quite capable of taking care of herself, and didn't appear to be in dire straits at all.

Giving himself an internal shake, Reno knew that his precognitive dream was to be taken seriously. And this woman had some connection with it. Having to sit on his impatient urge to blurt it out to her, Reno decided just to wait and see how things unfolded between them.

For the first time in years, he managed to hitch the corners of his mouth upward. Maybe it wasn't a full smile, but he knew it could soften people's initial reaction to him. He'd realized a long time ago that people were easily threatened by his countenance. Not to mention he was six foot five and two hundred thirty pounds of pure, hard muscle. Maybe, if he attempted a little more of a smile it would ease the hard planes of his face and she'd stop frowning at him.

It worked! Instantly Reno saw her eyes flare with surprise. That full mouth softened a little, too. Maybe he needed to learn to smile again. With her, it would be something he'd attempt to remedy very quickly. Reno watched as she gently deposited the young child on the ground. The little girl laughed and scampered away.

"Hello!" Reno greeted her in Spanish, lifting his hand. "You on a morning ride or did you come to see me?" He wasn't sure who was who yet here at this mining operation. Knowing that Cruz was underhanded by nature, Reno decided to trust no one. What he would trust was what he saw with his own two eyes.

"Good morning," Calen responded. Her stomach clenched with anxiety and her heart pounded heavily in her breast. She was raw with fear, yet as his deep, husky tone washed over her, Calen felt amazingly calm. She knew from having tea the other day with the wives of the mine owners that they had hired this man, a world-class sniper, to come here and kill El Espanto. When she found out he'd arrived in the early morning hours, Calen had wanted to check him out. Personally.

She forced a social smile she didn't feel. Pulling Star, her gelding, to a halt about five feet away from this tall, powerful-looking man who was her sworn enemy, Calen kept her face pleasantly arranged. "Good morning. I'm Magdalena Calen Hernandez. I live near here."

"Nice to meet you. Welcome to my humble abode. I'm Reno Manchahi, the paramedic who's just been hired by the Guild to run this clinic." He touched the brim of his hat and acknowledged her with a salute. Dama Calen seemed guarded, not wanting to hold his gaze very long. Why?

Calen watched as Manchahi swept his hand toward

the ramshackle hut that was supposed to be a clinic. Of course, she knew it was all a ruse to hide his real purpose here: to kill the people's night guardian, El Espanto—her. The sniper was tall, his shoulders wide beneath the white cotton T-shirt that clung to his highly masculine body. His chest was broad and deep. She watched the flex of his biceps as he settled his hands on his lean hips once more. The jeans he wore outlined long, solid thighs. The cowboy hat only emphasized his rugged look.

She remembered hearing how this man had been a prisoner. He must have exercised daily to have a sculpted body like that. But it was his work-worn hands, long fingers and pronounced knuckles that drew Calen's interest. He was used to hard manual labor, no doubt. There were many pale, thin scars across the tops of his hands. What had caused them?

Calen knew enough about snipers to understand they would lie for days out in the wilds, waiting to target their quarry. He was more animal than human; she sensed that strongly. And she was stunned at the attraction she felt toward Manchahi. How could that be? Her jaguar nature told her he was similar to her. But that was impossible.

Deciding she must be rattled because of the fear she felt toward this man who wanted to kill her, Calen ignored her driving inner yearnings. In the past when adrenaline was running high in her bloodstream, it often confused her jaguar senses. Trying to live in a human and animal world simultaneously was very, very tough. And right now, this unexplained attraction was fighting with her very real fear. She didn't want to be here, but she knew she had to come. If she didn't check out her enemy, it could mean her demise out there on the slopes some night.

"I came over to look at the new clinic that Senor Cruz said was going to be available for the *esmeraldos*," Calen lied to him. She shifted her weight in the saddle, unwilling to dismount.

With a grimace, Reno turned and glanced at the hastily assembled shack. "Well, I don't know about you, Senora—"

"I don't stand on protocol, Senor Manchahi. Just call me Calen. Everyone else does." She added a quick smile to punctuate her request. Seeing his eyes widen momentarily with surprise, and then narrow to inspect her more closely, Calen tensed inwardly. He possessed the look of a dangerous, feral hunter. Reno Manchahi had large, cinnamon-colored eyes. She could easily see his deep black pupils. Under any other circumstance, Calen would say he had beautiful eyes for a man: inquisitive, filled with intelligence and alertness. But she couldn't go there, not when his real purpose in Ecuador was to take her life.

"Well, okay, sure, no problem." Caught off guard by her unexpected friendliness, Reno mumbled, "My friends call me Reno. So far, everyone I've met around here hangs on to their labels and aristocracy as if their lives depended upon it. Classism is alive and well down here, it seems." When he swung his head back to her, he saw Calen's wry smile widen for a moment. But the smile went no further than her soft, beautifully formed mouth. Her spring-green eyes assessed him like a hawk. Reno felt simultaneously wary and drawn to her. It was a crazy reaction. Was it her body language that put him on guard? She sat easily on the horse, her hands resting on the withers, reins in her long, artistic-looking fingers.

"Ah, yes. The Guild. Well, Reno, I'm afraid they do cling to their classism, as you've already seen."

"It feels like I stepped back into the eighteenth century," he drawled good-naturedly. Calen must be a superb athlete, in Reno's estimation. He was entranced by her natural grace and honeyed voice. She was not the usual Ecuadorian woman, he felt sure. Most South American women seemed relegated to being housewives and mothers because of the powerful patriarchy still alive and well on the continent. Seeing the gold Rolex peeking briefly from beneath the cuff of one brown glove, he said, "I take it you're from the upper crust, too? Even though you're not a member of the Guild?" He managed a sour smile to go along with his challenge. Maybe his question was too personal. But maybe not.

Calen sat back on the horse and rubbed her nose, while a grin faintly curved her mouth. "I see you have typical *norte americano* bluntness."

"I see I can't fool you."

Her smile was genuine, and Reno felt warmth sheet down through him like heat lightning on a hot, muggy desert night. An ache sprang into his chest and then caught fire in his lower body. Thrown off guard, he was momentarily distracted by the traitorous response. Yeah, he'd been without a woman for a damn long time. And Calen Hernandez sure as hell was stoking the fires back to life. Just that one dazzling smile made Reno fantasize about taking her into his arms and kissing the hell out of her—and more....

"Let's just say I've lived around here for two years, and I can't bear to see people starve to death. With the help of my foreman and his family, I do what I can to aid those who have much less than we do."

Reno gave her a thawing smile. "Music to my ears. A compassionate rich person. That's novel in Ecuador, I bet." He supposed she could take his sarcasm wrongly, but all she did was chuckle softly, as if understanding his black humor.

"And is that why you are here?" Calen inquired. "To help the *esmeraldos?*"

"Yes, I was hired by the Guild to provide medical services to them." He didn't like to lie, but it was necessary. He managed a lopsided grin. "I'm as poor as they are." That wasn't untrue. And Reno found himself not wanting to lie at all to Calen. She felt too important to him, to his life, to do that. Frustration ate at him. He certainly had not expected to be smitten by a beautiful, rich Ecuadorian woman. Or, for that matter, to have his precog show up in real life on his doorstep!

Calen raised her brows. The man appeared genuinely upset. How could that be? He was here undercover. Why should he care at all about the poor? Stymied, she murmured, "Not very generous of them, was it? This clinic of yours is little more than a hovel, *señor*." Calen was working quietly behind the scenes to create a small hospital for the suffering *esmeraldos* at the river. The blueprints were ready and actual building would begin in about six months. No one knew of her planned project—yet. The Guild would oppose it because their arrangement would be that building such a hospital in the jungle would only bring more of the poor from cities to the mine region since free health care was available. There might be a legal battle as well, but with her billions, Calen felt the Guild would have to bow to her needs eventually. Besides, the hospital would be placed on her property and she had a right to do it. Right now, however, Calen wasn't breathing a word of the project to anyone, and especially not to Reno.

"Call me Reno," he reminded her gruffly. For whatever reason, he wanted to be on a first-name basis with the exotic and mysterious Calen Hernandez. She was the woman in his precog, yet she seemed not to know him. Or did she? There was a distracted look in her eyes. And he continued to feel a lot of turmoil around her. Why? She was old enough to be married, but she had leather gloves on so he couldn't see if she wore a wedding ring. Down here in South America, Reno knew, many women married early and had a lot of children very quickly. Calen was certainly old enough to be hitched. Who was the lucky bastard that shared his life with her? Probably a rich man.

Women and individuality did not go hand-in-hand in many parts of the world, Reno knew. Wives and mothers were often treated like second-class citizens at best, and at worst, abused property by the man of the house. Reno sensed Calen would never bow to any man. Maybe it was the proud set of her shoulders, that beautiful posture as she sat in the saddle, or the defiant tilt of her chin. She was treating him as an equal— nothing more and nothing less. That suited him, but also made her an enigma.

"Okay, Reno," Calen said, her tone teasing, "the reason I came over here this morning was to see if you needed help of any kind."

"This place is a sorry excuse for a clinic," he muttered. "They gave me a gurney that was obviously thrown out into the jungle for a couple of years, an old wooden table that wobbles every time you walk by it and a very old first-aid kit that's got half the supplies missing from it."

"Knowing the stinginess of the Guild, I figured that your dispensary would be little more than a shack." Calen critically studied the dilapidated wooden structure. "I was right."

"I can't help the *esmeraldos* like I want." Reno studied her. No longer smiling, the woman appeared to be deep in thought, and he could feel her retreating somewhere inside herself. He tried not to stare at the circular birthmark partly visible near the back of her slender neck. In his world, a birthmark symbolized something important, a map for the person's lifetime. He had one himself: the vesica piscis symbol of two circles overlapping. His mother had told him it was a sign that he had a mission to carry out in this world. She had never said what the mission was, but that Reno would discover it at the right time. Unconsciously, he rubbed the back of his neck where the birthmark was situated, beneath his shoulder-length black hair.

What did the Calen's birthmark mean to her? Did she even care? Reno wanted to ask, but bit back the question. His curiosity was eating at him. Deciding to become more personal, he spoke up. "Calen is an unusual name. It's not Spanish, is it? Does it have a meaning?" In Reno's world, names all meant something.

She smiled slightly. "My mother loved Mary Magdalene, so gave me her first name, Magdalena. My father, who loved the stories of Britain that he'd read as a child in the Catholic missionary school, wanted me to be called Calen." Shrugging, she added, "It's an English name meaning 'powerful in battle.'" Her father must have seen her becoming a Warrior for the Light, as did her mother; the name was subtle, yet a powerful reminder of her mission in life. Calen obliquely wondered if her parents had sensed that she would, one day, be El Espanto, fighting for the rights of the poor. Surely, they must have. But Calen didn't share that with anyone, much less Reno, who would be stalking her shortly.

"That's a mystical name, if you ask me," Reno commented. "I like it. I've never heard of anyone called Calen before. But it sure fits you." Indeed, she looked like a proud warrior. It didn't take much for Reno to imagine her like a modern day Joan of Arc.

Again, Calen gave him a slight smile. "You aren't the first to ask me about it, and I doubt you'll be the last. At least my parents didn't call me Apple or some other stupid name I'd be hung up on for the rest of my life."

Chuckling, Reno nodded his head. She had a good sense of humor. Buoyed by her friendliness, he asked, "What can you do to help me here with this pitiful excuse for a clinic?"

Calen sat up straighter in the saddle. "How about if I dismount and take stock of what you really need to help the *esmeraldos,* Reno? I've been after the Guild for two years to set up a clinic down here. I have some contacts in Quito and I know where we can probably get you medical supplies at cost. Who knows? They may donate them to you." Calen was going to see if this spy would keep his cover. She sensed he was genuinely upset by what he'd been given by the Guild. Could she believe that Reno was earnest about helping the poor?

If so, he was proving to be interesting. After all, his real job was to find and kill her.

"To tell you the truth, I can use all the help I can get, Calen." That strange happiness riffled through him again. Caught off guard by the unbidden emotion, Reno blinked once to assimilate it. As he watched Calen gracefully dismount, his throat constricted. Unexpected tears jammed his eyes.

Turning away, Reno gave himself an inner shake. He couldn't figure out his overwhelming emotional response toward this willful, alluring woman. What was it about her that was reviving his cold, dead heart and bringing it back to life? The precog he'd had? Oh, there was no question that, in it, Reno had felt an incredible desire toward her, as if they had been lovers across time. That was the feeling surrounding the vision. And that was why he'd felt torn up as she'd pleaded with him to come and help protect her.

Reno, for the first time in his life, felt vulnerable.

Chapter 5

"Not inspiring," Calen commented as she followed Reno into the clinic. Because she was a shape-shifter, she was supersensitized to anyone's aura, the energy that emanated from around the body. Reno's aura was a throbbing, vital and powerful force to be reckoned with. Calen continued to fight the instant attraction to him and was nervous at being so close to him, even though six feet separated them.

Reno turned and stopped by the dilapidated gurney. Just the two of them were there, and she felt the space between them shrink. Calen reminded herself that she was staring into the eyes of her killer. He was after her, although he didn't know that yet. And if she had anything to do with it, Manchahi never would. Still, the look in his unguarded eyes made Calen wish she could be open around him.

"I can't be so diplomatic. It sucks," Reno agreed grimly, running his hand across the deeply scratched aluminum top of the gurney. What was it about Calen that was drawing him like a magnet? He had to resist staring at her like the slavering jaguar he was beneath his skin. His heart pined away for her. His lower body ached like sin itself. He felt such an avalanche of sexual desire for her that it caught him completely off guard. And yet Calen had done nothing to invite this response from his traitorous body. She was no flirt. In fact, just the opposite: she was cool and detached.

When she'd turned, Reno had seen the rest of her birthmark. With her thick, black hair caught up in a ponytail, it was easy to see the vesica piscis symbol. Stunned, Reno realized that it was the same as his. He searched his memory and recalled his mother telling him there were others like him in the world, but that they were rare. And they were all Warriors for the Light, people who had incarnated into this lifetime for the good of the earth and all its inhabitants. Did Calen know this? Reno itched to ask her a hundred personal questions, but he would be out of line to do so. Better to keep conversation focused on the clinic for now.

Placing her hands on either side of the doorway, Calen nodded. "Senor Cruz was going to stock this place for you?"

Reno studied her as she stood with one booted foot resting over the other. "He said that what I saw was what I got." Drawn irresistibly to Calen, Reno couldn't understand why he was feeling such turmoil in his heart and gut. She was beautiful in an arresting kind of way. She wasn't model attractive, but the slight tilt of her pale green eyes, the way she reminded him of a graceful willow moving with the wind, all conspired to make Reno want to know a great deal more about her. She had to be married. Reno found that assumption disheartening. But then, why should he care? He was down here to find El Espanto. One shot, one kill…

"Pity," Calen murmured, looking around the hastily constructed shack. It was comprised of three rooms, the one they stood in being the largest. She forced herself to think despite the haze of yearning in her body. Why was she so attracted to him, of all people? He would murder her the first chance he got. What dark, wounded part of her was drawn to her killer? That upset her even more. Calen swallowed hard. "You need chairs for your patients, a gurney to examine them on, a desk, file drawers…many things. Not to mention medical supplies."

Frustrated, Reno shook his head. He noticed her assessing gaze. His instincts told him this was a woman who thought a lot but said little. "I'm going back to Cruz to ask for more," he stated.

"If I know Senor Cruz, he'll tell you to find what-

ever you need on your own. He's not given to generosity, from what I've seen in my two years here."

"You're just a fount of good news, you know that?"
One corner of his mouth lifted as Reno teased her. The
look on her face thawed momentarily as their gazes
met, melded and...something happened.... Reno
wasn't sure what. It was like a meeting, a molding,
setting off a flash of recognition so deep that it stunned
him for a second. He had no idea what the hell was
going on between them. Or why.

Calen felt it, too. For a pregnant moment silence
stretched. Fighting it, she forced herself to move
around the room and inspect it. "With Cruz there is
never any good news," she told Reno in a husky voice,
trembling inwardly. She could feel his stare, her skin
prickling wildly beneath it. The man was powerful in
unknown ways. His gaze burned a path from her head
down to her toes, lingering on the back of her neck,
where her birthmark was. His eyes then roved like
welcome sunlight across her breasts, over her hips and
then down her legs. Wanting to escape, Calen quickly
investigated each of the other rooms. One could easily
be an examination room, the other, a tiny office. She
forced herself to walk back to where Reno stood. He
continued to watch her from hooded eyes that seemed
to glow with some unearthly force or energy.

"You're a qualified paramedic?" Calen couldn't
help but notice the irony. Taking lives...saving lives.
Which was it with him?

"I am."

"Don't paramedics carry a medical pack with them? Where's yours? If you knew you were being hired to come down here and service a clinic, I'd have thought you would bring one along." Holding his darkening gaze, she waited for his answer.

"Because…" Reno dragged in a breath of air and realized he was tired of lying to her. "I was in prison until just lately. I kept up my paramedic skills in there. The bag I used to have is still at the brig. I was not allowed to take it with me." He smiled dryly. "Too many items in there to kill someone with, I suppose." Not that he would, but that was the reason the brig officials wouldn't allow him to take it on the airplane.

Reno carefully watched for a change in facial expression, but Calen didn't bat an eyelash. And this shocked him.

"What were you in for?" she demanded.

"I was thrown in the brig for planning revenge. A U.S. Army general murdered people I loved, and that's all you need to know. I didn't carry it off, but I wanted to. And if I can in the future, I will."

"Revenge?" she repeated, gazing directly into his eyes.

For some reason Reno felt compelled to elaborate. "The general stalked my wife, Ilona, while I was doing a second tour of sniper duty in Afghanistan. He plotted to get her to go to bed with him. When he went to our house, Ilona was there with our daughter, Sarah. The general raped Ilona. She put up a hell of a fight, but he murdered her." Touching his brow, tears burning in his eyes, Reno looked down at the floor and muttered, "And then he murdered my little girl, set fire to our house.... I heard about their deaths two weeks later. There was DNA evidence that he'd killed them, but it disappeared from the forensics lab. All kinds of evidence pointed at the general. When I went to him and accused him of their deaths, he had me thrown in the brig for twenty years for threatening a superior officer."

"I'm so sorry." Calen could see the anguish banked in his darkened eyes. His deep voice was raw and guttural. She understood what it was like to lose one's family. What she couldn't fathom was the loss of a child.

Reno's honesty threw her off balance. This was her hunter, she reminded herself sternly. The man who wanted to kill her.

Searching his hard face, Calen realized he'd suddenly closed up like a proverbial safe. Feeling nothing as she sent out invisible energy to read him, Calen released her grip on the riding crop, shifted it to her left hand and began to gently tap it against her boot.

Reno wondered why the hell he'd suddenly come clean with her. Normally, he never spoke of his wounds, his losses. There was something about her that made him open up and he found himself not only wanting to spill his heart and guts to her, but to be held by her. Calen was strong. He sensed it with his jaguar knowing. He saw it in the firmness of her tall, proud body. And he saw it in the quiet strength in her pale green eyes, now bright with unshed tears.

Tears? Suddenly, Reno realized they were tears for the loss of his wife and child.

Deeply touched, he found tears stinging the backs of his own eyes—for the second time today. It was an unexpected reaction, completely unlike him. He *never* cried. Had never wept over the loss of his wife and child, his mother, his father. Instead, he'd funneled his grief into revenge against the general who had taken their lives. With Calen's calm, anchoring strength, however, Reno felt as if he were loosening inside, unraveling like a ball of yarn. What magic did this woman possess over him? Blinking his eyes to shove the tears away, Reno responded gruffly, "Yeah, it's a real shame. But my revenge keeps me going. I'll get that son of a bitch someday." And he would.

Calen heard the steel quality in his tone. She was seeing the hunter once more. Eager to get away from such a morbid topic, she said, "I fly into Quito once a week. I can find you a paramedic bag there. I'll ask Godfredo Santos, my manager, to make some phone calls to medical service companies in the capital. He will ask them to donate items such as dressings, tape, gauze—that sort of thing—to your efforts here. I have a friend who owns a pharmacy in Quito. I'll make a call to her and ask for the type of drugs you'll need to keep on hand. This is the jungle, so medications are a little different than perhaps you're used to."

Nodding, Reno studied her. She was talking out loud, not necessarily to him, her eyes fixed on the floor in front of her. "That sounds good. Are you sure Senor Cruz wouldn't help foot this bill?"

Giving him a cutting glance, Calen moved back toward the door. "You'll find out soon enough that the man is coldhearted toward those who suffer around here." She gestured toward the slope of the mountain, where hundreds labored in the hot, morning sun.

"I think I've already come to that conclusion," Reno said. The woman seemed to know a great deal about medicine. A nurse by training? Maybe a doctor? The questions begged to be asked, but now was not the time.

Reno's face had softened a great deal as she studied him. No longer was it hard and closed. The gentle look in his eyes touched her as nothing else had. Gulping, Calen realized the man beneath the armored plating was terribly human—and vulnerable. Her heart beat once to underscore that fact. Reno was a sniper. He killed on orders, Calen reminded herself grimly. Cruz had paid him a lot of money, and Reno *wanted* to kill her. She hated taking a life, and doing so would burn in her conscience for as long as she lived. Yet he was different. He killed for a living.

"All help is appreciated," Reno said, deciding there was nothing he could dislike about Calen. For whatever reason, he kept sensing cat energy around her. In South America, the biggest cat predator was the jaguar. In fact, she had the look of a jaguar, with those huge, tilted green eyes that shone with life and curiosity. He took a ragged breath, trying to control his responding body.

"What do you need by way of medical supplies?" she asked.

After the list was made, Calen remained at the door. A part of her wanted to be done with this man. Another part wanted to stay. She wanted to know her killer, to understand how Reno Manchahi thought. How he saw the world. The more she could get inside his head, the better her chances of staying alive. He'd been in prison. He'd had his family murdered. And he'd plotted to kill an American general.

Calen wanted to call him a murderer, but the idea didn't gel within her. She had so many psychic impressions about Reno that she couldn't conveniently peg him. He had allowed that hard mask to dissolve in front of her, and he'd told her the truth about his past. He was that much more dangerous to her because she couldn't label him or fit him neatly into a convenient category.

Soon enough, Manchahi would be stalking her nightly. And that would make her forays across the mountain to protect the *esmeraldos* even more perilous than before. No, he was a man to watch, understand and avoid.

Few men had ever drawn her, and when they had, Calen could see through them, evade and walk away before she got entangled in a relationship. But not now. Not with this male, who dominated the room with his height and athletic muscularity. Indeed, Reno seemed like a mighty warrior, with his rugged good looks, his bulk and the power that swirled like a thunderstorm around him.

"I'll get those supplies for you within a week," Calen promised him.

"You're a guardian angel in disguise, Calen. Thank you," he said softly.

Bitterly, Calen rubbed her brow and turned to look out toward the mountain slope. "I'm no one's guardian." She hadn't counted on his warmth and grateful attitude.

"Don't take that image away from me, okay? You *are* a guardian angel. I saw you with the kids earlier. You help the poor. If that isn't being a guardian, I don't know what is."

She couldn't stop herself from turning toward him again. Was this how he looked when he peered intently through a rifle scope at his target? "I'm a very busy person. Every day I have a lot to do to run my business. So taking time out of a very heavy schedule like this, well, that is why I hesitated. But I'll fly to Quito later this week and pick up medical supplies after I meet with my business team. "

"You're a pilot, too?"

"I am."

"What kind of business do you run?" Reno found himself helplessly fascinated with her. Calen wasn't an obsequious woman, that was for damn sure.

"Oil."

"Oh. Your husband runs the company?"

Giving him a tight smile, Calen leveled her gaze on

him. "I'm not married. I run my own business. What's the matter? Don't you think a woman can run a billion-dollar empire?" Her voice was cool.

Reno actually seemed pleased with her reaction. His eyes lost that hunterlike quality. They widened and became almost… What? Warm? Calen could swear she saw happiness in them. No, she had to be making it up.

"I see." Reno glanced at her left, gloved hand, then focused again on her face. She gave him a lethal smile, her eyes suddenly cold and hard. Yeah, okay, he had it coming. He shouldn't have put his foot in his mouth like that with Calen. Of course she'd take his comment as an insult. "Where I come from, the women of my nation, the Apache, were warriors right alongside their men. So I have plenty of respect for any woman who wants to run an oil empire. I'm all for it."

"Apache?" Calen found herself hungry for any information on Reno. "Are you related to Geronimo?"

Reno gave a thin smile. "No, but on my mother's side, Lozen, a woman Apache warrior, rode with him. Lozen was one of my relatives."

"So," Calen murmured, "you come from a long line of women warriors?"

"Yes, I do. And I'm proud of it. So was my mother." Reno's voice softened a little. "My mother was full-blood Apache, a medicine woman. I grew up on a reservation in Arizona. She taught me of our proud lineage, that women are far stronger and, more than likely, smarter than any man." Reno held up his palm.

"Lozen had a special talent, and that was another reason Geronimo wanted her with him as the U.S. Army chased him all over the Southwest and Mexico, trying to capture his band. Lozen would hold up her hands like this—" he raised both hands, palms out "—and she would close her eyes and slowly turn in a circle. When her palms grew hot, she knew that was the direction the soldiers were coming from. She would tell Geronimo, and he would avoid capture because of it. Lozen was never wrong. She had an incredible gift and used it to keep her people free."

"She was clairvoyant," Calen concluded. "Gifts like that come from spirit."

Reno nodded. "Yes, that's what we believe, too." He didn't add that Lozen was a shape-shifter, like the rest of the family. He was sure Calen wasn't capable of accepting that tidbit of family heritage. And yet, Reno decided to risk it all. "I see you have a special birthmark on the back of your neck. Do you know anything about it? What it means?"

A warning flashed through Calen. Unconsciously, she rubbed her neck. How much should she tell this man who was studying her so intently? "The *esmeraldos* say that it is the mark of the Warriors for the Light. They call it the vesica piscis symbol. My parents bore the same birthmark in the same place." Calen wasn't about to tell him she was a jaguar shape-shifter.

"I was wondering if it meant anything. The Apaches put great stock in birthmarks as a symbol."

He was getting too close to her for comfort. "My mother told me it meant I had a mission on earth to help bring peace to the world. That's all I know." That wasn't a lie; it was just a tiny part of the rest of the truth.

"Seems like you do that now," Reno said, looking out the door at the *esmeraldos* working on the mountain. "You're doing what you can to help the starving here."

"I do what I can, Reno." Calen lifted her hand in farewell. "I've got to get going. I'll be back in touch with you in less than a week."

"Thanks for your help, Calen. I know the people who come will be grateful."

Calen was damned if Reno was going to find out anything else about her. Giving the enemy information was a stupid and dangerous thing to do. Tonight, she had to ride once more. And she knew this hunter would be out there looking for her…to kill her.

Throat closing with fear, her heart pounding, she saw Reno give her a slight, heartwarming smile. The gratitude burning in his eyes nearly undid her. He wouldn't be looking at her like that tonight….

Chapter 6

It was time. Calen knelt on a small gold pillow in an alcove of the cave, where Godfredo was saddling her black Arabian. Her heart began pounding slowly, something it always did shortly before her ride into the darkness to help save lives on the mountain. Several lit candles on her small mahogany altar flickered. On the circular dais were two other objects.

Settling on her knees, and already wearing her black spandex bodysuit, Calen picked up a small hand-carved jaguar. Her father, Galvez, had fashioned this fetish for her while her mother still carried her in her womb. And when Calen was five years old, Gina had sat her down one day and given her the wooden carving. Calen could still remember every word:

Daughter, you are a Warrior for the Light. Your papa was led to a mahogany tree and told to take a small branch. From that branch he was guided to carve this jaguar for you. I have painted it yellow with black spots. It is to remind you of the heritage that you carry in your blood, as a shape-shifter who works with this special guide. Take this fetish. Never be without it. Carry it in your left pocket. It will protect you....

No matter how many times Calen picked up the small fetish, which was two inches long and about an inch high, her fingertips tingled wildly. Placing a kiss upon it now, she held it against her heart. Her lips moved as she whispered, "Great Mother Goddess of all, I pray you keep us safe tonight as we try to help the *esmeraldos*, my people. I ask for your cloak of protection to hide within. I ask that your boundless courage infuse me in my moments of terror when I wonder if I can do this at all. I pray that you guide me to those who need help this night. This, I ask in your name...."

Calen placed the fetish in a small leather pouch and slipped it into her pocket. The other article on the dais was a dark leather thong with the claw of a jaguar suspended from it. This, her mother had given her at age six. She had once again sat her down and told her its story:

Darling girl of mine, this is the claw of a female jaguar. She was dying of old age in the forest near the river. I heard her call me by name. I kept following the bank of the Esmeralda River and there, on some moss near the water, she waited for me. When I approached her, she told me that when she died, I was to take the first claw on her right front paw and give it to you. At the time this happened, I did not know I was pregnant with you.

I stayed with this beautiful old jaguar until she closed her eyes, and a last breath shuddered out of her spotted body. Then I took the claw from her paw. I said a prayer for her spirit and thanked her for this gift. It was only later, when I discovered I was carrying you, that I realized the old jaguar knew.

Take this claw. Always wear it in recognition that you are a proud priestess of the Inca traditions. The Quero blood runs strongly through you. Even though you were born in Ecuador, your blood comes from the royal lineage of the Incas of Peru. Never forget this. For the Incas considered the jaguar the most powerful animal spirit on the face of Mother Earth, and it is considered the mightiest Warrior for the Light. Always wear this necklace. If you are in trouble or danger, call upon it and you will be protected.

Calen brought the curved claw to her lips. She kissed it lightly, then pressed it against her heart. It was this second gift that had allowed her to enter the world as a shape-shifter. Since her parents taught her how to move from human to jaguar form and back again, she'd had many years of practice, and her dual lives were seamless now.

After slipping the necklace over her head, Calen lit two more white candles. Their light flickered in the small alcove of basalt rock. Feeling an incredible calm come over her, Calen knew that some kind of invisible magic was at work. It always amazed her that, when she wore these articles from the jaguar, she became confident, her fear dissolving.

Calen rose and dusted off her knees. The sense of centeredness and quiet resolve bestowed by the jaguar spirit always soothed her pounding heart.

Turning, she saw that Godfredo had Storm saddled. The black mare pawed restlessly, her front hoof digging into the hard-packed clay floor where she was tied. As Calen moved toward the horse, she noticed the saddlebags behind the cantle. One contained grenades, the other, ten clips to put into her 9 mm pistol, just in case. The quilted Kevlar fabric was in place around the Arabian's broad, deep chest. It hung over her hind quarters to just above her hocks. Storm was as protected from bullets as she could be. In the past, the mare had been hit three times, but the Kevlar had saved her life. Calen had never been wounded. She understood the horse was a helluva lot bigger target, and the foreign mercs would rather shoot her mount than her. That way, they could get to Calen a lot faster, to capture or kill her.

Calen slid her fingers along the animal's sleek, arched neck. Her manager had brushed the Arabian until she shone like polished ebony. Storm's long, thick mane was like fine silk. Moving her fingers through the clean stands, Calen looked up to see Godfredo standing by, his hand on the black leather bridle.

"Everything in place?" she asked, unsnapping the ties and letting them fall against the thick teak posts.

"Yes." Godfredo handed Calen her Kevlar vest. "Storm is frisky tonight. She must feel what is coming—a busy time."

Smiling tensely, Calen took the vest and put it on. She mounted her restive steed. "I hope you're wrong about a busy night. Manchahi is out there. I can feel him. And he's hunting me." There was a whisper of fear in her voice.

Godfredo nodded. "Be *very* careful, Dama Calen."

When Calen pressed her heels to Storm's sides, the Arabian snorted and leaped toward the tunnel. Time to get on with the business of saving lives.

Calen's entire being shifted as she rode the trotting mare toward the winding lava tube, a quarter mile in length. There, she dismounted and walked the animal through it. As they emerged into the forest, Calen remounted. Storm remained at a walk. The brush was thick here. There were three different paths out of the dense vegetation that kept the opening away from prying eyes. Calen took a different one every night. Changing her habits was important. Never take the same path twice. Go against the mercs' expectations. Calen stopped and reset the alarm after leaving the tunnel.

Her face grew damp beneath the fabric mask. A slight trickle of perspiration started at her hairline and rolled down her jaw. Guiding Storm with only her knees and calves, she rode silently through the jungle, the path barely visible. Fortunately for them, when rain came, it erased their tracks. And rain happened almost nightly, with thunderstorms moving throughout the area. Wiping her jaw with her gloved hand, Calen looked up as they left thick brush. When she sat back in the saddle, Storm halted abruptly. Calen had schooled her many years earlier in the art of dressage. The Arabian was never used on the dressage circuit, even though she was one of the best in South America. No, Storm's talents and skills were used to save lives, not earn medals—quiet heroism that would never be known by anyone save for Calen and the Santos family.

Storm splashed across the shallow river and leaped up the bank to the other side. As Calen scanned the trail in front of them, she felt her eyes adjusting, the night goggles hanging around her neck to be used later. It always happened this way. At first, the jungle seemed unfathomably dark. But then Calen would feel a tingling where the jaguar claw lay between her breasts. In a matter of seconds, that curious feeling would move quickly upward and reach her eyes. This was when Calen would see the jungle revealed. It was a remarkable and magical process, thanks to her shape-shifting talent. Her perception improved to the point where she could see the jungle as if standing in it on a cloudy day. She could only attribute her amazing ability to the spirit of the jaguar coming over her physical body.

She pressed her right knee against Storm, and the horse instantly turned to the left. With a slight squeeze of Calen's calves against the barrel, the mare broke into a slow, graceful canter. This trail would lead to another. Tonight, Calen felt strongly she should utilize the third trail.

The jungle was a thick wall on either side as they went, Storm snorting with each rhythmic stride. It was about one mile to the main track around the bottom of the mountain. The barbed wire fence was on one side of that path, with No Trespassing signs hung every hundred feet.

Reaching the main trail, Calen turned to the right, toward the fence. Dismounting, she quickly snipped through the wire with a pair of cutters. She put the handy tool back into her saddlebag, mounted and rode through the broken fence line. They were now on mine property. And she knew three to four different merc units were patrolling it right now on horseback.

Calen remembered Reno's story about Lozen, his relative who could hold up her hands and feel the enemy cavalry's location. Calen grinned tightly as she steered Storm up the winding trail through the trees and brush on the lower slopes. If only she had that psychic ability, she'd be able to find where the mercs were instead of having to rely on her mare's alertness. A horse could hear sounds a mile away, and Calen relied heavily on Storm's abilities to hear or smell other horses in the vicinity. If she were in jaguar form, she, too, could hear faraway sounds, but not in human form.

The wind whipped around them. The trail was steep and rocky. Storm grunted and leaped again and again over exposed roots that would trip her if she didn't spot them first. The vegetation was not like a wall, but more scattered. Looking up, Calen could see the ghostlike blanket of humid clouds just below the summit of the ten-thousand-foot mountain.

Reno Manchahi was out here. Snipers would hide, unmoving, and watch for their quarry until just the right moment, then squeeze off one killing shot. Calen had done her homework on snipers. Manchahi was a huge danger to her. Unlike the careless guards, a sniper remained concealed. Could Storm pick up his presence soon enough? She wasn't sure. If they were downwind of him, then yes, it was possible. But if the Apache were laying out here somewhere near a tree or bush, covered with leaves and sticks, and upwind, they would not see him.

Her heart pounded in her chest as they rose higher and higher on the slope. They were now about four thousand feet above their starting point. The *esmeraldos* often used this area because it was on the north side of the quiet volcano. Moonlight never bathed this portion so the darkness cloaked them as they dug tunnels.

Running her fingers along her mare's sweaty neck, Calen knew the Arabian was working hard. She was in peak condition, with special shoes and a special feeding program to keep her up to the task two to three nights a week. To give her mare a well-deserved rest, Calen would shape-shift into her jaguar form another two nights. During the dry season, which they were in, she rode much more often. In the wet season, they could rest, because rain and muddy conditions stopped many *esmeraldos* from trying to dig. The tunnels would just get saturated and cave in on them. Many times, she'd saved lives during such tragedies. The drive to find one emerald to feed their family and get them out of this starvation cycle put the *esmeraldos* in constant jeopardy.

Without a word, she shifted her weight, and the mare skidded to a halt. Calen narrowed her eyes. This was the area where *esmeraldos* usually came. She watched Storm's small, fine ears flick back and forth. They were both listening for whispered voices.

There! Calen twisted in the saddle. The mountain had many swales and knolls, sweeping grades covered in trees and brush. The mare's ears were pinned back. She heard the noise, too.

Guards or *esmeraldos?*

Calen wasn't sure as they trotted silently across the slope. Standing in the saddle and trying to see over the top of the rise, she felt her heart start to pound again.

And then she smelled cigarette smoke. Guards!

Instantly, she halted Storm. The mare sensed the danger, too, and stood like a statue. Calen quickly lifted the rifle from her back, put a dart into the chamber and held it in her hands. The smoke was strong. Where was it coming from? Turning, she lifted her head and sniffed several times. No, not the north. The breeze, what little there was, came from below. Eyes narrowing, Calen leaned forward to try and see between the trees.

A movement!

Storm's ears had pricked up. The mare had located another horse, Calen was sure.

She spotted a husky merc on horseback as he rode from behind a small tree and out into the open. She saw the red glow of the tip of the cigarette in his mouth. His partner, a smaller man, rode behind him. Calen picked up the reins in her left hand, resting the butt of the rifle on her right thigh. Storm moved forward at a brisk walk. The horse was incredibly quiet as they approached the guards from above. Using the brush to hide behind, Calen wove closer and closer to their unsuspecting quarry. She and Storm now stood twenty feet above them on a protruding shelf of rock. The sentries were completely unaware of their presence.

Dropping the reins, Calen quickly shouldered the rifle. She just wanted to disable the men. The darts she would fire would render them unconscious almost immediately. Storm stood very still.

Her sweaty cheek against the stock of the rifle, Calen steadied her breathing. She brushed the trigger with her finger, blinked several times as perspiration ran freely down her face inside the mask. Mouth compressing, she got the first guard in her rifle sight, and fired. The rifle had a muzzle suppressor on it; no one would ever see the flash or hear the explosion.

She heard the guard yelp in surprise as the dart hit

him in the left shoulder. Calen lowered the rifle and, with shaking fingers, pushed the second dart into the breech. Quickly, she hefted the weapon, the second guard now in her sights. He moved toward his partner, confused. *Squeeze, don't jerk....* She brushed the trigger again with her index finger. The stock jolted her shoulder; the dart was fired! It hit the second sentry in the thigh. Calen knew they wore Kevlar vests. She had to know where to shoot so the dart wouldn't bounce harmlessly off the armor.

The first guard groaned, flailed and fell from his horse. The animal instantly took off at a frenzied gallop down the mountain. The second man cursed loudly and jerked the dart out of his thigh, but it was too late. Calen watched as he pitched over in a nosedive from his own horse, landing headfirst, unconscious, on the ground.

Without hesitation, Calen put her heels to Storm, and they raced off the ledge and down the slope. When they reached their destination, they skidded to a halt. Calen dismounted, her pistol drawn as she approached the unmoving guards. The larger of the two still had the dart sticking into his thick shoulder. Calen pushed him onto his back with the toe of her boot. Leaning down, she divested him of the pistol at his side and took the rifle he carried. She went through the same routine with the second sentry.

Once she'd removed their weapons, she pulled off the guards' combat boots so that they'd have to walk barefoot for miles back to their base camp. She remembered to grab their radios, too, so they'd be out of communication and unable to call for help. After stuffing the boots in her saddlebags, she slung the rifles on her left arm.

Storm stood still, her ears flicking. Smiling beneath the mask, Calen whispered into her radio headset to Godfredo, "Two down and unconscious. I'm coming home...."

With the three rifles, Calen remounted. She quickly replaced her own weapon on her back, then spun the Arabian around, grasping the two AK-47s as they galloped down the slope to the trail. The wind pounded against them as the mare picked up speed, moving a lot faster than she had on the way up.

As they careened onto the main path around the mountain, Calen decided to head home on the fourth trail. Leaping over several roots, the Arabian grunted, then sped down the narrow corridor. Leaves and branches slapped against Calen as she clung with her thighs and calves. She kept the AK-47s in front of her. Any other way, they'd be ripped off her arm by a protruding limb and she'd be knocked to the ground.

And then, in a split second, Calen felt something like a huge fist punch her in the center of her chest. Torn out of the saddle, the rifles spinning wildly off to the side, she was tumbling, tumbling...and then began to shift and change. Arms and legs shortening, Calen felt the power of the jaguar come over her as never before. As she fell to the muddy earth, she landed on all four feet. Breathing harshly, her rib cage flaring out and sinking inward like huge bellows, Calen looked down at her jaguar form. She saw her thick gold, spotted paws, her claws sunk deep into the mud.

What had just happened? There was an ache in the center of her chest. The area burned deeply. Then, Calen smelled *him*. She recognized Manchahi's male odor. Lifting her nose, she scented the humid air. Yes. It was him. Her killer. Calen's mind spun, trying to remain detached from her emotions. She had been shot—by Reno. One powerful shot to the chest. To her heart. The bullet had struck her Kevlar vest and knocked her off her horse.

She heard a man coming; her acute hearing picked up his soft footfalls heading in her direction. Reno thought he'd killed her. Not this time!

Calen wheeled around silently and stretched her long, fluid body into a ground-eating gallop. As a jaguar, she could run at speeds up to twenty-five miles an hour and easily outdistance her human assailant. He would find nothing, just horse and jaguar tracks in the mud. Almost smiling, Calen moved like a whisper among the leaves and ferns off the trail. She headed directly for the lava tube, which was a good five miles away. How she savored the power of her jaguar form, the deep breaths, the silence of her cat feet meeting and molding with the soft floor of the jungle.

Tonight, Manchahi had tracked and found her. This

told her how skilled he was at his job. But all he would find were the AK-47s that belonged to the guards, nothing more.

Within thirty minutes, Calen was traversing the lava tube. She halted there, took a deep breath and willed herself back into human form. The sensation was always uncomfortable for her, as if the jaguar were peeling itself off her human body, much like removing a skintight latex glove. For fifteen seconds, the time it took to make the change, she was vulnerable. Dizziness assailed her as the process began.

Calen opened her eyes and looked down in the dim light. She saw her muddy hands, not her jaguar paws. Quickly, she touched her Kevlar vest. The bullet had dug a crater right over her heart. Fear oozed through her. Reno was good, all right. If she hadn't been wearing the vest, she'd be dead. Shaking off the slight dizziness, Calen forced herself to move.

Pale and worried, Godfredo met her as she exited the tunnel. "What happened out there, Dama? I couldn't get you on the radio. I heard a shot! Storm came running back here to the cave without you. Are you all right?"

She nodded. "Y-yes, I'm okay. That *norte americano* sniper shot me in the chest." She relayed the rest of the story as she limped up the slope to the small dressing room near the stall. Storm was already there, brushed, cleaned up and eating her well-deserved flake of hay.

The first thing Calen wanted to do was get rid of the

damn mask. She jerked off the hood. Fresh air! "Oh, this always feels so good," she whispered, leaning back, her eyes closed as she took in several deep, welcome breaths. She quickly shimmied out of all her gear. After divesting herself of the dark garments behind an opaque fabric screen, Calen studied her chest. The area between her breasts was deeply bruised, swollen and throbbing. She got into a pink cotton T-shirt and jeans, sat down on the stool and pulled off the knee-high boots, trading them for liberating sandals. The last thing Calen did was remove the jaguar fetish and necklace, and place them back on her altar. Tonight, they had saved her life.

So now she had another party hunting her. And of all of them, Reno Manchahi was the deadliest. A shaky breath left her lungs. Fear etched her like a knife. She pressed her hand against her pounding heart, closed her eyes and hung her head. Her parents had said that at age twenty-eight, her life would change forever. Her birthday was less than a week away. Calen wondered if it would bring her death.

Worse, even though Reno had nearly killed her, Calen could feel no rage over the assault. Remembering his cinnamon eyes, his look of loss, vulnerability and loneliness, she could not be angry. After what happened tonight, how could she still be so magnetically drawn to her killer?

Chapter 7

It was time to check in on Reno Manchahi. Calen dismounted from her gelding, Star, and tied him up to a post on the porch of the clinic. She was afraid, and took a deep, cleansing breath to control the sharp sensations in her gut. It was early, 7:00 a.m., and already there was a line of mothers with children patiently waiting to receive medical help. Two weeks had passed since the undercover sniper had shot her. It had taken this long for her to work up the courage to face him. Calen had postponed her birthday party, as well. Until she could resolve the present situation, she didn't feel like celebrating anything.

So far, Calen's eyes and ears among the *esmeraldos*

had reported that, since receiving the promised medical supplies, Reno worked from 6:00 a.m. to as late as 9:00 p.m. every day.

She couldn't avoid him forever. If she didn't show up, he might get suspicious. Rubbing the area between her breasts, where the bruise still lingered, Calen tried to quell her mounting anxiety.

Because of her wound, she had not ridden out since that fateful night. But on four different occasions, she shape-shifted into a jaguar to continue her work on the mountain slopes of the mining property. While Reno was stalking her, she'd been safe at home in human form in her villa. The break had been welcome, but it didn't stop the foreign guards from finding and killing trespassing *esmeraldos,* and as a jaguar, she continued to save lives. Calen hadn't slept well since being hit. Wrestling with cowardice and guilt that others were being harmed because she hid in her villa, she didn't think much of herself of late.

As she mounted the porch, Calen removed her leather gloves and called a warm greeting to a number of the poorly dressed women. She knew many of them by name. Her heart ached for them, for the sick, cranky babies in their arms, the small children clinging to their mothers' worn cotton skirts.

First things first. She distributed the hard candy she always carried with her to those waiting in line. Calen had kind words for all of them. She saw the depression in the women's eyes turn to hope as she touched each on the shoulder and whispered words of greeting. In the past, some women had reported that Calen's touch healed them. They whispered that she had the magic of a jaguar healer, someone who could restore an ailing person to health. The children, who knew her well, waited with outstretched hands and smiles.

As she gave a wrapped candy to each, it took everything Calen had not to feel the rage burning deep down inside her. If fate had been different, she would be here herself, standing in line with a sick child of her own. But fate had pulled her out of this misery and given her a second chance.

Straightening up after she gave away the last bit of candy, Calen quickly walked up onto the porch. The clinic was in better shape now, with new plywood, and painted. It was obvious Reno had been working hard. Jose Santiago, a friend of Calen's, lived close to the new clinic. Phelan Santiago, the patriarch of the family, and considered a saint by the *esmeraldos,* had left to explore the southern end of the river and never returned. No body was ever found. Many thought Phelan had been killed by the local jaguars, but no one could prove anything. He simply disappeared from their lives, as many did who lived in the wilds of this mysterious jungle. His grandson Jose was growing into the old man's shoes.

According to Godfredo, Jose had come over every day to help Reno rebuild the clinic. The man gave an hour of his precious time, away from sluicing for emeralds in the river, to help make the clinic a reality. The Santiago family had been one of the first to come here after the Santa Maria vein had been discovered. And they were a bulwark in the poor community, greatly respected and loved by all.

Calen eased between the doorjamb and a mother with two young children. As she entered the clinic, her gaze went to the center of the room, where Reno had a small baby lying on the gurney, now fixed, the anxious mother standing nearby. He blew on the stethoscope before placing the metal on the infant's naked chest.

If Reno was aware of her entrance, he didn't show it. Calen stood quietly and watched. Her senses were open, like radar, and she was absorbing every bit of energy within the room and processing it.

Reno was dressed in a bright red polo shirt that showed off his masculine physique. Oh, Calen didn't fool herself; as a woman, she was absolutely drawn to this man. What was wrong with that picture? Giving herself an internal shake, she forced herself to take in the scene with the most objective eye possible. As big as he was—and he was a giant, towering over the shorter, pathetically thin *esmeraldos*—he was incredibly gentle with the squalling infant.

She saw the intensity of his features as he closed his eyes to listen to the heartbeat of the infant. The mother, barely out of her teens, looked on, distraught. Calen could see the infant's ribs. The diagnosis was going to be chronic diarrhea, for sure. Her heart bleeding for the crying infant, Calen approached, giving the mother a gentle smile.

When Reno opened his eyes, he blinked. Calen Hernandez, dressed in her usual riding outfit, stood there looking back at him. Her black hair was loose this time, tousled and soft around her glorious golden features. But it was those mesmerizing, light green eyes of hers that pulled his heart out of the deep freeze. He could feel it thudding with…what? Reno didn't have time to examine his feelings at the moment.

"Hello," he managed to say, pulling the stethoscope out of his ears and draping it around his neck.

"Hi. Looks like you have a baby with a severe case of diarrhea."

"Yeah, the kid needs an IV of Ringer's lactate." Grimacing, Reno shook his head. "I have no IVs."

"You have to tell the mother to boil the water she gives her baby," Calen told him in English. "One of the awful things we constantly work against here is the filthy water. New people keep coming from the cities, pouring into this area. The *esmeraldos* have been instructed to boil the water they get out of the river before they drink it or use it to cook with. Otherwise, their children can die of diarrhea and loss of fluids."

"This is my fortieth case in a week. I hear you," Reno murmured, gently turning the baby onto his tummy and running his hands lightly across his prominent rib cage. He pinched a tiny bit of skin on the infant's back. It didn't return to normal when he released it. "He's really dehydrated," Reno said worriedly.

"Those baby bottles we bought?" Calen said. "Where did you put them?"

"In the back room. Why?"

She smiled. "Tricks of the trade. Let me find them and bring them out here." Calen went quickly to the back room, but found the door locked. She felt Reno approach her from behind, his energy powerful and oddly comforting to her. Her fear miraculously and inexplicably dissolved. It was a shocking turn of events. How could her killer calm her? Take away her fear? Gulping, Calen turned and held out her hand.

"If I don't keep the supplies under lock and key, folks will steal everything we got from Quito," Reno murmured. His fingers tingled as he placed the key in her open palm. He was taken with how long and delicate Calen's fingers were. Hands of a healer, his mother would say.

"I know." She turned and quickly unlocked the door. Like a drug she craved, she wanted Reno close to her, holding her and… She shook herself, squelching the insane wish. To her relief, Reno went back out to the gurney, where his little patient was still pitifully crying. His mother tried to soothe him, to no avail.

Having found the box she wanted, Calen carried it to the exam room. Placing it on one end of the gurney, next to Reno, she opened the box, pulled out two bottles and a set of nipples and handed them to the mother.

"You must tell her to boil enough water to fill these two bottles. When she finishes feeding one to the infant, she has another on standby."

Reno dutifully related that to the mother who was now holding her infant in her arms. She nodded eagerly.

"Senor Reno, I have no pot with which to boil water. What am I to do?" she cried softly, giving her baby a stricken look. "I already lost my little girl a month ago to diarrhea. We just came here. We are poor…."

Reno felt frustration as never before. Switching to English again, he looked down at Calen, who looked hauntingly tortured by the woman's plea. "What can I do? Do you have any ideas?" He was more than glad to see Calen, for many reasons. He had found out in the two weeks he'd been here that Calen Hernandez was one of the few people who got things done when she said she would. Further, her word was her bond, unlike the Guild's empty promises.

"I'll call and have Godfredo drive up here. I have several boxes of cooking pots at the villa that just arrived yesterday to be distributed to the camp. Tell her to come back for one later this afternoon. And tell her that if she knows any other mother in the camp who doesn't have a pot, to come and get one, too. I'll send all I can, but we won't have enough for everyone."

"That's better than nothing," Reno said, feeling admiration for Calen. She was practical, another plus in her favor. He told the young mother the good news. Her eyes filled with tears and gleamed with sudden hope.

She bowed her head and kissed the back of Reno's hand, thanking him over and over again.

"Don't thank me," Reno told her, embarrassed by her actions. "Dama Calen is doing this for you. Thank her."

Calen smiled and went around the gurney and gently hugged the thin woman. It hurt her to see the woman had sores all over her arms, a sign of chronic malnutrition. "Reno, do you have any bottled water around here?"

"Uh, yes." He realized what Calen wanted to do. It was a brilliant idea! He went to the corner where he kept plastic bottles of water. Picking up two, he grinned at her. "You're a pretty savvy woman, you know that?"

She tried not to allow the warmth in Reno's eyes, the admiration in his tone to touch her. But it did. Profoundly. Calen felt like a thirsty plant without water, and he was like life-giving drops, reviving her. "We'll try to get more boxes of bottled water up here for you, now that I know you need them," she murmured.

Nodding, Reno found a plastic bag and put the two bottles of water and the two glass baby bottles in it. He handed it to the mother, who was crying again—this time in relief and joy over Calen's ingenuity and generosity.

"Thanks," Reno told her in a conspiratorial tone after the woman had left. "The people here love you, you know that? They call you a saint. I can see why. You're just about all that stands between them and starving to death or dying of dysentery."

Calen tried to ignore his praise. Just being near Reno made her heart beat with a joy she'd never felt in her life. Even more confused by how her body ached for him, she managed to answer in an off-key tone, "I do what I can."

As he held his hand out to help his next patient, an elderly woman, step up on the overturned wooden crate that served as a stool, so that she could ease up onto the gurney, he said, "I tried to tell Cruz we needed IVs. We got into a helluva fight about it."

"Yes, I heard about that last week."

"Oh?" Reno glanced at her. "Word travels fast around here, doesn't it? We might not have many phones in this jungle, but word of mouth works better than Ma Bell." He chuckled.

"Nothing is secret." That was a lie, but he didn't need to know that. She should leave, but something coaxed Calen to stay. Why? "But don't let Cruz get to you. You're a savior to the *esmeraldos*. They love you. I've heard nothing but praise from them for the help you've given them these past couple of weeks."

Except for the elderly patient, they were alone. The other waiting women stood stoically outside the door. His breath stole away at the gentle warmth of Calen's soft smile. She was attractive in a mysterious way—in Reno's view, exquisitely beautiful. His hands itched to caress her mussed black hair, which shone with reddish highlights. He'd had more than a few torrid dreams about kissing this enigmatic and generous Ecuadorian woman.

His brow furrowed. "I'm no damn savior, that's for sure." Not with forty-two men dead under his gun sights. "If they really knew me, they wouldn't come near me." Especially the part about being a jaguar shape-shifter. That would scare the hell out of them and they'd never come back for treatment.

Buffeted by the energy and emotion with which he bit out those words, Calen said, "The greatest saints were at one time the greatest of sinners." The hard planes of his face seemed to ease at her whispered words.

"I'm too much of a sinner to ever be thought a saint in the same breath," Reno countered. An unexpected tenderness and apparent understanding flared in Calen's large, liquid eyes. Eyes a man could lose himself in, body and soul, and come out healed and whole. Calen possessed such a mysterious strength. A woman's strength that flowed out to him like the gently lapping ocean on a peaceful night.

"Have coffee with me tonight? After I close the clinic?" The words flew out of Reno's mouth before he could stop them. Truth was, he wanted time alone with this alluring woman with a heart of gold and the soul of a saint. She was like nurturing, life-giving sun to Reno, bringing him back to life in ways he'd never thought possible. And yet, despite the chemistry, the connection, he steeled himself to be rejected.

She drew the fine leather gloves from her belt, and her full mouth softened. "What time?"

"Nine?"

"All right. I'll be here. Want me to bring anything?

A good cup of hot coffee? I don't see any around here."
She glanced about the clinic.

An unwilling grin flexed the corners of Reno's
mouth. "Yeah, I'd like that. Sleeping here nightly
doesn't leave me much time to run down to Cruz's
villa and ask for a cup of java. Here I am in one of the
premier coffee-producing countries on the planet, and
I can't drink a cup a day even if I wanted to."

"You sleep here?" Stunned, Calen pulled on her
gloves and snapped them closed on her wrists. Why
had she accepted his sudden invitation to coffee? She
didn't know who was more surprised, she or Reno.
Calen knew this was a chance to get to know her
hunter-killer better. It had to be done to ensure her
continued survival, she told herself.

"Yeah, I sleep here on the gurney after I shut the
doors for the night," Reno told her, running his fingers
through the long dark hair that grazed his shoulders.
During the day, he wore a red bandanna around his
head to keep the hair out of his eyes. It definitely made
him look like an Apache.

Shedding the latex gloves, Reno dropped them into an
old oil can serving as a wastebasket. "Cruz told me I'd
better stay here or I'd find all the equipment gone in the
morning. I took him at his word." Reno hitched his hands
on his hips and looked around. "Cruz was right. The first
three nights, men tried to break in. When they found me
here, the break-ins stopped. They know I stay here. It's
the only way to protect the drugs and medical supplies."

"Well, let me see what I can do to get you set up with a few things, since you're living here, too. I'll see you later tonight. And I'll bring you a thermos of good, hot Ecuadorian coffee."

With that, Calen left quickly. It would take some time for her to prepare for her coffee date with Reno. But something told her that even with her steely resolve to keep on guard, one look at Reno would distract her. She hoped it wouldn't lead to her downfall.

Chapter 8

A flutter of anxiety coursed through Reno as he heard a Jeep growling up the slight hill, then coming to a stop outside his clinic. It was 9:00 p.m., so that was her. Dama Magdalena Calen Hernandez. As he disinfected the gurney, Reno scowled. All day, since his damn invitation came roaring out of his mouth, he couldn't have been happier. Or more scared.

Shaken by the feelings running rampant in him like galloping mustangs, Reno quickly finished the last of his cleaning then threw the rag into a nearby basket.

The door to the Jeep opened and then shut. His heart leaped with anticipation as he peeled off the latex gloves and dropped them into another container. The screen door was propped open to allow the sultry, humid air into the sweltering confines of the clinic. The rusted screen prevented hungry mosquitoes from getting into the room, but he'd rather swat at them and have a breath of fresh air. Hurrying to the doorway, Reno reached it before Calen appeared. He found her mounting the porch steps, her arms filled with packages. Reno picked up two large bags from her arms.

"Helluva big coffee thermos you have in here!" he said, grinning down at her. The feeble light from the kerosene lamps indoors cast deep shadows across her face.

Calen smiled a little unevenly. "Thanks. Yeah, you looked like you were starving, so I thought you might like some of the leftovers from the meal Eliana fixed for us earlier tonight." She pointed to a small table and two chairs on the porch. "How about we sit over there?"

Nodding, Reno balanced the paper sacks in his arms. "Well, you're right about not eating." He could smell the wonderful odor of lamb wafting up from one bag. His mouth watered. "I ate some of my own grub this morning, but things got real busy and I didn't stop for lunch today." He pulled out the ancient wooden chair. This time, Calen was dressed in a revealing pink tank top and loose jeans. He could see the swell of her breasts, the tempting outline of her hips and those magnificent legs. In his mind, there was nothing sexier than a woman who rode horses. Her legs were finely curved, taut and beautifully sculpted from the daily exercise.

Feeling nervous, Calen sat down. She saw the look in Reno's darkened eyes. The lamplight was weak out here, the night surrounding them. The croak of frogs calling to one another, the buzz of insects, provided music for their meeting.

Clenching her hands beneath the round wooden table, she watched as Reno opened the first bag. All day long she'd waffled between coming and not coming tonight. Fear marched right alongside her desire to be with him. It was torture to Calen because she knew she was loco to want to be anywhere near her killer. And yet here she was. Unable to explain the addictive desire to be with Reno, she had finally given in to the yearning of her heart.

She nervously licked her lower lip and spoke. "I brought leg of lamb, potatoes, carrots and onions. Eliana is the best cook in the world. There's a plastic container of gravy in there, too."

"Heaven!" Reno muttered gratefully, taking out everything carefully. She helped him arrange the items, and he opened the lid to the gravy. Salivating, Reno realized she'd even brought him dessert, and his heart opened in appreciation. She'd provided real flatware, too, not plastic utensils. As he sat down, Calen pulled the thermos out of the second bag, along with two ceramic cups.

"This smells so good," he said, slicing into the thick rosemary-braised lamb. His stomach growled. How long had it been since he'd had a real, home-cooked meal? The answer made him wince inwardly. The little things in life, like his wife cooking him a meal, made him feel the pain of loss so sharply that, for a moment, Reno hesitated. Swallowing the unexpected emotions, he took a deep breath and started to eat.

Calen grinned. "You were starving. I'm glad my intuition said to bring the leftovers along. What have you been doing for food? If you're sleeping here, you have no kitchen facilities."

Shrugging, Reno chewed on the succulent meat, closing his eyes and relishing the taste. How nice to simply savor good, home-cooked food! He opened his eyes and responded, "I brought a stash of protein bars with me from the States."

"What? That's *all* you've been eating since you got here?" Calen was alarmed. She tried to tell herself she shouldn't care, but she did. Reno gave her a one-shouldered shrug as he continued to eat hungrily. She knew that he probably hadn't had the greatest food in prison. Ignoring her worry, she poured them the freshly made coffee. Her hands shook slightly. Above all, she had to appear cool and collected for this casual meeting.

"Cruz promised me a heating element and some other kitchen stuff," Reno said between mouthfuls. "It hasn't appeared yet. I'm finding out he talks big and delivers little."

"Mmm," Calen said, setting a cup of steaming coffee before him. "The Guild tends to be arrogant and deliver empty promises. It's their style." She looked around the porch. In the distance, beyond the curve of the dirt road, she could hear the *esmeraldos* down at the river. This was dinnertime in South America, and she could smell the odor of rice and beans cooking, along with wood smoke from their fires.

"I feel damn guilty eating like a prince when those people down there—" he pointed his knife toward the river "—are subsisting on rice and beans, if that."

"I know," Calen said softly, picking up her coffee and sipping. She leaned back, pleasure thrumming through her as she watched Reno wolf down every morsel of food. Why should she care if he wasn't eating right? He was her killer.

Her heart, however, said otherwise. If the man was a brutal murderer, why had he cared for the people these past two weeks? Maybe he wanted to insinuate himself so the *esmeraldos* would tell him all about El Espanto. Not that the people knew that much. Reno would get a lot of myths about her, but that was all.

"I have to tell you, Calen, these are mighty fine vittles. Like my mother used to cook. We had a sheep herd on the reservation where I grew up. That's how we made enough money to survive from one year to the next. My female relatives carded wool and my mother wove beautiful blankets and sold them to the trading posts. We ate lamb and mutton almost daily. And I've sure missed it."

"How many sisters do you have?"

"None."

"Any brothers?" Why should she care? Calen chastised herself, but she wanted background on this guy.

"No," Reno said, pushing the plate aside at last and reaching for the freshly made loaf of banana bread. He slathered a slice with softening butter. "I'm the only kid they had. My father was a mechanic. He worked at a small gas station about twenty miles from our homestead."

"Your voice changes when you talk about home."

"Yeah, I guess I'm homesick."

"Is that your Apache blood talking?" She saw him give her a half smile. Sensing his pain, she waited.

"I s'pose. My parents died a few years ago. I miss them. They had a lot of wisdom. I find myself wishing I could pick up the phone and talk to them, ask them things and get good, honest answers in return." Biting into the thick, warm bread, he savored its nutty sweetness. "What about you?"

"Me?" Calen shrugged, on guard. "My life is somewhat dramatic, I'm afraid. My whole family was slaughtered before my eyes when I was a child." She gestured toward the mountain in the distance. "My family were *esmeraldos,* Reno. Very poor. And we were caught up on the slopes of the volcano one night, searching for emeralds. I was the only one to escape being killed by the mine guards." Calen would never forget that horrifying night. Even now she had recurring nightmares about it at least four or five times a year. Between them and her other nightmares of having to kill foreign guards, and seeing their faces in death, Calen often got less sleep than she wanted.

His brows fell. "I'm sorry," he said. Searching her pensive features, Reno could feel her anguish over such a horrific loss.

"Things got better," she reassured him. "I found my way to a Catholic orphanage after it happened. I walked into Ibarra, where I was adopted three months later. Most people think I was born with a silver spoon in my mouth, as they say. My adopted parents owned a bunch of oil rigs out in the Pacific Ocean off the coast of Ecuador. I have no siblings, either, so we have that in common." Calen's heart ached. Folding her hands around the hot mug, which felt good because of the chill within her, she forced a smile she didn't feel. "I grew up with the best of teachers and schooling in Quito."

"At least you got out of this squalor," Reno said. Inwardly, he knew that Calen had probably never gotten over the loss of her parents. Who would? He tried to steer her to a less painful topic. "And your love of horses? I understand from Jose Santiago that you are a world-recognized dressage rider."

Reno liked looking at Calen across that rough circular table. Her profile was etched by lamplight from the window. Her mussed hair lay across her shoulders, giving him a wild urge to tunnel his fingers through those thick, silky strands.

"That? Well, my adopted mother realized I loved horses the first time she introduced me to them. She was a national dressage rider herself, you know. She won the Pan-American gold medal in dressage for Ecuador many years ago."

"I heard you did, too." Reno finished off the bread. He reached for the steaming mug of black coffee. Watching for her reaction, Reno noticed how she remained heavily guarded, and wondered why. Maybe she didn't trust him. Fair enough. Reno resolved to earn her trust over time.

"Yes, I've won the Pan-American gold medal, too."

"Going to the Olympics, then?"

"I'm going to work to make a spot on the Ecuadorian dressage team. Yes. That's three years away."

"You got a horse who can take you there?" Reno imagined that, with her billions, she could afford the best bloodlines and conformation in a horse to do just that. He saw her smile pensively as she stared down at the mug resting on her knee.

"Yes, I do." It was her black Arabian mare, Storm; she was world-class, but she'd never see the inside of an Olympic dressage ring. Her mare had other talents Calen needed in order to help keep her safe and alive out on the slopes of that mountain in the dark of night.

"That chestnut you rode up on this morning? He's a big, well-conformed dude."

So Reno knew horses. Calen wasn't surprised. "Yes, Star. I try to get him out of the ring daily. Horses get bored just working in a sandlot. I like to ride him on trails to relax him. He's happy just plodding along." It wasn't a complete lie. Star was her backup horse during the Pan-American trials.

"Good thinking. He's a nice-looking animal." And Calen was a nice-looking woman. Curiosity was eating at Reno. "The *esmeraldos* say you are a saint. Jose, who seems to idolize the ground you walk on, said you've been here two years?"

"Yes. And I'm no saint." The furthest thing from it. Calen lifted her lashes and absorbed Reno's shadowed, roughened features. She saw a slight hint of a smile playing at one corner of his well-shaped mouth. For whatever crazy reason, she had the urge to lift her fingers and run them gently against those shapely lips. The man exuded energy, warmth and caring toward her—like a veritable power station.

Maybe her celibate life was getting to her. Maybe she needed to look at men differently. Until now, Calen's entire focus had been on revenge. It had to be. That, and keeping the *esmeraldos* somewhat protected against the murderous Guild.

"Well, you're saintlike," Reno said. He raised his head and glanced into the clinic. "Without your help and support, I wouldn't be able to help these folks like I am right now. Again, I am grateful." And he was. He noticed Calen was giving him a funny look, one that he could not intuit. She had up a lot of walls to keep him out, energetically speaking. What was she hiding?

"I do what I can, Reno."

"Why did you move back here two years ago?" he

wondered, sipping his coffee. Instantly, he saw her eyes narrow a bit. And again, he felt that wall keeping him away.

"I had a villa in Quito and lived the good life, while my people were starving out here. I came back to Ibarra with Godfredo and Eliana. They were very supportive, helping me and advising me in designing the villa I have now. They've been instrumental in me channeling charity donations to the people here." None of this was a lie. Calen smiled inwardly as she watched Reno digesting the information. It was becoming clear he wanted this little tête-à-tête just for that: part of his snooping around to find El Espanto. Her silly, naive heart thought Reno was attracted to her, hence his blurted invitation earlier today.

Fool, she chided herself. He was just finding out the lay of the land. Okay, that was fine with her. Nostrils flaring, she said, "Does your name have meaning? I understand Native Americans are very conscious of symbolism in their daily lives."

Sitting back, Reno said, "*Manchahi* is Apache for *wolf.*"

"That fits," Calen said wryly. Wolf, yes. The ultimate North American hunter. Her gut knotted briefly. Reno Wolf. That was more like it. With his wolflike instincts, he'd nearly killed her already. "And Reno? I understand that's a large city in the state of Nevada."

Chuckling, Reno said, "My parents got married and spent their honeymoon in that gambling center. That's when she became pregnant with me."

"Fitting," Calen said.

Moving the chair so he could stretch out his long legs, Reno said, "What do you know of this El Espanto?"

"Mostly heresy, Reno. He's seen as a savior to the *esmeraldos.*"

"So, El Espanto does what, then?" He heard profound passion in her low, husky tone and saw fire leaping to life in her eyes. Reno guessed that she was glad for El Espanto, as well.

"He protects them from being cold-bloodedly murdered by the hired mercenaries." She held Reno's thoughtful, dark gaze. "The mine guards murder them, Reno. It's awful."

"It is. After our talk, I found out that the mercs shoot anyone caught on mine property," he said, almost apologetically. "I'm sorry to upset you." He could see suffering in the way her full mouth compressed. Wanting to reach over and touch her hand, which was curled into a fist on the table, Reno had to stop himself before he did just that. "So, El Espanto saves lives?"

"Of course he does! It isn't right that the Guild gets away with murdering poor, hungry people." Calen took a long, ragged breath. "There is no law out here, Reno, in case you haven't figured that out yet. The Guild will never be brought to justice for what they are doing out here nightly." She jabbed a finger toward the tall, dark mountain just ahead of them. "How would you like to be one of these families? Dreaming of finding one emerald that would lift you out of horrible poverty and

starvation? Put flesh on your starving children's prominent ribs? Have your babies sleep at night instead of
crying incessantly because they are hungry? No, I think
El Espanto's presence is a response to this terrible
atrocity that the Guild has set into motion. Yes, the *esmeraldos* see him as a protector. Without him, they are
defenseless. Do you know how many families have
been murdered this year? Ten. My God, that's seventy-
five people."

Absorbing her impassioned and righteous rage,
Reno digested her trembling words. How much he
wanted to get up, go to Calen and lift her into his arms.
Reno's automatic urge to protect women and children
was working big time. His arms ached to hold Calen.
She was such a strong, confident woman. She would
feel wonderful against him. Would the fire burning in
her narrowed eyes translate into passion, as well? Reno
thought so.

Gently, he tucked all those reactions away. He had
to focus on what she knew about El Espanto.

"Have you ever seen him?"

"Me?" Calen snorted. "Of course not."

"He rides only at night."

"Oh? Is that what the *esmeraldos* tell you?"

"He rides a black horse. It's a small horse, but a very
spirited one. And the ghost is tall and thin. Several
have said he has green eyes that sparkle in the dark.
They say he is magical, that he can appear and disappear at will. That he's not real, but an angel from God

come to save them from the sentries. They say he is Michael the Archangel come to earth with a sword to protect them."

Calen realized she was too impassioned. Sitting back, she gulped down some of the hot coffee, burning her tongue and throat. "I wouldn't know. I spend all day working on business and attending my charities in the evening. By the time my head hits the pillow, I sleep deeply. My villa is surrounded by a ten-foot wall. We've never seen El Espanto."

"Yet, as I understand it, you have four villas around this mountain?"

"Yes, I do. One large one on the western flank of the mountain, and three smaller ones on the north, south and east."

"Why?"

Calen could feel Reno searching. Trying to get a handle on her escaping feelings, she murmured, "I rotate my two dressage mounts at different villas each month. I want them fresh. I want them interested in the changing surroundings. Horses do better when they have something new to look at. They don't get bored out of their skulls being in the same old place or paddock. I had Godfredo and his men make dressage rings at each of the villas. That's why."

She glared over at him and hoped her quelling look would stop him from asking questions. Actually, she used the villas and trailered her black Arabian mare to reach different trailheads that led up the mountain.

Would Reno figure that out? Calen would put nothing past this intelligent sniper. He was a wolf, after all. And damn savvy. He might look like he was relaxed, sitting there with his legs crossed at the ankles, the coffee cup resting on this hard thigh, but he didn't fool her at all. Sensing that he was putting all this information into his memory, Calen warned herself to be careful about what she shared with him.

"Patrón Cruz said El Espanto has killed four Guild guards in the last two years. Is that true?"

"I believe it is." Calen felt bad, but if the foreign mercenaries were not going to stop murdering her people, then something drastic had to be done. Now, those guards' wives were without a husband, their children without a father. All that ate daily at Calen's conscience. She tried to justify her actions, and on some days it worked. On others, like right now, it didn't. She had murdered them.

"You'd think the Guild would get it, wouldn't you?" Reno said, looking down at his half-empty cup of coffee.

"Get what?" Calen played dumb.

"That El Espanto wants them to stop this wholesale slaughter of trespassers and maybe do something less drastic." He shook his head. "I don't think Cruz comprehends. Or maybe he doesn't want to."

"Cruz is greedy."

Reno glanced at her dark features, her eyes filled with fury. "He wants El Espanto's head."

"He's got a million-dollar reward out for him," Calen agreed.

"That's a lot of money. Any *esmeraldo* could live like a king off that. Why do you think they haven't turned the ghost in?"

Shrugging, Calen said, "I don't know."

"Or maybe El Espanto really is magical. No one seems to know where he lives. Or where he goes. He just suddenly pops up out of the dark to challenge the guards and save a family. The people I've talked to say he doesn't always kill the guards, that in most situations, he's hit them with a dart that renders them unconscious." Reno watched her gaze down at her feet. He wasn't about to confess that he'd shot at a dark horseman on the slope two weeks ago.

Reno roused himself. "That tells me that El Espanto doesn't really want to kill, but send a message to the Guild and to the mercs. I've talked to several guards who were knocked out by one of those darts El Espanto fired at them. Their shoes, weapons and radios were taken. That means El Espanto isn't always the killer that Patrón Cruz wants me to believe."

"It sounds like you're very interested in El Espanto."

Reno shrugged. "I just like to hear about local legends, is all." Only Cruz knew about his taking the shot a couple of weeks ago. The man wanted weekly reports on his sniper activities. Reno was sure he'd nailed the rider, but when he'd tracked to the spot, he found only horse and jaguar tracks, plus two AK-47 rifles. And no blood. That incident provoked more questions than answers. No one had shown up at the hospital in Ibarra, either. So if he had wounded the rider, the bullet hadn't penetrated his body. That, or the rider was wearing a bulletproof vest. Because Reno never missed a target. Ever.

Calen bit her lower lip. She'd had enough. Feeling as if Reno were trying to crawl inside her head and heart, she stood up abruptly. "I have to go, Reno. It's been nice, but I have a lot of paperwork to catch up on tonight." Actually, it was nearly time for her to get ready for her first ride since being shot. Gathering up the sacks, she stepped past Reno before he could get up. She saw the surprise on his face. "I'll see you around. I'm glad you liked the lamb. I'll tell Eliana. That will make her happy. Good night…."

He reached out, his fingers wrapping around her wrist. "Wait. We have a secret we share…and I want to talk about it before you leave. Give me five minutes?"

His long, strong fingers felt like red-hot brands on her lower arm. Stunned, feeling fear zigzag through her, Calen lost her normal coolness. "What?" The word was torn raggedly from her lips, driven by surprise laced with terror.

Reno saw her eyes widen when he touched her, so he released her arm. Why such a knee-jerk reaction? He didn't know, but he was determined to forge a closer link with Calen. His body, his heart and mind were howling at him to bond with her. And he felt helpless to do anything but acknowledge that he craved Calen's nearness, her mellow, husky voice melting over him and her miraculous way of dissolving the ice around his heart. Reno didn't fool himself—he wanted Calen. In every possible way. And yet she was like an unreachable dream. Or was she?

"Come closer," he urged her. "I want you to see something." He lifted the back of his thick hair.

Unsure of what was going to happen, Calen did as he instructed. Reno turned his back to the lamplight. When he lifted his thick, blue-black locks, she gazed down at the back of his thick, powerful neck. A gasp escaped her. There, just below his hairline, was the vesica piscis birthmark! Just like hers! "Oh," she murmured, her hand flying to her parted lips.

Dropping his hair, Reno turned and looked at her. Calen's face was drained of color. He worried that she was going to faint, so he tentatively gripped her hand again. "Calen? You okay?"

Shaking her head, she jerked away. Touching Reno was like finding a luscious sweetness she'd never experienced before with a man.

The worried look in his cinnamon eyes washed through her, healing her fear. "No, no. I'm fine, really." She went over and sat back down before her knees buckled beneath her.

She watched as he came and sat at the rough wooden table. His chair scraped the porch floor. "You've got the same birthmark as I do," she stated in a hoarse, unsteady voice.

"Yes," Reno said. He crossed his arms on the table

and held her startled gaze. "That's our secret, Calen. My mother had always told me there were others out there like me. I didn't disbelieve her, but I never saw anyone else with that kind of birthmark until I met you." He managed a raw smile of sorts. "You shook my world in more ways than you could ever realize. I was attracted to you, by your beauty, Calen. Any man in his right mind would look at you and desire you. But when I saw that birthmark, it explained, at least to me, why I feel so drawn to you."

Opening his hands, his voice filled with awe and frustration, Reno added, "Here you are. Beautiful. Rich. Powerful. Doing work to help your people. All the things my mother said of the Warriors for the Light—that they helped humanity in many different but good ways. Even though you went from abject poverty to wealth, you live the mission ordained by your birthmark. I find that incredibly heartening. Hopeful. And inspiring."

Her emotions a tornado of despair, joy and anguish, Calen tried to think through it all. Reno's face had lost that implacable and unreadable hardness. Instead, here was the man she'd always yearned for but never believed existed: warm, open, vulnerable and gut-wrenchingly honest with her. Reno was drawn to her. He'd just admitted it. Feelings swinging violently like an executioner's ax within her, Calen sat very still and tried to harness her runaway emotions. The swelling and bruising between her breasts throbbed, reminding her he'd nearly taken her life out there two weeks earlier.

Reno saw so many emotions clash in Calen's face that he gave up trying to read her. Energywise, it felt as if a violent, chaotic tornado had entered the dispensary. He understood it was her emotional reaction to him, since he'd laid a lot out to her without preamble. "Look, I need to say some things to you. Things that my mother told me when I was a child. And maybe none of this will make sense to you, but maybe it will. Will you let me share it with you?"

"Go ahead," she said, and pressed her hand against the column of her throat.

"From the earliest time I could remember, my mother told me our family were descendants of the Warriors for the Light. Anyone who bore this birthmark—" he jabbed a finger toward the back of his neck "—had a responsibility to help, in a good way, all our relations here on Mother Earth." He lowered his brows and clasped his hands on the table in front of him. "My mother said there was a necklace called the Emerald Key that would one day be rediscovered. And that a noble Incan woman from the northern part of that empire would be born someday when the world was in utter chaos. She'd be charged with trying to find that emerald necklace, which has seven golf-ball-sized hand-polished spheres on it. Each sphere was marked with a word in an ancient language. As each sphere was recovered from a power spot somewhere around the globe, the necklace would once again be reassembled."

Reno sighed and sat up. "It is said, in stories handed

down through my family, that this woman, if she was successful in finding the seven spheres, would wear the necklace when she was pregnant. And by wearing it, a thousand years of peace would begin to filter into our earth, taking us out of this chaos, darkness and greed."

Heart hammering, Calen could do nothing but stare like a stunned child at his shadowy features. "Yes, that is what I was told, too. This is…amazing." Shocking. An earthquake of dread and joy exploded through Calen. Her killer was a Warrior for the Light, just as she was! And yet, he was hunting her. How could that be? A Warrior for the Light did not kill people like this.

Swallowing against a dry throat, Calen searched his eyes, which held confusion and questions. "But there's more to the legend, Reno. My mother said that the dark side will be in charge of the earth when this woman is born. That there will be more wars, pestilence, plague and killing going on than ever before in our history."

"We're there now," he told her flatly. "Don't you think?"

"I wouldn't disagree. But the dark side is hunting for those spheres as we speak. That's my understanding. And if they find the seven spheres of this emerald necklace, they will hold the key to the future of our planet, instead."

"Yes. And there is supposedly a woman from the dark side who, if she reassembles it first, will send the earth and its inhabitants into a thousand years of darkness, wars, greed and, eventually, self-destruction."

Calen nodded. "That is what I was made to understand, too. That there will be a battle to locate the Emerald Key and that women play a prominent role, on both sides, in finding it. The first side to find all the spheres will decide the fate of the earth."

"So," Reno growled, "why have I met you now? Why here?" He gestured around the shack. "I know enough about Inca history to know that Ecuador was once a northern province of that empire."

"So it was," Calen agreed softly. She felt the sizzling, intense inspection of his gaze. It was uncomfortable and yet simultaneously warming and protective. She was in a schizophrenic dream of ridiculous extremes. The bruise between her breasts ached, as well, a reminder that his sniper bullet had already nearly found her heart. And yet, as she sat across the table from him, he had no clue as to what he'd nearly done to her. Or that he'd try to kill her in the future. On the other hand, he was one of the Warriors for the Light. And so was she.

Stomach churning with nausea, Calen didn't know how to react or what to do. It was one of the few times in her life when she felt completely trapped, like a bug in a spiderweb, and there was no way out.

"Maybe," Reno mused, "we're meeting like this because we're here to help one another. If we work together, maybe we can help bring earth the peace it so desperately needs."

Her nerves frazzled, Calen grabbed a glass of water

and gulped some down. As she set the glass back on the rough surface of the table, she rasped, "Or maybe it's to look for the first sphere? My mother told me that it would be found in a cave here in Ecuador someday. She didn't know where, just that she had a feeling it would be discovered here."

"That's possible, I guess. But you've lived in Ecuador all your life. Do you have any idea where it might be?"

"No." Wiping her mouth with the back of her hand, Calen struggled mightily to keep her emotions under control. "My mother told me that, at the right time, the spirit of the sphere would come to the person in a dream, and reveal where it was located and how to find it."

"Maybe we should start paying attention to our dreams more?" One corner of his mouth hitched upward. Reno wanted to soothe her, since she seemed deeply affected by this conversation. Even her hands were trembling. Why? Was it because two warriors had finally met? Reno had no idea how many were on earth right now. Calen was the first he'd encountered.

"For sure," she stated, her voice off-key. "Did your mother tell you the rest of the story? That a man and woman would come to the first couple who found an emerald sphere? That this second woman was one of six people, all Warriors for the Light, who would be in-strumental in battling the dark side?"

Nodding, Reno said, "Yes. That all in all, there are six people who will form an allegiance, or society, to fight the darkness. And at the same time, they'll try to find the Emerald Key before the dark forces do. It will be a race, and my mother said there is no guaranteed outcome. That the earth could plunge into darkness and destruction or, if the light were lucky, move it into a thousand years of peace."

"Correct. And amazing," Calen murmured, "that you're Apache, and through your traditions the same story has been handed down, as it was through my family before they were murdered."

"That is how things are passed on, Calen—orally. The Native Americans have a long verbal history of much knowledge. We didn't invent writing or books, but we had good memories, and the stories were told to each new generation."

Shaking her head, she looked at Reno in a new light. "Perhaps that's why I feel so close to you in some ways," she finally admitted. "When I first met you, I was drawn to you so powerfully that it scared me. I didn't know why. And maybe this birthmark we both carry explains it."

"I felt the same toward you," Reno admitted quietly. He wanted to share much more of how he felt toward Calen, but she looked rattled enough. "My mother said we'd always recognize our own kind, that our genetics were unique from other humans. That's probably why we have this strong connection, which binds us to one another for better or worse."

Calen couldn't disagree. *Better or worse.* Oh, if Reno only knew how bad it was! But he didn't. She could see that in his face now, which was completely open and accessible to her. Her ache to reach out and slip her hand across his scarred one, to feel his power, his protection, was nearly overwhelming. And yet that hand would pull the trigger to kill her one night.

"It's time for me to go, Reno. I'm very tired and I have a long day ahead of me tomorrow." That wasn't a lie.

"Of course," he said, rising. "I laid a lot on you. I'm not known for my diplomacy. Here, I'll help take the sacks back out to your Jeep."

Calen had to think. Think! As Reno made short work of the items, she walked to the vehicle. The darkness was complete, a hazy fog lingering just above the treetops. Monkeys cried out in the jungle and frogs croaked and sang. As she climbed into the driver's seat, Calen knew she could no longer ride Storm across the mountain. No, she'd have to shape-shift into the jaguar to continue to protect her people and avoid Reno. She doubted he'd kill a jaguar even if he saw one. He would be looking for a rider on a horse instead.

Still, as she lifted her hand in farewell to Reno, who stood in the headlights, Calen knew her plan wasn't fool-proof. She could die. Being a Warrior for the Light was no guarantee that her life would be spared any more or less than any other human being's. Her days were numbered.

Chapter 9

Where the hell was El Espanto? Reno padded softly in the darkness, his jaguar vision making the night seem like dawn. Dressed in typical sniper garb, he carried his rifle and waited for his mind to churn up some answers. Five weeks ago he'd shot at a horseman galloping along this same trail. And every night since then, he'd hunted the slopes, trying to intercept him again. To no avail.

Stopping, he heard the snort of horses above him and to the left. They belonged to the two mine guards who rode nearby. He was well aware of their rounds, and discounted them.

Had he gravely wounded the ghostly rider? Was

that why he hadn't found him since then? With the cool night air damp with earthy odors of decaying leaves and fallen trees, Reno scanned the area. Normally, the sounds of crickets and frogs made the jungle seem alive. But not now. Why not? Hand tightening around his rifle, Reno began to inspect every patch of nearby real estate.

As he searched for signs of intrusion, he recalled that on four different occasions since he'd shot at El Espanto, a jaguar had raised hell with the guards. Cruz believed it was probably a rogue cat trying to move in and claim another jaguar's territory. He'd said that a jaguar family owned the mountain and usually left humans alone.

Nothing. Damn. Reno's fingers tightened briefly around the cool stock of his weapon. As he pivoted and perused the wall of jungle nearby, his mind moved to Calen—again. Always. How badly Reno ached to see her. Since their coffee together three weeks ago, she'd all but disappeared from his life. Reno imagined he'd scared her away by impulsively showing his birthmark. His mind understood the logic: she was rich and of another class. He was a criminal and poor. Even if she came from a poor family, Calen had ascended to the heady realms of the superaffluent. More than likely, she wanted nothing to do with the likes of him.

Reno couldn't really blame her. But his heart ached and pined away for her anyway. His dreams of her were torrid in the dawn after a night of hunting for the ghost on the slopes of the mountain. In these dreams, Reno made long, slow, passionate love with Calen as he explored every inch of her lush, golden-skinned body. Shaking his head, he told himself he had to stop hoping for the impossible. As a sniper, he couldn't afford to be lulled into complacency. To do so could mean his death. Reno didn't fool himself; El Espanto had killed before, and if they met, he could die.

The sudden yelp of a guard above broke the silence. Whirling, Reno heard another scream. It was the second guard, coming over the radio Reno carried.

"Jaguar! There's that jaguar again! Shit! Shoot him! Shoot him!"

Then Reno heard gunshots shatter the stillness— wildly fired shots. Digging the toes of his boots into the damp clay, he lunged up the slope, rifle ready in his right hand. His radio shrieked and squawked as the two guards yelped and shouted. Rushing upward, slipping and scrambling, Reno dodged a riderless horse careening down past him. The second horse exploded out of the brush to his left. It, too, was riderless. Had the rogue jaguar attacked the foreign mercs? Did they fall off their startled mounts?

As Reno leaped onto a well-trodden guard path, he spotted both sentries on the ground. A huge, stocky gold jaguar with black half-moon spots crouched over one of them. Its mouth was very close to the sentry's exposed throat.

The cat saw Reno.

In a split second, the animal turned and raced down the hill toward the jungle, a quarter of a mile away.

Jerking to a halt, Reno saw that the guards were shaken but not harmed. They didn't realize he was nearby, their night vision nonexistent compared to his. Breathing heavily, Reno willed himself to calm down. Concentrate! He had to concentrate! The only way to follow that rogue cat was to become a jaguar himself.

Moving out of the line of sight of the mercenaries, Reno willed his jaguar guardian to come over him. Like a tight glove fitting over his body, it happened. There were sensations of expansion, changes in the length of his arms, hands and legs. Animal strength tunneled through him. And fifteen seconds later, the morphing complete, Reno was on all fours, hurtling silently down the slope after the other jaguar.

Running full tilt, his stride long and swift, Reno scented the air. It was easy to pick up traces of the cat who had just left the scene. To his surprise, he could smell that she was female. That was unusual, because normally, only males went to claim new territory. Reno's human mind mixed uneasily with his primitive animal mind. It was always a struggle to keep the human elements in charge.

Leaves and brush swatted at him as he continued his charge toward the female. He couldn't see her, but her scent grew stronger and stronger by the moment. He was closing in on her. Reaching a trail, Reno rushed downward. He picked up speed as the path canted through the twisted jungle growth.

Along the trail, the vegetation rose like walls, high and thick. Nothing could penetrate it at this point. The foliage was so dense it kept everything out but small birds and animals. Reno veered around a curve, running full bore, his hind legs pumping like tireless steel pistons. The trail snaked to the right around a hairpin turn. Skidding, Reno felt the mud flying back beneath his belly and coating it as he galloped on, trying not to trip or fall.

The trail finally straightened out. He smelled the female very close now. Was she slowing down? Tired? Probably. She felt safe in here, Reno thought. No one would follow her—or so she figured.

Reno's plan was to scare the cat out of the area. He had no intention of killing a jaguar. After all, it was his guardian's people. If this was a rogue cat trying to establish a new territory, she might leave once and for all confronted and threatened. That would make Reno's job up on the mountain easier as he continued to hunt for signs of El Espanto.

The trail thinned and curved to the left. He slowed, knowing he'd never make the bend at this speed. As he ratcheted down and made the turn, he saw a dark shape in the middle of the path just ahead of him. It was the female jaguar. She was standing and facing him.

Reno skidded to a halt, not expecting to be confronted by her. And then something happened that startled the hell out of him. The beautiful female jaguar began to waver like heat waves in a hot desert. Blinking, Reno tried to grasp what was happening.

Like shimmering waves rising from a blisteringly hot asphalt highway, the jaguar began to change shape— into a woman. And not just any woman. It was Calen!

Hissing in surprise, Reno tensed. Calen stood there in a black, body-hugging spandex suit. In her right hand a rifle appeared. She wore a black baseball cap, her hair pulled back into a ponytail. She was breathing hard, her chest heaving. The look on her face was grim as she saw him struggle to stop no more than ten feet away from her.

She lifted the rifle toward him, mouth flattening.

Breathing hoarsely, Reno reeled in shock over what he'd just seen. His mind whirled, trying to grasp this stunning truth. It was Calen! Reno willed himself back into his human shape. The morphing process took a long fifteen seconds—seconds that seemed like horrible, slow-moving hours. Changing from one form to another was always a period of vulnerability. The process left Reno dizzy for several seconds afterward.

"Reno!" Calen gasped. She instantly lowered her rifle. Eyes widening, she stared at him and his ragged sniper outfit. She couldn't believe what she'd just seen.

"You…" Reno gasped. He scowled and searched her shocked eyes. "You're a shape-shifter. You were the jaguar up there. You attacked the guards."

Nodding, Calen felt her heart thump violently in her

chest. "Yes…yes, I did." She gulped. What was she going to do? Reno now knew her secret. As she watched him, the barrel of his weapon remained pointed toward the ground.

Calen did not want to kill Reno. She wanted to run. To hide. But that was now impossible.

"What the hell is going on here? What were you doing out there on the slopes? You attacked those two guards!" he repeated, his voice thick.

Perspiration trickled down her overheated body. Calen shakily wiped her mouth with the back of her gloved hand. "Yes, I did attack them." She saw Reno's eyes narrow speculatively. Calen didn't wait for him to put it together. "Reno, I'm El Espanto. You might as well know it." Hand tightening on her weapon, she wondered if he was going to lift his rifle and shoot her. She wore Kevlar, but snipers preferred head shots, and she wore no protection there.

"Dammit!" he growled. Pulling off his ragged cap, his long, dark hair damp with sweat, he glared at her. "You can't be!" Everything in him screamed that was impossible. Yet Reno stood there looking at Calen's proudly held shoulders, her luscious mouth set in that thin line and those willow-green eyes of hers blazing with courage he'd seen in few men, much less a woman. She was telling the truth. He shook his head in utter disbelief, then forced himself to lock on to Calen's burning gaze.

"I shot you." It hurt to say those words. To realize

he'd nearly killed the only woman since Ilona to make him feel alive, to make him feel hope since the tragic loss of his family. Heart squeezing in terror at those realizations, Reno could barely breathe. Faintness momentarily rimmed his vision, and he took a step back to steady himself.

He sharply recalled how his commanding officer had pulled him aside, gripped his arm and told him, with tears in his voice, that Ilona and Sarah had been murdered. The same harrowing sensations—the feeling of the floor dropping from beneath him until he was falling, falling, falling into a bottomless pit of hell—engulfed him all over again. He'd nearly killed Calen....

Calen's smile was mirthless. "Yeah, you nailed me, Reno." She touched her Kevlar vest over her heart. "Right here. I was riding Storm, my black Arabian, when you shot me. Your bullet knocked me off my mare and as I fell, I changed into a jaguar. By the time I hit the ground, I was in cat form and got away from you."

Rubbing his wrinkled brow, Reno muttered, "That's why I saw horse and jaguar prints."

"When my life is threatened like that," Calen told him in a low voice, "I automatically turn into my jaguar form." Worry crept into her husky tone. "More to the point—what are you going to do now that you know I'm El Espanto? Cruz is paying you big money to kill me. What are you going to do, Reno?" Her hand remained firm around her rifle. Calen watched with a profound wariness as Reno scowled, looked down at his own weapon, disgust clearly mirrored in his features. Would he kill her? Would he fulfill the contract with Cruz? Her throat ached with tension and her mouth went dry as she watched the sniper.

Wiping his brow with his hand, Reno shook his head. "Hell no, Calen. I'm not going to kill you. I couldn't...wouldn't! And I'm so damn sorry I almost took your life." His mouth curled with savage pain. "I wish I'd known. I wish..." His voice trailed off as he searched her wide, haunted eyes. "How long have you been doing this? Leading three lives?"

"Two years. Ever since I moved back here from Quito."

Reno walked toward her. Calen stiffened warily. "I'm not your enemy, Calen. Not now. Not ever. So relax. I'll never lift my hand or weapon toward you again. I understand better why you're back here. You might be rich, but your heart and soul are with your people, the *esmeraldos*. You've come back to help save lives."

He understood. Tears burned in Calen's eyes. A sob caught in her throat as he drew close. "I—I didn't think you'd understand, but you do...."

Setting his rifle on the ground, the barrel leaning against the trunk of a tree, Reno turned toward her. There was no way he was going to take her life to get his life back.

Only a few feet separated them. Reno watched as she set her own weapon next to his. It was a truce. The night enclosed them, the spicy fragrance of orchids surrounded them. Far out in the jungle, the animal sounds joined together in a musical chorus. "Do you know what this means?" he demanded.

"No, Reno, I don't." Swallowing hard, Calen whispered rawly, "I'm scared. And I'm confused. I'm relieved. Thank you for not taking my life."

Reaching out, he grazed her damp cheek. Her flesh was so smooth and firm beneath his exploring fingertips. "Of all the people I've ever met, Calen, I would never intentionally hurt you. Not *ever.*"

Reno saw his entire life change in that moment. Cruz would be furious. He'd contact that spook, James, in Quito, and Reno would be going back to the brig again.

Absorbing the tender look in Calen's searching gaze, the soft parting of her lips, he realized he would never have her, either. Whatever crazy, idealistic dreams he had of them together were now gone. Forever. "I'll be sent back to the U.S. Back to prison."

"What?" Calen's voice snapped as she drew in a ragged breath of surprise. Her skin tingled sweetly where he'd lightly touched her cheek. How badly she wanted Reno. On every level. In every possible way. She ached for him. "What are you talking about?"

"I'll have to tell Cruz I refuse to hunt down El Espanto. The CIA will escort me back to the U.S. and back to the brig. I'll be there for another seventeen years to fulfill my prison term. The only way for me to gain my freedom was to haul El Espanto's body back to Cruz so he could verify the kill." A sad quirk came to Reno's mouth as he held her tear-filled gaze. "And that isn't going to happen, Calen. I'm walking away from this assignment. It will be the only time as a sniper that I won't finish a mission I've been given."

Uttering a cry, Calen threw her arms around Reno's proud, broad shoulders. She clung to him, her lips pressed against his sweaty flesh. "No! No, there *must* be some other way, Reno! There just has to be."

The sensation of her warm, firm body meeting, melding and sliding against his was such an unexpected surprise that Reno automatically embraced Calen. Her lips against his cheek ignited a powerful yearning within him. Turning, he met and slid his seeking mouth against her parting, waiting lips. As he tasted the salt upon them, he realized Calen was crying—for him. For them. After all, they were jaguar shape-shifters. They bore the birthmark of the Warriors for the Light. They were part of a clan, a group of people who were on a rare and sacred mission. More than that, Reno realized he was falling deeply in love with this courageous woman who risked her life for others.

He felt Calen tense, her breasts pressing insistently against his chest as he moved his mouth more surely across hers. There was a moan of pleasure, like the low growl of a jaguar, coming from deep within her. The reverberation of sound spread outward like tiny ripples, as if a stone had been thrown into a still pond. Her mouth grew soft and hungry as she met his sweet assault. Oh! For too long Reno had pined for the nurturing, loving caress of a woman who made his heart race, his blood turn to boiling, churning lava. And now, miraculously, Calen was in his arms.

One kiss. And then, Reno knew, he had to go away and leave her—forever.

Calen's mouth was pliable and lush, a blossoming orchid beneath his own starving lips. She tasted feminine, sweet, and, like a thief, Reno stole selfishly from her. Their punctuated, ragged breaths mingled, their emotions soared, and each moaned with pleasure as their mouths clung to one another. Their lives had always been entwined—sacredly, secretly—and they knew that now.

As his tongue traced the tip of hers, she trembled violently within his grasp. Arms tightening, Reno felt her knees suddenly give way. Yes, their kiss was sealing an age-old legend, now come to brilliant, vibrant life. His parents were both shape-shifters. They had told him it was rare they'd ever find mates like themselves. Now, Reno had found his mate. The terrible tragedy was he had to walk into Cruz's office and turn himself in, that the mission to find and kill El Espanto was canceled.

Calen tore her mouth from Reno's and gripped his shoulders. As she leaned back, she saw his eyes burn for her. The knowledge thrilled her. How fiercely her body throbbed with yearning, how brightly her heart glowed. "Wait, wait. There has to be a way around this…." she whispered unsteadily.

"I don't see any, Calen. None." Reno gave her a sad

look. "I just found you, I just got my life back, and now it's gone again." His voice cracked as he stroked her wet cheek, which glistened with spilled tears. "This explains so much to me. Why I was so drawn to you. I didn't know why. Now, I do. We're alike, you and I, in so many ways. We're shape-shifters. We carry the vesica piscis birthmark. We might come from different countries, different backgrounds, but on a deeper level, we are the same. Most important, we're both from the jaguar clan. No wonder we were helplessly drawn to one another. Like draws like."

She had to think! Calen pulled out of Reno's arms, which was the last thing she wanted to do. "There's more to this, Reno. Listen to me, will you?" Her voice was desperate as she moved to the other side of the narrow path, her breath coming in gasps. This man was full of contrasts—so terribly masculine and yet so heart-wrenchingly vulnerable. Hopelessness shone in his eyes. His face held so much anguish that it hurt her soul. "I need to tell you what else is happening."

"All right." Reno watched as she removed her baseball cap and touched her furrowed forehead.

"You need to come with me, Reno. We have four miles to go to reach safety. I can get you to a place where Cruz will never find you. We need to talk as we walk. Come on." Calen settled the cap back on her head, positioning the bill low over her eyes. Picking up her rifle, she slung it across her back. "We don't have much time. Let's go."

Reno followed her lead. It was hell to tell his body, his soul, to stop kissing this woman whom he'd been looking for all his life, whether he knew it or not. He'd wanted to lay her down, stretch her out on the trail and make wildly passionate love with her. Yet Reno knew this wasn't the time or place.

Slinging the rifle over his back, he quickly caught up with her. The trail was wide enough for them to walk side by side. Roots stuck up everywhere, but with their remarkable night vision, they could avoid all of them.

His heart pounded when Calen reached out and gripped his hand. "Hurry," she repeated in a tremulous whisper. "We don't have much time."

An hour later, after having showered and changed into casual clothing Godfredo lent him, Reno was inside Calen's massive bedroom at her villa, a cup of hot, delicious coffee in hand. She sat on the edge of her bed, which was covered by a colorful Peruvian quilt of red, black, yellow and purple. His head spun with information that she'd shared with him about her triple life.

The coffee settled his taut nerves and her presence calmed him. Meeting Godfredo, her foreman and friend, in the cave had blown Reno away. The tactics Calen employed showed her to be a brilliant military strategist in her own right. Proud of her plans to keep the *esmeraldos* safe, Reno just watched her and absorbed her unique energy.

Calen was no ordinary woman. But then, she was a

Warrior for the Light, so why should he be surprised? As he gratefully sipped the hot coffee, Reno burrowed his bare toes into the thick softness of the sheepskin rug beneath his feet.

"I had a dream last night, Reno," Calen confided to him in a low voice. "Remember the legend? It was said that a woman in the northern province of the Inca empire would find the first emerald sphere when the world had plunged into the final days of darkness before ultimate destruction?"

"Yes," Reno said. "I recall the same information being passed down through my family."

Nodding, Calen tried to keep her focus on what was most important. But every time she looked at Reno's mouth and remembered the branding, heating quality of it sliding across her own, she became liquid, could barely think coherently. "I had a dream that showed me where the cave is located. I was shown a stone altar. On top of it was an old pouch. Then I saw the first emerald sphere inside an old leather bag. I know how to get to this cave to get the emerald."

Calen saw surprise flare in Reno's cinnamon eyes. "We need to go there today—as soon as it gets light enough," she urged. "It's time, and we're the two people who are being asked to go retrieve it."

Shaken, Reno asked, "What about Cruz? When they find me gone, they're going to hunt me down and haul my ass back to the States."

"I don't know. Not yet. I do know you need to be with

me, Reno. In my dream, you were at my side. So I know
you're a part of this discovery." Calen gave a strained
laugh. "When I woke up, I couldn't figure out why you
were there in the dream. Now I do know. You're a jaguar
shape-shifter just like me. That vesica piscis means
we're from the same family." She rubbed the back of her
neck beneath her mass of hair. "We're in this together."

Giving him a searching look, Calen said, "I'm not
going to lie to you, Reno. I've yearned for you with my
heart and soul since we met." She felt heat rush into
her face. "I'm not usually so forthcoming in personal
relationships, but we don't have the time to be anything
but honest with one another right now. All my past relationships were missing something. Now I understand
why. My parents told me that when I was twenty-eight
years old, my mission and my life would join." Gazing
at Reno, she said softly, "The mission is to get that first
sphere. My life is better because you've walked into it.
If our kiss means anything, Reno, it gives me hope,
because you make me feel whole." There, the words
were out. The feelings behind them, powerful.

After setting the cup aside, Reno got to his feet
and moved over to where Calen sat. He saw hope
glinting in her clear green eyes—hope for them, for
a future together. Great Spirit knew, Reno wanted the
same thing. Sliding his hand along her jaw, he
rasped, "I had a wonderful marriage to a woman I
loved with my life, Calen, so I've been luckier than
you in that sense." His fingers lingered near her

parted lips. "I never thought I'd ever meet another woman who could fill me like Ilona did. But I have, and you do…and more. If nothing else, the last month here has taught me that you make me whole, too, in a way I've never known before."

Closing her eyes, Calen absorbed his exploring touch. How she wanted him, body and soul. Heart to heart. The human and animal parts of him melding with her. The sensation was sharp, startling, beautiful and scary to Calen. She gazed up at Reno, who now sat beside her. "I've never known love like you have, Reno." Not until now, but Calen was too frightened to say those words to him.

Reno removed his hand, because if he didn't, he was going to bed her. Instead, he leaned over and picked up the coffee cup from the nightstand. "Let's take this in steps, Calen. First, let's find the cave and that sphere. Next, figure out a way to keep me from getting tossed back into prison."

"All right," Calen agreed huskily. "Let's get some breakfast and then we'll ride to that cave. One step at a time here. Warriors for the Light stick together, through thick and thin…."

Chapter 10

"There it is," Calen called softly, twisting around in her saddle. Reno rode behind her on Star, the chestnut gelding.

"I see it," he called back, keeping his voice low.

After she settled back into her saddle, Calen rode Storm down a steep, muddy slope on a barely visible trail. This was a path more than likely used by wild pigs over the years. She had spotted a rounded mound of black basalt below what was part of the mountain. The area was near a shallow, slow-moving stream, the rock mound thickly covered with trees, ferns and other vegetation. Although the sun was high overhead, the light was dim due to a thunderstorm rumbling toward them.

Calen dismounted near the well-shielded opening and waited for Reno to do the same. They carried knapsacks that contained flashlights, a radio, water and food. When she looked up at the sky, Calen saw a bolt of lightning zigzag above them. Thunder followed, a resounding clap, shortly afterward. Any moment now it would start to pour.

"Let's get inside," Reno said, adjusting the black baseball cap over his eyes. Carrying his covered sniper's rifle on his back, he jogged behind Calen toward the entrance. The ferns held large amounts of dew, and as he waded through the hip-deep vegetation, his jeans quickly became soaked. The fabric clung to him like a second skin, outlining his muscular limbs.

Once she'd slipped through a barrier of spindly trees and reached the entrance, Calen waited for Reno to join her. She was surprised that the cave felt drier than the dank jungle outside.

Though walls of vegetation protected them, Calen was thankful for her pistol. There was no way to tell if locals knew of this cave, or if someone from the dark side was following them. And she wasn't willing to take chances.

"Flashlights," Reno said, looking around. They opened Calen's pack and he pulled out two. After handing her one, he studied the dark cave. "Pretty dry, isn't it?"

"Amazingly so," Calen said. "The stream is just outside. I thought for sure it would be a wet, high-humidity cave. Most of them around here are."

"But the one you use isn't, either," Reno reminded her. "It's fairly dry."

Calen nodded and switched on the light. While it was true they had jaguar vision, even in a completely dark cave, their abilities could not probe the interior and flashlights were necessary. "That's true." The quiet was unnerving after the rising wind from the storm outside. She didn't want to spend any time exploring, just locate the entrance tunnel she'd seen in her dream. Sure enough, an opening appeared at the rear of the oval cave. The roof was jagged, of gray, rust-colored and black basalt. The formation came from lava that had been spilled by a volcano millions of years before. As it cooled, it took on the appearance of what to Calen looked like sharp dragon teeth.

"That's where we're going." She nodded up ahead. "In my dream I was shown a narrow tunnel at the rear of the cave. If my dream is right, it will wind like a snake even farther back, but not go any deeper into the earth."

"That would explain why it's not damp," Reno said. His senses were wide-awake, almost screaming. The smell of guano was strong. He guessed that bats made their home in the front part of the cave. At least, in this entrance area. On the ground, which was composed of hardened clay, he saw mounds of droppings, a few bleached skeletons of smaller animals that had crawled in here to die and sharp triangles of basalt that had fallen from the ceiling over time.

"Right. Let's go." Calen's hushed voice echoed

softly. Just as she stepped forward, a huge boom of thunder caromed across the jungle. The air in the cave literally trembled from the loud rumbling. Cringing, she hurried toward the tunnel.

Anxiety, fear and curiosity flared in Calen. The space was narrow and only one person at a time could traverse it. She felt Reno right behind her, however. It was a comforting feeling. Would they really find a stone altar at the end of this tunnel?

The air inside was fresh, not at all dank or musty. As Calen trained the light on the floor, she realized there had to be another entrance through which such clean air could flow. They continued in a twisting, snakelike fashion for nearly ten minutes. Touching the rough wall of rock as she walked, Calen finally saw the path widening in front of her.

"I think we're nearly there," she called over her shoulder to Reno. He was almost too large for the narrow passage and had to bend over as he went.

"Good," he growled. "I feel like a pretzel that's been pulled out of shape."

As she stepped into a huge, circular room of hard-packed red clay, Calen knew they'd arrived. Moving her light around the space, Calen spotted the altar. Her breath snagged.

"Look, Reno." She pointed excitedly. The light revealed more than she'd seen in her dream, and it kept her anchored in awe. Unmoving, they both studied the waist-high, rectangular altar in the silent chamber.

"Interesting," he finally murmured. "Did you see all of this in your dream?"

"No, just the altar and what was on top of it." Calen gulped. The cave's temperature was cool, the air dry and fresh, though she couldn't see another entrance to the room. "Look. The vesica piscis circles have been dug out of the clay around the altar. Do you see that symbol, Reno? There are no bats back here, either."

His eyes narrowed as he ran his flashlight over the two intersecting circles. Indeed, it appeared as if someone had patiently dug them at least three inches deep into the soil. In the center, where the circles overlapped, stood the altar.

Silence cloaked them. He felt safe here and absorbed the calming quiet. "This cave energy feels good to me. How about to you?"

"There's no question it's a healing sensation. Not threatening at all. I don't feel anything bad in here." Calen focused her light on the altar. It wasn't made of basalt as she thought it would be. Instead, smooth rocks of all colors, shapes and sizes created the four-foot-tall and six-foot-wide altar. The stones appeared to have been worn and rounded by water action. The altar was beautiful and celebrated all of nature's colors.

"What do you make of it being situated in the center of the vesica piscis?" Reno asked.

"My mother trained me in the circles, Reno. We were very poor, but she had bought a ball of red yarn from a trading post in Ibarra. I wasn't more than four years old when she showed me how to work with them. I had to cut two sixteen-foot pieces of yarn, then lay one in a circle. Next, I laid out the other piece of yarn in a second circle, covering about half of the first. After I'd created the double ring symbol, she told me to step into either circle outside of where they overlapped.

"I stepped into one. She asked me what I felt. I told her nothing. Then she told me to step into the area where they overlapped. My mom told me they called this the 'Eye' area, and when I stepped into it, I got so dizzy I fell!"

Calen chuckled fondly at the memory. "My mother helped me stand up. She told me to stay in the Eye, ground myself, bend my knees slightly—not lock them—and close my eyes, take a few deep breaths of air and then just feel the energy."

"Interesting," Reno said. "My parents did the same thing, only they used an old ball of white string for me to form the intersecting circles and work with the energy."

She looked up at his deeply shadowed face. "And did you feel it, too? The power in the Eye?"

"Oh, yeah," Reno responded wryly. "Without a doubt. My mother had me sit in the Eye every day and meditate for at least twenty minutes. I had to keep a journal of what I experienced. How about you?"

Smiling softly, Calen wiped her perspiring brow. "Same here. I just find this so amazing, Reno. We're from two different continents, yet our training was identical."

"It validates everything we were told and taught,"

he agreed huskily. Reno studied her intently. "What happened next in your dream?"

"I walked up to the altar to look at the items that rested on top of it."

"We need to be careful," he murmured, pointing to the vesica piscis. "We know from a lot of experience that the power is in that overlapping space. How strong is the power, I wonder? What will it do to you? Is it too powerful to enter without harming or even killing you?"

Shrugging, Calen said, "I was wondering the same thing. When I was meditating in the Eye, I would see a lot of things. Future events. Faces. Places I didn't know. I saw galaxies. I went to other constellations and star systems. I saw many of my past lives here on earth and on other planets. People's faces I didn't recognize—at least, not then—would appear in front of me. Looking back on that training, I realize that many of the faces I saw then were people I knew later in this life."

Wiping his mouth, Reno said, "Same here. Although…" he turned to her with a slight grin, "…I never saw your face. Not until I had that precog of you a day before they cut me loose from prison to come down here." Reno told her the rest of the dream he'd had. Calen's eyes widened beautifully and he found himself aching to kiss her once more. Again, it wasn't the right time or place.

"What a beautiful dream about me," Calen whispered, deeply touched. "The jaguar skin I wore over my shoulders was to clue you in that I was a shapeshifter, like you."

"Yeah, but I didn't interpret that part correctly. Dreams are funny," Reno said. "You have them but that doesn't mean you can accurately read or understand what they're trying to say to you. Dreams speak in the language of symbolism. And I don't know many people who are expert interpreters."

Groaning, Calen said, "You're right about that." She shone her light on the altar once more. Curiosity was eating at her. She wanted to run over and check it out, but years of training cautioned her to be conservative in her approach.

"This is a very, very sacred site," Reno said. "We need to try and understand the power that's here and not screw it up or get hurt by it."

"Right," Calen said as she continued to glance about the chamber.

"Let's keep looking around before we do anything." He raised his light to the ceiling. It seemed just like the outer chamber. For the next five minutes, they continued to stand, observe and search. They found nothing else. Reno liked the energy of the space; it seemed to throb with a quiet, nurturing life force. Did it have to do with the emerald sphere that might be in that old, dark brown leather bag sitting on the altar? He wasn't sure.

"I'm going to approach the altar," Calen told him. She shed her pack and leaned it against the basalt wall. "You stay here."

"Be careful," Reno warned. "Take your time. Test that Eye very carefully."

"I will," she promised softly. With careful steps, Calen drew closer to the multicolored stone altar. Her breath hitched as she neared it and the overlap. Closing her eyes, she grounded herself by picturing silver tree roots gently encircling her ankles several times, and the tip of each root going down through her feet and sinking at least a hundred feet into Mother Earth. That was something she'd been taught from the beginning. Without proper grounding, people could find themselves in trouble if they entered any place of power.

The energy emitted from a sacred site could overwhelm them, dizzy them, knock them unconscious or worse, kill simply because it was so potent. Calen obviously wanted to protect herself from such a reaction.

After proper grounding, she opened her eyes and took several deep, calming breaths. The altar was less than eight feet away from her. Looking down at the symbol carved into the floor, she lifted her foot to move into it.

As she stepped into the Eye, Calen was instantly seized by the power. If she hadn't spread her feet farther apart than normal, she'd have been bowled over by the fierce waves of energy radiating and pulsing within. Holding her hands out from her body as if she were on a tightrope high above the ground, she gulped and struggled to rebalance herself.

"Calen?" Reno's voice was urgent. Worried.

"I'm okay. The energy's really powerful here. I'm just trying to come to grips with it. Give me a minute to let my aura and body adjust to it." She closed her eyes and visualized the power coming into the center of her head, or crown chakra, then flowing down through her body, into her legs, feet, and following the silver roots into the earth. As soon as she did that, the dizziness stopped.

Breathing raggedly, Calen waited. The whirling sensation quickly dissolved. Now she felt light, happy and in ecstasy instead of like a ship being tossed in a violent storm. Instead of fighting the energy that throbbed vitally within the Eye, she was now a part of it.

"Everything's settling down now, Reno." She slowly lowered her arms back to her sides. "I'm hooked into the energy. Now I'll see what's on the altar."

"Just be careful," he pleaded from where he stood near the tunnel opening, his flashlight trained on her.

Calen approached the altar. Colorful, rounded pebbles lay next to a rotting llama-skin pouch wrapped with gold wire. Her heart pounding with anticipation, she slowly opened her hand, palm flat, and ran it above the pouch several times.

"What are you picking up?"

"A whole lot of energy. My palm feels like it's burning. But it's a cold sensation."

"Feminine energy, then."

"Yes." Calen flicked the accumulated energy off her hand. She had garnered the invisible yet palpable energy by moving into the space above the pouch. Masculine energy was always hot or warm, feminine energy gave a cool or cold sensation. "Whatever is in this pouch definitely has only feminine energy in it." Part of the container was cracked and open. Calen leaned over and shone her light into it. What she saw stole her breath.

"What?" Reno demanded, concerned. "What's wrong?"

"Oh, this is just incredible, Reno. There's a beautiful emerald sphere inside this pouch! I can see it! When I flash my light into it, the light reflects. The color is so…awesome…magnificent…."

"Do you want to pick it up? Or does it feel like there's too much power to it?" Reno had seen medicine objects that his parents would handle only during ceremony. And he understood that the Emerald Key was a consummate ceremonial tool. A global one. The energy around it would be potent and perhaps fatal if a person handled it incorrectly or without profound respect or proper metaphysical training.

Reno's throat tightened as he watched her continued investigation of the pouch. Calen did not attempt to touch the object yet. A well-trained metaphysician was always cautious around energy. Especially energy like this. And yet, despite his confidence in her skills, he couldn't help but be scared for her.

Calen's pulse quickened. Her breathing became shallow. She rubbed her right hand against her damp jeans and prepared herself to pick up the pouch. Would it knock her silly? Kill her? Calen wasn't sure. Just as she got ready to slide her fingers into the pouch, she saw the emerald begin to throb and glow from within. Instantly, she froze, her fingers inches from the object. Gasping, she whispered, "It's alive, Reno! It started glowing with an inner light just as my fingers got near it, like someone switching on a lightbulb."

"Okay, just be careful. Can you telepathically get in touch with the spirit within it? Tell the spirit that you come in peace? Not to harm you?"

"I'm doing that right now." Calen closed her eyes and sent a friendly message of introduction to the spirit of the sphere. She knew that everything on Mother Earth was alive. Each rock contained a spirit whose personality was as diverse as that of people. As she communicated her name and why she was here, there was an instant reaction from the emerald sphere. Feeling coolness and excitement touching her mind, Calen relaxed. The sensation was feminine, gentle and incredibly nurturing, much like a mother holding her infant to her breast.

May I pick you up? I mean you no harm, Calen told the spirit within the emerald sphere.

You have my permission, daughter of the Inca people. I have waited a long time for you to appear. Please, pick me up, Warrior for the Light.

Calen was familiar with that name. Grinning, she eased her fingers into the cracked leather pouch. After curling them around the golf-ball-size sphere, she carefully removed it. The emerald rested in the palm of her right hand and an explosion of energy poured through her.

If she hadn't been grounded, Calen knew that she'd have dropped to her knees like a felled ox. Instead, the sphere blazed internally like a beacon, throbbing with shimmering, dappled gold-green light. The gemstone felt cool, peaceful and centering to Calen. She heard Reno shifting restlessly behind her. "It's stunning, Reno," she said. "And it feels so good." Turning, Calen held it out toward him. "Look. It's just so miraculous to be holding this."

Reno stepped forward, but stayed outside the over-lapped circles. Calen's whole body seemed to glow. The powerful light emanating from the sphere infused her aura, brightening the cave with its greenish hue. He felt privileged to witness the emerald's effect on her. Respectful and awed, he stood a few feet away from her and stared. The emerald sphere was huge, roughly rounded and shaped by human hands sometime in the ancient past.

"It's beautiful," he managed to murmur. "I've never seen anything like it, Calen. Ever."

"Me, neither," Calen whispered. "Would you hand me that pouch we brought in my knapsack?"

"Right." Reno hurried back to her pack to retrieve the bag. After handing it to her, he watched as Calen gently deposited the glowing sphere inside and tight-ened the thongs at the top. The light in the cave fell back into blackness as soon as the sphere was safely deposited. Reno switched on his flashlight once more, and she handed the pouch to him.

"This emerald rocks with power," she warned. "We can't wear it on our bodies or we'll be so spaced out we won't know what's going on. We need to put it in the leather saddlebag on Storm when we leave here. Storm has four feet solidly connected to Mom Earth. She'll be able to handle the energy, send it to the earth without being stunned like we are."

Reno agreed. As the soft, buttery leather filled his left palm, he felt the incredible cool, feminine energy instantly flow up his arm. It surprised him as nothing else ever had. Oh, he'd grounded himself, for sure, but he didn't know what to expect from holding such a sacred object. The energy tunneled through him like a green-gold tsunami wave and ended up in his chest, encircling his racing heart.

Then, to Reno's shock, he began to see flashes of his wife and daughter in his mind's eye, or brow chakra. The pictures staggered him. He saw happier times with them before he'd been sent to Afghanistan to hunt down terrorists.

Calen saw Reno's face change. As he held the sphere, she heard a low gasp issue from between his compressed lips. What was going on? She stepped out of the Eye and over to his side. His expression shocked her. First, she saw his pain, and then tears gathered and finally rolled down his face. Reno was crying. He was the last man on earth Calen expected to see break down and weep.

"What's going on, Reno? What's the sphere doing to you?" She gripped his arm to steady him.

With brimming, hot tears running down the weathered, hardened planes of his face, Reno couldn't speak. All he could do was feel and then feel some more. He felt the utter helplessness, revenge and rage associated with the general who had murdered his family. Then he felt the soothing, calming beauty of the emerald's energy flowing through him, erasing his pain. And, like waves lapping an ocean shore, Reno experienced the rage and hatred and vengefulness again, to be washed away once more by a wave of healing, profoundly loving energy from the sphere.

Calen tightened her grip on his arm. He'd closed his eyes, his fingers wrapped tightly around the pouch he clutched to his chest. Something good was going on between Reno and the emerald sphere. Calen wasn't sure what it was.

Urgency thrummed through her. In that moment, she realized that she loved him.

Chapter 11

"Take it. I can't handle this energy anymore." Reno thrust the pouch back into Calen's hands just before they reentered the tunnel. His voice was thick with emotion, unsteady and raw sounding even to him.

Calen took the pouch containing the sphere and quickly dived back into the tunnel. Reno followed, flashes of his past with his family continuing to hit him, shake him to his core. The memories were poignant and filled with love. Somehow, they erased his agenda of hatred and revenge. Never had he felt so much since Ilona and Sarah's deaths. Reno rubbed his chest and struggled to focus on getting out of this place in one piece. The dark side could be around, and he had to remain alert.

When they reached the outer chamber, Calen saw a gray light leaking through the thick, heavy wall of rain-soaked foliage that covered the entrance. Something in one corner of the cave caught her eye. She flashed her light in that direction and saw what appeared to be an old leather pack, rotting and falling apart. A shiver went down her spine. There was also a body, long dead, the clothes rotting off the corpse. Choking, she turned to Reno, who came to a halt when he saw the body, too. "I didn't see this in my dream."

Reno studied it from across the room. "Looks like a miner's pack, maybe. There's a pickax next to it. Can you make it out?"

"Barely. I saw a tool." Who was it? Someone who'd came across the cave by accident? Did whoever it was know of the sphere on the altar?

"I wonder if someone got lost and stumbled in here by mistake," Reno said, his voice low. "Disoriented, maybe? Sick? Dying? Let's go find out."

Calen shivered, put the pouch in her left pocket and followed Reno over to the nearly hidden corpse. The light revealed a very old man. There was no rotting odor; the body had long ago dried out, the skin and flesh eaten away by insects, revealing gleaming white bones. Calen saw long white hair and recognized a leather miner's hat. "He was an *esmeraldo*," she whispered. "Very old."

Reno tried to ignore the ongoing war of emotions the sphere had stirred up within him. Crouching down, he carefully removed a leather sack that hung around one of the man's whitened scapulas. "What's in here? Shine the flashlight on it for a sec." Reno opened it up. Inside was a piece of rolled up paper tied by with a leather thong. The leather fell away as Reno removed it, the paper cracked and powdery with age. Carefully, he opened the thin, brittle sheet. "Looks like some kind of official stamped deed. A miner's claim, maybe?"

"Let's get it out into better light to look at it," Calen said, gazing over his shoulder.

"Good idea." Reno handed the paper to her. "I'm going to search this dude to see if he has any identification on him." He went through the rotting fabric of the man's peasant shirt and cotton trousers. "From the looks of it, this gent was elderly when he died," Reno said, continuing his search. "He might have died of malaria or some other disease."

"*Esmeraldos* die of starvation more than disease," Calen told him grimly. "And dysentery." She felt deeply for the man who had died alone in this cave. Who was he?

Reno found no identification on the skeletal remains, and soon gave up the search. "Let's get outside," he coaxed, rising to his feet. Right now, Reno wanted to get out into the light, into the greenery of the jungle. His heart ached with such grief and joy that he struggled not to be overwhelmed by it.

The thunderstorm had passed. Above him in the hazy blue sky, a few strands of humid white clouds drifted silently by. He and Calen moved to where the horses were tied. The animals' coats were darkened from the rain, the saddles damp from the earlier downpour. Calen deposited the pouch with the emerald into Storm's saddlebag and then buckled it shut. Reno joined her as she opened the brittle piece of paper found on the old miner.

"Oh…" Calen whispered, shock in her tone. "This is Phelan Santiago! Oh, dear."

Frowning, Reno scrutinized the deed, written in Spanish. "Who was he?"

"Phelan was a legend here at the Santa Maria mine. He and his family were among the first *esmeraldos* to settle here two generations ago." Calen rapidly read the official-looking paper. "There are latitudes and longitudes on this, describing a piece of property that is deeded to him and his family. It's near Ibarra, because the town is mentioned. Phelan had gone into Quito, to the recorder's office, to have this deed stamped. He's the owner of something around here, but I can't tell what from this deed. Surveying descriptions aren't my forte." She glanced up at Reno. "Do you know what this describes?" She handed the paper to him.

"Not really. We'd have to go to Quito to find out. They'd have this claim on record. I don't know if it's a mining claim, or maybe he bought a piece of land to live on near Ibarra." He searched Calen's willow-green eyes—eyes that gave him a profound sense of peace.

"No *esmeraldo* owns land here," Calen said,

scowling. She rolled up the paper, her voice tensing. "Tomorrow, I'm going to send Godfredo and some of his men back here to pick up Phelan's remains. The man was considered a mystical person and a healer, Reno. Everyone at the *esmeraldo* camp along the river loved him. His grandson, Jose Santiago, is the patriarch now. I need to tell Jose and his family about this. I know they'll be shocked but happy to get Phelan's body back for burial."

"Was Phelan one of us?" Reno asked, looking toward the camouflaged opening of the cave.

"That's what I was wondering. My mother told me that those with the vesica piscis birthmark have different metaphysical talents. Some are healers. Others are telepaths, or know how to teleport things or themselves from one place to another. They aren't all shape-shifters like us. She mentioned that a person might have a strong ability as an empath, able to feel others and help them. Or a medium who speaks to the spirits of the dead and brings their messages back to the living."

"My parents said our kind could be shamans, too, able to traverse the invisible dimension and bring back messages, information or retrieve lost pieces of a person's spirit." Reno looked around. The sharp squawk of parrots, along with screeches of nearby monkeys, brought the jungle into focus for him.

Calen tucked the paper inside her vest and zipped it shut. "My father said some of our kind had telekinesis, the ability to move things and make them appear

and disappear." Touching the damp skin at the back
of her neck, she added, "Whatever we are, Reno, we
are distinctive. But I've always felt different—and
alone. Having my parents explain to me why helped
me so much."

"We have a lot of other things to worry about right
now," Reno warned her. "I'm a wanted fugitive. I have
to report to Cruz every morning on what I did the
previous night, patrolling the mountain slopes of the
mine. I didn't show up this morning. I'm sure he's
already placed a call to that spook in Quito and he's
got the local law enforcement out looking for me."
Reno's mouth became a determined line. "I'm not
going home in chains, Calen. Never again. I'll die first."

Alarmed, she reached out, her fingers tentative on
the bulging muscles of his upper arm. "You're staying
with me, Reno. No one will think that I, the local rich
woman, would hide someone like you. Don't worry
about that for now. And Godfredo and his family will
keep your secret. They won't turn you in."

"Cruz probably thinks I took off and am hiding in
the jungle somewhere." Snorting, Reno added, "Not
that the bastard would go after me. He's too soft and
too much of a wimp. But he would send his mercs out
lookin' for me." Her hand on his arm sent waves of
longing through him. How much Reno wanted to kiss
Calen again! The urgency and danger of their situation
was primary, however.

"Good," Calen said. "Let him. That will keep him

occupied. Let's mount up and get back to the villa. There's a lot of planning we need to do."

Sated by a lunch of white rice, red beans and savory curried beef, Reno followed Calen to the massive library in the center of her stucco villa. They'd showered, he'd shaved, and Godfredo had found another set of clothes near his size to wear in lieu of the ones that were muddy and stained from their jaunt to the cave that morning.

Calen sat down at her mahogany desk and Reno pulled up a chair opposite. She had made a document copy of the deed and faxed it to the Quito recorder's office for confirmation and explanation of what it was.

Calen placed the pouch containing the sphere between them on the shiny desktop. As he eyed the small sack, she could see he was wary. "We need to look at this in good light," she told him. Opening the pouch and pulling over a high-intensity desk lamp, Calen cradled the sphere in her left palm and looked at it closely. "I see the vesica piscis symbol on it, Reno. And there's something else….a script or some kind of writing engraved on it."

Turning, Calen picked out a book, an old leather-bound one, from a shelf. "When my family was murdered by Santa Maria guards, I was ten years old. I wasn't at the Catholic orphanage for more than three months before my foster mother and father adopted me." Calen opened the book, her fingers gently turning the yellowed, brittle pages. "My adopted parents loved me like their own. I got the best education and lived in a home that was like a castle.

"One of the things I did as a child was to try and write down everything my real parents had taught me about my birthmark. As I got into my teen years, I began scouring antique stores in Quito for old books on the topic. And this is one of them." Calen lifted her head and looked across the desk at him. "My biological father said that the Emerald Key was a necklace that contained seven huge emerald spheres with gold spacers between them. The necklace had been deliberately taken apart. He said the spheres were hidden around the world to keep them from being found by the dark side. One day, he told me, a woman born in the northern provinces of the Inca empire would come along and she would find the first one. She would then create a building where she would draw others like herself together, in order to help the world.

"In this building, the sphere would be safe, and she would send people around the world to find the other emeralds, one at a time. My mother said each sphere had a word plus the vesica piscis sign engraved upon the surface. She called them the Seven Virtues of Peace." Calen found the spot in the leather book, her hand gracefully splayed across the yellowed pages. After Calen stood, she turned the book around and placed it in front of Reno to read.

Reno cradled the old book. The leather casing was

cracked and aged, several places ragged and split. He quickly perused the Spanish. When he turned the page, he saw the somewhat geometric script that did, indeed, match what was inscribed on the sphere. "Do you know what the virtues are?" he asked, returning the book to her.

Calen shook her head. "No. My parents were training me every day, and I'm sure at some point I would have learned that. But they were taken from me before I was taught it." Her voice ebbed with old grief. She saw the tenderness burning in Reno's eyes, and when he gripped her hand, her sadness lessened.

"I'm sorry, Calen. I can't imagine losing one's parents so young." And he couldn't. Clearing his throat, Reno added hoarsely, "But I know what loss of loved ones is, and in that way, we seem to be alike. We've both lost those who meant the most to us." Reluctantly, he eased his grip from her cool hand. He didn't want to, but it was necessary. "Maybe because we're shape-shifters or maybe because we are jaguars, this kind of awful loss has to be experienced or lived through the best we know how. Jaguar medicine brings tragedy as a way to develop our spiritual strength. I don't know." He shrugged his shoulders.

Her hand tingled with the delicious heat of his touch. "My parents said the path of the jaguar was about life-and-death issues. My life mirrors that in all respects. My parents and brothers were murdered as I hid in the bushes and watched them being shot to death by foreign mercenaries. And then I'm taken and reborn, given a new life as an adopted daughter to the richest oil baron in South America. I return here, to Ibarra, to help my people, and I end up killing four mercenaries."

Shaking her head, Calen uttered in a mournful tone, "I never meant to kill them. I hate killing. All I wanted to do was drug the guards, scare them into quitting so that Cruz would stop murdering the *esmeraldos*." Touching her heart, Calen gave Reno a trembling half smile. "I can never forgive myself for having to kill another human being. I…it just isn't part of my makeup. Yet here I am, riding the slopes with a rifle, ready to shoot any guards who try to kill my people."

"I've killed forty-two men," Reno told her, his deep voice contemplative. "Listen to me, Calen. In my mind, I rationalize their deaths by reminding myself that those terrorists won't cause another 9/11 somewhere else in the world. I see what I've done as something positive, not negative. And you have to do the same."

"I was raised to believe that killing was wrong, Reno. No matter what the reason."

"I wasn't. My parents said that Warriors for the Light had the right to defend themselves against the dark side. That included killing, if it became necessary," he growled. "Sometimes you can't fight the darkness by wishing it away or being nice, Calen. You can't make nice to something that doesn't recognize nice."

"Yet we are the unforgiven, Reno. You cannot forgive the general who murdered your wife and daughter. I doubt I could, either. And I can't forgive myself for killing those guards to save lives I felt were equally important." Sighing, Calen spread her hands. "I know jaguar medicine is about life and death. I guess I never realized how brutal and real things would become. As a child, I heard my parents speak of jaguar medicine. And when they were murdered, well, I remembered that it was about violence and transformation. My parents were shape-shifters, too. They died terrible, violent deaths. So did my brothers. I'll never forget it." Calen's lips quirked as she searched Reno's hooded eyes. "Am I a killer, too? A murderer by nature? Is that why violence follows my life path?"

"Listen to me," he demanded harshly. "Jaguars are primal animals. They are at the top of the food chain here in South America. Their *nature* is to kill to eat or to defend their territory. Don't you think that among the Warriors for the Light, there must be some who battle with the dark side? Not everyone is on the front lines as we are. There are many roles to play in bringing peace to this world. My parents said there were people in all walks of life, all careers, of both genders, who were Warriors for the Light. Most do not know who they are. Some do. But not all defend and kill. That is the role of the jaguar clan we are a part of. We are on the front lines, Calen. That is our nature, and we're here to fulfill it. That doesn't mean we enjoy killing, because we don't. We see it only as a necessary end product when nothing else—diplomacy or arbitration—will work.

"We're not all jaguars, to be sure," she added. "And not all shape-shifters are warriors. But there have to be warriors among us to do the dirty work." Calen smiled. "I try to look at us as if we are Jedi warriors from the *Star Wars* movies. We always defend. We never attack. And we're in this huge global battle, locked into a death-spiral dance with the dark side. My parents told me I was born into this time and body to be a Warrior for the Light. To put my life on the line to bring a thousand years of peace to this earth of ours. They never told me how that would come about or what part I'd play. But I did grow up knowing I had a mission, and that I was a warrior for Mother Earth and all her relations."

"Sometimes," Reno confided, his voice husky with feeling, "we have to meet the dark side at their level, and fight for the *right* reasons, not the wrong ones. More of us should put our lives, even our family's lives, on the line in the hope that our world will choose peace instead of destruction. That is why we are the way we are. Every army has to have soldiers, and we're all of that."

"Great logic," Calen muttered, sitting back in the chair and studying him. "My conscience eats me alive over the four men I've killed. I hate going out two or three times a week to confront those guards. I know the possibility is always there that I'll have to kill them if I can't drug them first. I guess I don't want to believe I have to kill in order to bring peace to the world. There's got to be a better way."

"There is," Reno said, trying to help her feel better. He jabbed his finger toward the sphere resting on the desk. The unearthly orb throbbed constantly with a golden-green glow. "The Emerald Key is part of that cosmic plan for peace for our planet. If we find the rest of the spheres before the dark side does. It is said that once the necklace is worn by this special woman who is pregnant with child, the earth will be showered with the energies of love, peace and compassion. This is the trigger for the earth to move out of the dark and head to the light, toward a dawning new era. Toward that thousand years, Calen. So, you've just taken the first positive step in that direction without using violence. You've found the first sphere."

"You're right. But there's much more we have to do. I thought a lot on the way back to the villa about building this place that the legend talked about. A special building to house this sphere. A place for the Warriors for the Light to call home."

"A base of operation." Reno nodded. "A place where we can marshal our forces to find the other pieces of the Emerald Key. It's a good idea. Did you ever have dreams about this?"

"Yes, many years ago. Shortly after my adopted parents died in a plane crash, and I was left with their oil empire, I had a series of dreams." Calen stood up and went to another row of books on the dark mahogany shelves. She pulled out one particular journal and set it on the desk, opening to a certain page. Tracing the handwriting with her finger, she said, "I was twenty-one at the time of their deaths. I kept a daily diary after that, Reno, because I was so devastated by their loss. I had to have someplace to express how I felt. I was three months into my grieving when I had a series of dreams." She turned the journal around and handed it to him. "Read these entries. See if any of my dreams make sense to you, or match what you were taught by your parents about who and what we are."

Reno pored over the entries, entranced by the information, by what she'd experienced. "Incredible…" he murmured after he'd finished. "Your dreams are a blueprint for what's to be done now." Shaking his head, he added, "Calen, do you realize you're the woman from the northern provinces of the Inca empire? You're the woman our legends have talked about." Reno gazed adoringly at her. There was no doubt she was attractive, accomplished, rich, but she was so much more to him.

"I don't know about that, Reno."

"Warriors for the Light are always humble," he said. "And you wear that trait well." He tapped the journal in his hands. "Calen, you're the one. You just found the first sphere. You were given the dream of where to find it, at the exact right time. And you were given a series of dreams or instructions on how to create the building for the light to fight the dark side. It's all in here. You have the money to do it, too."

"Don't forget," Calen said, unwilling to take on such a heavy responsibility, "the legend speaks of two more couples. A woman from the south, also part of the Inca empire, will come to me if I am truly the one. She carries the dark side within her, and yet she will know how to combat her own darkness and come to aid us, instead."

"Build it and she'll arrive," Reno murmured grimly. "And it will draw the third and final couple to help create the core of the Warriors for the Light."

"First things first," Calen said. "We need to get you a new identity and keep you out of sight of Cruz and his goons." She wanted to add, *I don't ever want to let you go, Reno. You're so much a part of my life.*

For the first time, Calen felt a breath of hope infusing her spirit, her heart. What she and Reno shared as shape-shifters was clearly a tie that would never be broken. It explained to her on so many levels why she had felt so irresistibly drawn to him even when he was trying to hunt her down, to kill El Espanto.

She saw Reno's eyes grow warm as she stood. "And how are you going to do that?" he asked.

Grinning a little, Calen said, "I have friends in Quito who can give you a new name, an Ecuadorian passport, driver's license and all the rest. You're going to need a makeover if you're going to help me bring all these dreams and ideas into being." She saw surprise in his eyes. "What? You don't think I will need help? I'm not about to let you walk out of my life, Reno. You're my partner in this, whether you like it or not. I can't do it alone."

Slowly rising to his full height, Reno rested his hands on his narrow hips. Calen looked defiant, a true warrior despite her soft cotton T-shirt, formfitting blue jeans and tousled hair. "To tell you the truth, Calen, it's nice to be wanted."

"You're more than wanted. You're irreplaceable." *To me. To my heart...* Calen bit back the words she longed to speak to him. Reno could run. He could leave. She couldn't stop him and she knew it. "I'm committed to this building, to finding the rest of the Emerald Key, to fulfilling my part in this legend now come to life. I hope you are, too." Fear gripped her stomach, making it ache with uncertainty.

She saw Reno's jaw flex. "My destiny is with you, Calen," he declared. "And unless you tell me to leave, I'm going nowhere."

Sheets of relief cascaded through her. Closing her eyes for a moment, Calen let the feelings roll through her. "Good," she whispered, and opened her eyes. "Because I don't want anyone else at my side but you." *Now and forever.*

But Calen couldn't say those words yet. So much had been violently torn from her in her life that she was afraid to dream of a warrior like Reno who could be with her, live with her. Not when she loved him with every breath she took.

The terror of seeing him violently taken from her stopped the words from leaving her mouth. No, Calen understood that every day would be a teeter-totter of loss or gain. There was no guarantee that Reno would stay, or for how long. Cruz could find him. A foreign mercenary could spot him and shoot him on sight. Life was so tenuous. So unsure.

Taking a deep, ragged breath, Calen said, "Come on, Reno, we've got a lot of work to do."

Chapter 12

"I don't believe this! Look, Reno." Calen handed him a reply to the fax she'd sent to the Quito recorder's office earlier that morning.

Reno was sitting at her desk, a number of papers spread out around him. Even with the danger swirling about them, Calen felt joyful. She had an ally, a partner, and her strong emotions toward Reno were reciprocated.

"What did they find?" Reno frowned and read the fax. When Calen was nearby, he found himself almost unable to concentrate on assigned tasks. "Phelan Santiago is the *owner* of the Santa Maria mine? The *emerald mine?*" He glanced up at her, disbelief in his voice.

She had a shining look of triumph in her eyes. "According to the recorder's office, he was the first to discover emeralds on the volcano, and went to Quito and filed the claim." Calen pointed to the fax. "He's the true owner, Reno. Do you know what this means? It means the Guild—Cruz and all the rest—have stolen it from beneath this old man."

Scratching his head, Reno leaned back in the leather chair. "If this is so, why didn't Phelan contest it, then?"

"Phelan was a poor miner, Reno. He had neither the money nor means to hire a lawyer. He was barely literate. Cruz and his bunch rolled into town and claimed the mine out from under him."

"But—" Reno waved the paper in her direction "—the Quito recorder's office couldn't just ignore Santiago's claim, could they?"

"Did you see the last line of the fax, where they say that they'd *lost* the copy they'd made and filed from the original document? My hunch is that Cruz slipped someone a lot of money to get rid of the copy of the deed there. Phelan had the original on him, or had hidden it so Cruz couldn't destroy it, I'll bet."

"But the old miner had the original deed all the time."

"Right. We may never know what happened or why Phelan didn't contest Cruz moving in on his claim. My guess is that he didn't mount a defense due to lack of money and lack of understanding of the legal system."

"Or," Reno said, his voice grim, "knowing what I know about Cruz, the bastard may have threatened

Phelan's family with death if he tried to fight for the land."

"That's true, too," Calen sighed. "When you come from a poor background, you're easily a victim. You don't think you deserve anything. And if Cruz did threaten the large, extended Santiago family, who have lived along the Esmeralda River since the mine was discovered, I'm sure Phelan would have wanted to protect them. So he just kept this document hidden."

Reno set the fax on the mahogany desk. He couldn't stop looking at Calen, admiring everything about her. Her hair was pulled back from her face now, exposing her high cheekbones and exquisite skin. But it was always her spring-green eyes that drew him like a thirsting soul. "So? What are you going to do?"

"Plenty." Calen folded her arms. "First I'm going to contact the Santiago family and show them the deed. Then I'll hire the best real estate attorney in Quito, and work with Jose Santiago to bring a lawsuit against the Guild and have the court award the property to the family. In the end, the Santiago clan will own the Santa Maria mine and Cruz and his goons will have to leave—permanently."

"Talk about twists and turns. Funny, how life is like that, isn't it?"

Just being in Reno's powerful, steadying presence was a gift to Calen. How badly she wanted to tell him that. But she couldn't, not with so many feelings to sort through and figure out. "We both know that better than most. I went from rags to riches. You went from free man to prisoner. And now you're free again."

"Not yet," he murmured. Reno knew she had put considerable time and energy into getting him new identification, a viable passport and other papers to make him a citizen of Ecuador. "I saw Godfredo in the kitchen. He just got back from Ibarra and said it's swarming with police and foreign mercenaries looking for me. They're showing pictures with my mug on them."

Calen reached out, resting her hand tentatively on his broad, capable shoulder. The blue polo shirt only emphasized the breadth and depth of his chest. "I know. And you are going to have to hide here until we can get things straightened out."

He settled his hand over hers. "Calen, I'm worried for *you*. If Cruz catches you hiding me, well, this guy is ballistic and out of control. If he gets even the faintest hint that I'm here, the bastard could send an army of goons down here and blast his way through your villa. Do you realize that?"

"I've thought of it, yes. I think the best thing to do is for you to work here in the library during the day and sleep in the cave at night. I know they'll never find the cave. They may well send guards to ask if you're here, but they won't find *you*."

Reno had other plans in mind. Dreams, actually. He wanted to sleep with Calen in her bedroom. Knowing that wasn't to be, he murmured, "Good idea. The cave will be fine."

"I'll have Godfredo put a bed there later today, with blankets, a pillow and other stuff. It's only temporary, but we can't take chances." She clasped his shoulder more firmly. "I just found you, Reno. I'm not going to lose you."

Hearing the tremor in Calen's voice, he squeezed her strong, warm hand. "Stop worrying. If I need to, I can escape out of the cave and into the jungle. You forget that I'm a sniper. I know how to fade into the background and live off the land. We'll take this a day at a time."

Reno released her hand, sat up and spread out several drawings on the desk in front of him. "Look at these, Calen. Drawings made from your dream journals. I've sketched them out. Tell me what you think."

She moved closer and admired his work. Just getting to bask in the warmth of his aura was enough for now. "Amazing, Reno. You've made my dreams a reality." Calen looked down at him, his face inches from hers. "I see you've put a sign on the front of the building— Vesica Piscis Foundation."

"Do you like it? I think the symbol should be the name of your foundation."

"I like it."

"You can start building wherever you want. And while you're constructing this place, this home for people like us, I can help you with ideas on how to create an Internet Web site, as well. This will give us global reach. I think that when people see the symbol, it's going to trigger a deep, hidden memory within them. A positive one."

"Genetic memory as well as archetypal resonance," Calen agreed, glancing at the points he'd written, a brief template for the Web site. "We all respond, in varying degrees, to ancient symbols because they are archetypes that reside in everyone's subconscious. The people who are supposed to work with us toward a peaceful planet will hear the 'call' and will be drawn to us. Even a person not aware of who or what she or he is will respond—that's the power of an archetype."

"And that's enough," Reno said, rubbing his chin. "It will call them to the Web site and get them in touch with us—I mean you."

"Reno, this *is* an 'us' gig. Not just me."

"I wasn't sure, Calen. I'm a stranger to you. And I have no money to speak of."

Calen rested her hip against the desk and looked down at him. "I found out a long time ago money is only a means to an end. And I can't think of a better place for my billions than erecting a foundation that would have teachers to teach people like us about our spiritual gifts. Or to be able to mount missions to help people who are beleaguered by the dark side. There are many who aren't like us, but who desire and pray for peaceful coexistence just as we do, Reno. We can use everyone's help. In turn, we can assist them in learning about their natural psychic abilities, because everyone was born with them to a greater or lesser degree."

Calen saw his eyes glitter in silent agreement. "I've thought a lot about this since this morning, Reno," she added. In my dreams I was with someone—and I'm sure it was you. Together, we could turn my vision into a reality."

"I bring the military mind-set to it."

"Yes, and I think it's going to be an important component of our foundation. Even though we want peace, we will have to fight for it. I'm not fooling myself. We are going to have to find the Warriors for the Light and draw them here to us. We are going to become responsible for training them, informing them and also trying to locate the other spheres of the Emerald Key."

"The foundation will have a lot of different aspects," Reno said. "Which seems to be why the other woman of Incan heritage and her partner will bring further assets and knowledge to the mix."

"Right. We're thinking alike on this, Reno. Don't forget, there's a third team, too. There will be six of us, three women and three men, to run this foundation fighting the dark side." Grimly, Calen added, "I don't know about you, but holding that sphere this morning changed everything. I realize now I was receiving a healing from it. I kept seeing flashes of my family being murdered. I felt all the old feelings I'd held so long in my heart." Calen touched her chest. "And now I feel cleansed. I feel lighter, Reno, as if the sphere was able to lift that wound out of me to start the healing process."

Reno leaned back in his chair. "I had a similar experience." And he told her about it. "All day, I've been processing a lot of feelings, mostly ones of revenge, of wanting to kill that general."

"That's why you handed the sphere back to me in the cave," Calen said. "You had such an odd look on your face. I didn't know what was going on."

"I was being battered by waves of feelings, good and bad," Reno admitted hoarsely. "That sphere did something to me, Calen. I can't describe it."

"That's a healthy sign, Reno." She gave him a tender look and touched his muscled forearm. "When I saw you crying, I knew that the sphere was helping you in some powerful way. Tears are always good. Better out than in, you know." She lifted her hand away, but oh, how she wanted to slide her fingers upward and continue touching him, absorbing him and seeing the wonderful changes in his cinnamon eyes.

"I never cried after my family was murdered," he admitted. "I was told of their deaths two weeks after it happened. My partner and I were out of touch in the Tora Bora mountains. When our C.O. finally got ahold of us, my wife and daughter had already been cremated." Reno stared sightlessly at the desk. "I never got to see them again. Never got to kiss them goodbye, nothing."

Unable to stand the pain in his face and voice, Calen eased away from the desk. She stepped behind Reno and slid her arms around him. Resting her chin on his shoulder, she pressed her head against his and whispered tremulously, "I'm so sorry, Reno. I'm sorry you didn't get to say goodbye to Ilona and Sarah. That must have been so terrible for you." Closing her eyes, Calen kissed his sandpapery cheek. His masculine scent entered her flaring nostrils. She felt his hands slide over her arms, which were crossed on his chest.

The world seemed to gently halt. Being able to salve Reno's suffering opened up Calen's heart. Hearing him groan sent a sweet reverberation through her. His fingers were strong and caring as they slid up her arms. The moment was pregnant, heated and filled with healing.

Smiling softly, Calen gave him a squeeze and pressed her cheek against his. "We know that when a person dies, their soul goes on living. That was the only hope left in me when I saw my family murdered before my eyes, Reno. They are physically gone, but I know they continue to live in the other dimensions." She sighed and felt his fingers curl gently around her forearms. "At night, in my dreams, they come to me. They love me and I love them. I can talk to them. My mother came to me last night in my dreams and told me that she and my father were now going to start to teach me more about my heritage that they couldn't pass on before they died. She said they couldn't do this before because I hadn't met you yet. Now that I have, my training and understanding will grow through my dreams, instead. I hope you have been able to see your family, to get some sustenance from them even though they are gone from this world of ours."

As he inhaled her spicy sandalwood fragrance, Reno

closed his eyes. Her husky voice poured through him. Did she realize her effect on him? The gentle strength of her arms, her courage to hold him like this. How he needed it! Somehow, Calen understood that the emerald sphere had triggered an avalanche of boiling emotions within him. Starved for a woman's caress, he sat there and absorbed Calen's nearness, her womanly strength healing his shattered heart.

"I don't dream, Calen," he finally managed to say. "Not anymore. I wish I could. I wish I could see Ilona and my daughter, but I don't."

Calen felt such a yearning to love Reno fully. Reluctantly, she eased away from him. The action tore at her heart, and she rested her hands on his shoulders as she stood behind him. "I feel that your desire for revenge, your urge to take the general's life, is blocking that gift for you, Reno. If you can forgive him, then I feel your dreams will allow you to be in touch with your family."

The second she pulled away, Reno missed her closeness. Hell, he was like a starving beggar. Until Calen had entered his life like sunshine, he hadn't realized how human he really was. For so many years, he'd hardened himself, feeling nothing but a fierce desire for revenge.

Her hands moved tenderly across his shoulders as if to soothe away his tortured anguish. Again Reno sensed that Calen could feel his grief and his rage. Was this what happened when two jaguar shape-shifters liked one another? An invisible line of communication stretched between them. Had Calen sensed his need to be held? To be cradled and lovingly protected in the worst moments of his suffering? Reno wasn't sure, but he was grateful nevertheless.

"I think you're right," he admitted gruffly.

"And that emerald sphere is healing the revenge within you." Calen eased her hands from his shoulders, for if she didn't, she was going to lean down and kiss his cheek again, and more. Her body responded torridly to what she really wanted to do: make wild, animal love with him. Unsure that Reno even thought of her in that way, Calen moved back to the side of the desk and held his narrowed, gleaming gaze. "What is the opposite of revenge but forgiveness, Reno?"

"Something's going on, that's for sure." He scowled. "I'm just not ready to give up planning to kill the son of a bitch for what he did to my wife and daughter."

"Maybe, sometime in the future, you will," Calen whispered. Blinking back hot tears, she added, "Perhaps the sphere is giving you a second chance. Grace is what my parents called it. When a person, through positive past actions, earned help from the Great Mother, they considered it grace. And maybe grace is being given to you right now, Reno—to help you review the past and change some of your attitudes and feelings toward it. To help you release it so that you can get on with your life and live in the present."

"For being only twenty-eight years old, you've got a lot of wisdom," he murmured. "What you're saying makes sense. My parents told me a long time ago that the wounds we carry stop us from living in the present."

Gazing into her serene face, Reno realized that if he wanted a relationship with Calen he would have to settle his past and release it once and for all. He smiled. "Thanks. This helps me more than you can ever realize."

So much was going on within Calen. She sensed Reno's dilemma and understood it as never before. He loved his family and always would. But the revenge, the rage and loss, held his heart captive. Calen knew Reno would always love his wife and child; that was as it should be. But the darker part, the revenge, would never allow him space within his heart to try to love again— until he was able to release that hatred toward the general. And until that happened, there was no room in his life for another woman. Even if that was what Calen yearned for, dreamed about and wanted more than the breath of life that flowed in and out of her body.

Unsettled, she held his turbulent stare. Despite her conflicting feelings, she was grateful to know what Reno was going through. In a broader sense, it helped her know how to support him. And that was something she wanted to do more than anything.

Why? Calen was afraid to admit it, to say the words even to herself yet. She hadn't known Reno that long. But it felt to her as if they were lovers reunited from many past lives they'd shared before—and they'd met once again in this lifetime. Swallowing, Calen stood up. "I need to contact the Santiagos. I'm going to drive up to where they live along the river and find Jose, tell him we've found Phelan's body and the good news about the mine ownership."

Reno nodded. "Go ahead. I can't go with you even though I want to."

He saw her smile as she brushed strands of dark hair away from her temple. "You stay here and work on our dreams for the foundation. You're doing a wonderful job, Reno."

"*Our* dreams?"

"Yes, ours. You know that. I need you here with me, whether you can accept that or not." There, she'd admitted it. At least, in the guise of the foundation and the vision for the future.

Reno's face changed, revealing an intense vulnerability. His eyes grew moist. His mouth lost that hard line that always told her he was pushing down his feelings. Most of all, that warrior's mask of his melted away.

It left Calen feeling stunned and breathless. Here was the man beneath the hardened armor of what life had dealt him. And what a man he was! Every cell in her screamed to turn, race back into his arms, kiss him senseless and feel him entwined into oneness with her—forever. Oh! Touching her flaming cheek, Calen was shaken to her core. "I mean, only if you want to be a part of this vision. This idea…"

"I do, Calen. We *are* a team," Reno stressed, his voice dropping to an emotionally charged rasp. "From the moment I saw you ride up to that shack, I realized we had a connection. That a miracle had entered my life." He eyed her shyly. "You're my miracle, Calen. And you give me hope when I thought I'd never feel hope again. I'm with you on this project. I'd like nothing more than to help you any way I can."

A shimmer of joy moved through Calen as she stood there, breathless in the wake of his words. The hope burning in Reno's eyes rooted her. "Maybe we're both having hope returned to us," she admitted softly. "In our own ways, we've never been able to forgive ourselves for not being able to help or prevent it when our families were torn from us. The emerald sphere has started a healing process within each of us, Reno." She drew a deep breath. "The essential thing right now is to keep you out of harm's way."

"Let's take this an hour, a day at a time, shall we? As a sniper, I'm pretty good at hiding, Calen. So don't worry about me."

Instead, Reno worried about her. He'd just found her, and he'd be damned if he'd lose her.

Chapter 13

"Reno, the mine area is crawling with Ecuadorian soldiers and police," Calen warned Reno when she found him at work in the library. The word is you're such a bad hombre they brought in military reinforcements to locate you. You're that big of a threat to the Guild. After setting the riding crop aside, she closed the door behind her. Worried, she looked across the quiet room at him. In the last two weeks, since discovering the emerald sphere, he'd worked nonstop with her dream journals to help create the foundation. Calen understood it gave him something positive to do, but she was concerned that he would eventually feel cooped up at the villa.

"More activity than usual?" Reno asked, setting the pen aside. Calen looked fresh and natural in her long-sleeved white cotton blouse, canary-yellow riding breeches and knee-high black leather boots. Her hair had been drawn back into a ponytail and he absorbed the exotic beauty of her face.

Rubbing her brow, Calen sauntered around the desk and sat down in the chair next to him. "I think there's twice the amount of law enforcement as last week. They're scaring the hell out of the *esmeraldos*. The soldiers are tearing apart their hovels, interrogating many people and frightening everyone." She picked up a pitcher of water from the silver serving tray and poured herself a glass. After taking a few sips, she added, "I even saw Cruz out there with the army colonel who commands the troops coming from Quito. He looked really angry."

"Anyone else with him?"

"Yes. A man in a white suit and Panama hat. He was Caucasian, perhaps *norte americano*. He was about six foot tall with gray eyes. I got close enough to check him out, but I didn't want to arouse suspicion."

"That's the CIA spook, Brad James," Reno said. Scowling, he put all the drawings and notes into a folder and set them aside. "They must think I'm still around. And you haven't been riding as El Espanto. For two weeks, things have been quiet in that regard. So why is James here now?"

"I don't know. He was your handler, right?"

"Yeah. I never trusted the oily bastard. I'm sure he's tied into Cruz and this mine, but I can't prove it. Probably getting some kind of kickback, would be my guess. Maybe he's upset because Santiago's lawyer has contacted Cruz. They just found out that Jose is going to sue him for ownership of the mine." Though they were discussing serious things, Reno couldn't help but appreciate Calen's loveliness. Her hair was slightly mussed from riding, her cheeks flushed. She'd probably galloped back to the villa from the river.

"That wouldn't explain James, though." Shivering, Calen said, "I get the feeling that the agent is just like Cruz—they both work for the dark side. They're into personal greed, prejudice and disempowerment of others. Powermongers of the worst sort."

"That's what the dark side does best," Reno agreed, folding his hands together. If he didn't, he was going to reach out and touch her. He looked down at her hands, how they gripped the desk. Hands he dreamed would someday run eagerly across his body, inciting flames, heat and desire within him.

Forcing himself to address her concerns, Reno said, "The dark side infects people, Calen. Most never know they've become hooked into it. That energy infuses them with a desire to lie, cheat and steal from others. It's also about power over others, too. I saw all those possibilities in James when he met me at the brig in San Diego. I could see he was on the take. I'm sure Cruz was paying him good money to bring me down here, pulling governmental strings in Quito and Washington, D.C. Could be that, with my disappearance, Cruz wants to sever ties with the spook once and for all."

"Could be," Calen said. "Reno, I have a plan. I've been thinking of a way we could make it safe for you to live in Ecuador and not always be a hunted criminal."

"Oh?"

"I think El Espanto is going to pay Senor Cruz a visit at his villa tonight." She tapped her fingers thoughtfully on the desk. "In order to prove that El Espanto killed the sniper, Reno Manchahi, I'm going to need your rifle. I will give it to him as proof that I've killed you. I'll tell him I threw your body to a jaguar. That way, he won't demand evidence of your remains. Cruz knows jaguars roam this mountain and kill humans from time to time, so that explanation won't be lost on him. Besides, he's going to be glad to be rid of you, the soldiers and this CIA agent, because he's going to be focused on trying to keep the Santa Maria in the coming court battle." She grinned. "What do you think?"

"That's a damn dangerous plan, Calen. What if James is there? I'm sure that army colonel will be, too. The place will probably be crawling with soldiers. You could get caught."

Chuckling, she said, "I'll ride to the edge of the jungle on a little used trail that leads directly to Cruz's villa. I'll tie Storm to a tree and then shape-shift into my jaguar form. I'll be able to get past any guards or situations because my hearing and smell will be a hundred times more powerful. Once I find Cruz, I'll shape-shift back into my El Espanto form with your sniper rifle in hand. I'll make sure he's alone. And when I leave, I'll change back to a jaguar until I get into the jungle. From there, I'll morph again, mount Storm and ride like hell out of there."

"The plan has possibilities. Even if Cruz buys it, I can't be seen in Ibarra." Reno pointed to his face. "My mug is rather recognizable."

"That's true. But what if we move you to my villa on the outskirts of Quito? You can keep working on our plans for the foundation. I can divide my time between here and there. Cruz will never see you, Reno. The two places he's going to be in Quito are his attorney's office and the courthouse. The chances of you meeting are minimal.

"Once we decide where we're building the foundation, you'll head up the construction project, working with all our contractors. We already agreed it should be away from Quito, someplace in nature, in the jungle. This minimizes your being found by Cruz or by the CIA. Besides, my take on government power and politicos is that James may be in hock over what has happened of late. Who knows? Washington could pull the plug on him down here. He might be reassigned to another country."

"And Cruz? What do you think will happen to him?"

Calen grinned. "Cruz is a little man, a petty potentate who stole the mine from the Santiago family. He grew up on the banks of the Esmeralda River, where it spills into the ocean. My hunch is he'll go back there, far away from you and me. All of his power, that exciting notoriety he loves so much, will be gone—along with his source of funds. Cruz will fade back into the anonymity from whence he came."

"You're a born strategist," Reno declared, proud of her abilities. "Maybe it's the jaguar genes?"

Laughing, and pleased that he liked her ideas, Calen responded, "Oh, I don't know about that. My adopted parents always thought I was pretty good at planning, too. I think it took root in me as a child on the slopes of the mountain. Learning how to strategize to avoid being caught by the mercenaries."

"Together, we can be dangerous," Reno stated in a thoughtful tone. "I was thinking of possibilities, how to keep Cruz from being able to identify me. I hate like hell giving up my rifle, though." He frowned.

"I know. I racked my brain trying to figure out another way to prove that you were dead. I thought about cutting off a hunk of your hair and giving it to him."

Touching his long hair, Reno said, "I'd do that in a heartbeat. Hair grows back. I'd do almost anything to keep my rifle, Calen. It's a part of me."

Calen tapped her fingers on the desk. "Okay. But I'll need more. What kind of identification papers did Cruz give you when you were brought down here to Ecuador?"

Reno pulled his wallet out of his back pocket and removed them. "If you give him these, he's got to believe you nailed me, Calen."

She studied them. "Then I need you to cut off a good hunk of your hair. I'll show Cruz it and this identification. I'll show him your sniper rifle, but tell him I'm keeping it as a trophy." She chuckled darkly over the foolproof plan.

"I can live with that," Reno said, relieved. "A sniper without his rifle is like a person without arms and legs. I'm married to that weapon." When he saw her smile, he added, "Well, after a fashion."

Laughing softly, Calen got up. "I understand. I'm going to ask Godfredo to get Storm ready for El Espanto's last ride tonight. I'll be in the cave. Bring me your hair and papers."

"Roger that." Reno grinned.

"Your only job is to locate that runaway bastard, Manchahi. You got that?" Carlos Cruz said as he stared through the thick smoke of his Cuban cigar. Comfortable in his overstuffed leather chair, his feet resting on his tiger maple desk, he hoped the *norte americano*, Brad James, understood his directive.

"I got it." James stood tensely.

Cruz's large office sat in the heart of the pink stucco villa. James noticed the man had two foreign mercs just outside the office door, both bristling with firepower. Cruz never went anywhere without such protection, for fear of being murdered by El Espanto. Or now, the possibility that Manchahi was on the loose.

James wondered if the sniper had left this area and

was hunting *him* down in Quito. Or maybe he'd hopped a flight and was headed back to the States to fulfill his plan to murder the general.

James didn't like Cruz's triangular-shaped face nor his close-set, dark brown eyes. He looked like a mean horse just waiting for the opportunity to kick someone. The man wore four thick gold chains around his neck, visible because he left his silk shirt unbuttoned halfway down his chest. Cruz reminded the agent more of a drug dealer than one of the richest gem czars in Ecuador. James guessed the man was in his midforties. He wore his black hair drawn back in a ponytail, a gold ring in his left ear, a gold Rolex on his wrist.

"You are to work with Colonel Perez from the Ecuadorian army to find that sniper." Cruz sucked repeatedly on the long cigar, the smoke wafting out of the corners of his full mouth. "And I want results. *Now.*"

"Understood," James uttered. The room was stuffy and airless, and he ached to step outside. "I want to know what my payment is. I already fulfilled the contract we had, Senor Cruz. I got you a world-class sniper down here to take out El Espanto. I can't help it if the bastard decided to turn and run." James glared down at the befuddled Cruz, who obviously didn't think he would ask for a thing.

The director of the mine jerked his legs off his desk and abruptly sat up. "How dare you ask me for more money, gringo!"

James felt his mouth pull into a faint smile. "You

need me, Senor Cruz. I want to be paid accordingly."
If he was going to hunt down the missing sniper, he
wanted enough money stashed away to make a new life
for himself after he retired from the CIA.

"You have no right to make any demands on me!"
Cruz stubbed the cigar into a crystal ashtray.

"You want this bastard found? Then you'll pay me.
And if you can't come up with a figure, I can."

"Gringo, you don't bargain with me." Jabbing his
finger at the CIA agent, Carlos took a deep breath and
exhaled angrily. "Get out of here and just go do your job!"

"I want one million dollars for my part in this."

"What?"

"That's the reward you have posted for El Espanto's
capture." He held Cruz's shocked gaze. "Isn't the
sniper—and silence—worth as much to you?"

Exhaling, Cruz whispered in fury, "Very well,
gringo." With a wave of his hand, he snarled, "I'll pay
your price, but only when the cold, dead body of the
man is lying across my desk."

"I'll look for Manchahi, but I don't promise his
dead body across your desk."

"Do not argue with me, gringo dog!" Cruz barely
controlled his ire at the CIA agent's cojones. "Get
out of my sight. You deal with Colonel Perez. Give
him whatever he needs to find this sniper among the
rabble."

James started to turn. The blinds were drawn across
the windows of the office, as dusk turned to night. Out

of the corner of his eye, he saw the large office door open. And what came next made him freeze.

A tall, lean man dressed in black from head to toe, a hood over his face, entered. He aimed a sniper's rifle directly at James. Behind him, James heard Cruz give a yelp of surprise. The stranger in black quickly shut the door and moved forward. On his back he carried an extra weapon, an AK-47.

"Both of you!" the man barked, "stand where you are or I'll shoot."

Cruz had barreled around the desk and slid to a halt next to the CIA agent. "You! El Espanto! You son of—"

"Save it," El Espanto snarled. "Sit down on floor. Both of you. Now!"

The barrel of the rifle swung toward the mine *patrón*. Breathing hard, Cruz glared at his enemy. "How did you get in here? How?" He petulantly sat down. The CIA agent knelt, then sat, legs crossed.

Chuckling, El Espanto said, "Come now, Senor Cruz, I am not of this world. You should know that by now. Your guards are stupid and insensitive. They go on their rounds not realizing I'm here among you like a jaguar among a flock of chickens."

Choking, Cruz stared up at the man. "Why are you here?"

El Espanto took a hank of hair from his waist pouch and threw it toward Cruz. "I heard your conversation. You can forget hunting for Reno Manchahi. This is his hair." He waved the rifle. "And this is his weapon." Digging into another pouch, all the while training the rifle on them, he threw some papers into the CIA agent's lap. "These are for you, James. The last of your *norte americano* sniper. He's dead. I shot him."

Cruz barely touched the thick black hair, which had been tied with a piece of twine. "*Dios!* He's dead?"

"You think anyone can kill me?" El Espanto laughed huskily. "When will you learn, Senor Cruz?" Holding up the sniper's rifle, he pointed to the CIA agent.

"And you, James. Do you recognize Manchahi's rifle here?"

James studied the weapon. "Yes, it's his weapon."

"Good. Because it's important you realize the man you hired to kill me is dead."

"He was the best! He said he could—could..." Cruz sputtered.

"What? Find me? Shoot me?" The dark-clothed figure chuckled again and slowly eased backward toward the door. "I will haunt you until you leave here, Senor Cruz. One of us is going and it won't be me. You either learn to treat the *esmeraldos* with respect or it's time for you to go."

Cruz glanced at the CIA agent, whose hands rested on his thighs. Cruz's own pistol was in the drawer of his desk. How he itched to put a round through this laughing masquerader!

El Espanto moved his hand to the doorknob. "Oh, one more thing, Senor Cruz."

"What?"

"Don't bother looking for Manchahi's body. I dropped it off at a local jaguar's territory. There will be several meals for the cat and her growing family of two cubs. Chances are the buzzards will make good on what's left of him after that."

Both men gasped, their faces becoming pale.

"Now, stay where you are for ten minutes. If either of you comes through this door before that, I'll kill you right where you stand. *Adios, hombres...*"

Calen opened the door and quickly slipped out. Looking down the hall, she saw no one. She closed her eyes and willed herself into jaguar form. Within fifteen seconds, the change occurred.

Once down on four feet, she padded silently down the white-tiled hall, her senses on high alert. She heard scrambling behind her from the office. Cruz and the agent were getting up. Then Cruz was screaming at the top of his lungs, "Get him! Call the guards! Call the soldiers to duty, dammit!"

With a hiss, Calen trotted down the quiet hall. At the T intersection, she halted and listened. The footfalls of a guard were coming her way at a leisurely pace. He hadn't got the call from Cruz yet. Turning in the opposite direction, Calen trotted swiftly down the hall to an exit.

She got up on her hind legs and placed her paws against the glass door. She had purposely left it ajar when she'd arrived. It swung open quickly beneath her jaguar weight.

Sniffing the air, Calen sprang down the concrete steps at the rear of the villa. And then, without warning, the night exploded around her.

Chapter 14

Mere seconds could feel like a lifetime. Calen crouched on the steps, her back to the wall near the door that she'd just emerged from. Bullets shrieked by her, peppering the stucco and sending up pinkish puffs, momentarily blinding her. All she could think was that Cruz had a secret buzzer he'd pushed on his desk after she'd left, alerting the guards around the villa.

Adrenaline screaming through her, Calen leaped off the steps and landed near a thick stand of hibiscus bushes next to the villa. More shots rang out, and sentries shouted to one another as they moved into position around the property.

Escape! She had to escape! At a gallop, Calen raced

along the wall, keeping near the bushes. Lights began
to snap on and shine down upon her as she scrambled
to escape. She raced around the corner of the villa and
skidded in a puddle of red mud. Shots exploded around
her, sending up geysers of clay.

Growling, Calen considered her options. On top of
the wall surrounding the villa was concertina wire
guaranteed to slice any intruders to ribbons. That was
not the way to escape. Panting hard, ears alert to the
sounds of the soldiers shouting to one another, Calen
slipped around another corner. Far at the back of the
villa property the trees and bushes were thick, and
would provide some cover. Should she head there?

She had to get out of here! Was that rear door in the
wall unlocked? Knowing she couldn't open it with her
paws, Calen figured she'd have to shape-shift back
into human form to twist the doorknob. In the time that
took, the guards could run around the end of the villa,
spot her and kill her.

Calen wasn't safe in her jaguar form, either. A well-
placed bullet could wound her, or take her life. Either
way, she was in trouble! Padding silently along the
base of the wall and emerging from beneath the
greenery, Calen saw the door. It was a smooth mahogany portal with a half-moon carved on it. The door was
protected from wet weather by a thick archway above.

Were there guards nearby? Calen whipped her head
right and then left. She saw no one. Behind her, however, she heard the heavy footfalls and gasps of sentries

trying to catch up with her. Did she have fifteen seconds? No. She knew she did not.

What to do? Skidding to a halt, Calen crouched, her large hind legs beneath her, then spun around. A good offense was sometimes the best defense. She had no idea how many men were coming after her, but knew they all carried rifles. All she had was the element of surprise, her fangs and claws. It had to be enough. They wouldn't be expecting a jaguar.

Digging her hind feet into the wet, well-manicured lawn, she headed back along the wall, galloping swiftly. Mouth open, breath rasping, Calen flew around the corner.

Her cat eyes easily penetrated the darkness. Three camouflaged Ecuadorian soldiers, M-16 rifles in hand, were barreling in her direction.

Calen saw surprise and then abject terror register on the first man's face.

"Look out!" he shrieked. Instead of raising his rifle when he saw her hurtling toward him, he faltered. His booted feet slipped from beneath him on the wet grass.

The other two soldiers screamed in unison.

Calen lunged forward, stretching her powerful body to its maximum. The first soldier was down and trying to stand. The other two gaped at her, clearly stunned by the ferocity of her assault.

She took a heavy swipe at the first guard, who was almost to his feet. Extending her claws, slashed at his right thigh, ripping the fabric of his uniform—and scoring his flesh. The man shrieked like a wild pig. Calen jerked her head up and focused on the other two.

Both had stopped, their mouths open, their rifles motionless. Calen figured she had mere seconds before they snapped back into professional mode to shoot her. Leaping over the wounded soldier, Calen dug her hind legs beneath her. Then she was sailing through the air, a deep growl emanating from her chest. Both paws opened, claws extended, she slammed into the guard on the left. As she hit him, Calen slashed a paw across the protective vest of the man beside him. Its fabric gave way with a satisfying rip as her claws gouged the Kevlar plates.

The impact of the collision sent the guard sprawling and knocked the wind out of him. His teammate cried out as he was flung against the wall of the villa. Calen rolled over, then scrambled to all fours. Jumping over her former pursuers, who by now were in shock and completely traumatized, she whipped back around the villa.

She had bought herself some time. Enough? Calen wasn't sure. Her sharp ears picked up the sounds of at least five other soldiers running toward her. Were they coming around the other side of the villa? If so, they would see her heading to that rear gate to escape. Calen couldn't attack them. The element of surprise worked only once.

The wind flowed past her flicking ears, humid and cool. Rounding the corner, she spied the exit.

What Calen saw stunned her. At the gate, which was open, stood a man dressed in dark clothes, with the El Espanto hood and hat over his head! Then she realized it was Reno. How? What? Her mind buzzed with surprise and questions.

The soldiers spotted her. Calen heard their shouts and commands. Bullets screamed past her. Dirt and grass exploded around her as she raced full tilt toward the doorway.

She saw Reno raise a pistol and fire methodically. More shrieks filled the air. In a flurry of movement, Calen tried to register all that was happening. Reno had come to save her, to save himself and everything they were fighting for. As she galloped toward him, the bullets whizzing around her suddenly ceased.

Good! Time to get out. Breathing hard, she lunged across the open lawn. She was most vulnerable to the guards' weapons right now.

The methodical pop, pop, pop of Reno's pistol continued. More yelps filled the air.

As she charged through the open gate, Calen felt a momentary sense of relief. Skidding to a halt, she forced herself to return to human form. Dizziness assailed her as the change ensued. She saw Reno dive through the door, slam it shut and then jam a large branch across the opening so no one could follow.

Morphing into her human form, Calen took the sniper rifle from her back and held it out to him.

"Thanks," Reno said, grabbing it. He pulled off the

black hood and grinned. "Thought you might need a little help."

Sweat ran down Calen's grimy features and she smiled unsteadily. "I did, thanks. Now come on! We've gotta vamoose!" She dug her boots into the earth, heading down the trail to the left, where Storm was tied and waiting.

Behind them, Calen heard the guards pounding heavily on the door, trying to force it open. Gunfire erupted. They were trying to shoot through the door in order to continue their pursuit! Gasping, she kept up a swift, steady pace down the muddy trail. Reno jogged easily alongside.

"How did you get here?" Calen demanded, her breathing harsh and ragged.

"Godfredo helped me saddle Star, gave me the extra El Espanto hood and hat and showed me how to get to this trail to find you." Reno glanced behind them. The soldiers were blasting away at the thick mahogany door. "Star is tied next to Storm. You okay?" Reno appraised her worriedly.

"Scared as hell, but fine. Thanks for being there."

"You're welcome."

Around the next curve, the horses came into view. "We need to ride like the wind. Follow me, Reno!" Calen quickly leaped into the saddle after untying Storm. The Arabian mare snorted and whirled around.

Leaning forward, Calen knew what she had to do to escape capture. There were four trails branching from the trailhead near Cruz's villa. Even if the guards got through the gate, they'd have a hell of a time trying to decide which one to follow unless they were good at tracking in the dark. She knew the soldiers were not experienced.

Had they seen Reno in the El Espanto costume? As she rode furiously onward, the breeze tearing past and cooling her sweaty face, Calen thought they must have. A grin erupted on her lips as she swiftly guided her brave, swift mare down a trail thick with tree roots. The soldiers would have seen El Espanto *and* a jaguar. That would confuse Cruz no end.

There had been stories whispered that El Espanto was a jaguar and not a horseman in black. Foreign guards had seen Calen in one form or the other. So now, tonight, Cruz would no doubt get reliable sightings by the Ecuadorian soldiers that both existed simultaneously! That would unhinge his theories. And it would serve to put him on notice that not only had El Espanto managed to enter his heavily guarded villa, but the ghost had a partner: a jaguar. Maybe, just maybe, that would be the straw to break the camel's back and he'd not fight the lawsuit. Instead, Cruz would slither back to where he came from.

Hunkered down, her face whipped by the flying mane of her stalwart mare, Calen flew across the mountain toward the wall of jungle a mile ahead. She pushed her horse to optimum speed across the brushy slope. Dirt clods flew up behind them as Storm dug her hooves into the soil.

The night was dark, with no moonlight. It was the time of the jaguar moon again—seven nights of darkness, when the lord of the jungle could walk without being seen. It was certainly a time of power for the jaguar, and perfect for fleeing undetected by armed guards. The only fly in the ointment was Calen's uncertainly over whether the mercs on the slopes were in touch with Cruz and the soldiers at the villa. If they were, word would spread fast, and she and Reno were still in trouble.

Calen twisted in the saddle to check on him. Star was moving at a fast pace as well. He was less than fifty yards behind her. And Reno had had the brilliant idea to put the other night-vision hood over Star's eyes, so that the steed could see where he was going and not trip and break a leg on one of the many exposed roots along the trail. Luckily, Calen always had a second set of night goggles on hand in case the first set broke. Calen was sure that Godfredo had helped Reno place protective Kevlar panels over Star, as well. Her dressage-trained gelding wasn't used to this kind of night foray, but he was a Dutch warmblood. That gave him sense and stability. Clearly he was taking this unexpected adventure in stride.

They whipped down into the jungle at last. Relief started to drizzle through Calen as she slowed her hard-breathing Arabian. They'd made a four-mile run at top speed; that was a lot of ground to cover while keeping up such a hard, unrelenting pace. Sitting back in the

English saddle, Calen slowed Storm to a ground-eating trot. She stood in the stirrups and looked ahead. This particular trail curved back to the shallow river two miles above the cave and safety.

The radio she kept in her waist belt crackled to life. She heard the mercenaries screaming out to one another over it.

"I saw two riders going down trail number two!" a guard shouted. "I picked them up through my night binoculars."

"Then get down there! Now! All guards on duty, head to trail number two!" Cruz thundered into the radio.

Damn. She and Reno had been spotted before they reached the screen of jungle. Mouth tightening, Calen figured there must be six guards on the mountain.

How far behind were they? The guards' small Spanish mounts were fast, but not as fast as Storm. Star was another matter. He was half draft horse, and not built for speed like her Arabian mare. That would slow them down. *Double damn!*

Calen whirled her horse around, and waited for Reno, who pulled Star to a halt. The chestnut's flanks were heaving and he had sweat gleaming across his neck.

"What?" Reno demanded. "What's wrong?"

"I have a guard's radio," Calen whispered hoarsely. She jabbed a finger toward the trail they'd just ridden down. "Six of them are after us right now. We were spotted going onto this trail by a merc who had night-vision binoculars."

Reno looked back. "What do you do when this happens? What's your plan?"

Wiping her sweaty brow, Calen said, "I've never been spotted before. And now we have six of those goons on our heels."

"Can we get off this trail and onto another?" Reno demanded uneasily. He gripped his sniper rifle. It felt good to have his friend back. Calen's face was tense and her eyes narrowed as she considered options.

"This jungle is too damn thick to penetrate, Reno. A human can't get through it, much less a horse."

Reno felt an urgency thrum through him. They'd gone about a mile down the trail. How close were the soldiers? Too close. The back of his neck felt cold and tingled, a sign of danger stalking him.

"No, the walls of the jungle are definitely too thick," Calen muttered. Worriedly, she looked down the trail toward the cave. "There's only one thing we can do, Reno. We've got to dismount, slap our mounts to send them home, and shape-shift into our other form. As jaguars, we can penetrate this wall."

"But the horses… Are you sure they can escape?"

"Storm knows the way home. She'll gallop down the trail toward the cave. Star will follow, don't worry." Quickly dismounting, Calen tied the AK-47 rifle to the cantle of her saddle. She kept the pistol that hung off her hip. "Come on, Reno! We don't have much time!"

Leaping out of the saddle, Reno refused to give up his sniper's rifle. He tied the reins around Star's neck so they wouldn't come loose and trip the animal. Looking up, he saw Calen doing the same.

"Ready?" she called to him in a low voice.

"Yeah."

Calen stepped aside and slapped her mare on the rump. Instantly, Storm scrambled, mud flying as she thundered down the trail at a gallop. Calen saw Reno slap Star in turn. Startled, the Dutch warmblood moved like an awkward giant, but lunged forward and quickly followed the fleeing Arabian.

Calen stepped off the trail and slipped the rifle across her back. "Let's do it. Let's get out of here." She willed herself into her jaguar form. The familiar dizziness came, along with the other sensations. Soon she had all four feet on the ground and looked toward Reno. It was the first time she'd seen him as a jaguar. He was a huge male with a massive chest and thick legs. The power around him was unmistakable, his huge yellow eyes wide and alert.

Calen had never had a jaguar partner. In animal form, she'd never had anyone to talk to. Now she did. In her mind, she sent out a telepathic message to Reno, unsure whether he would hear her or not.

Reno? Can you hear me?

Of course. This is cool—telepathy!

A satisfied growl came from her throat. Calen's hopes soared as he padded up next to her. He was a beautiful cat with black crescents scattered across his golden fur. But there wasn't time to appreciate the fact.

Calen picked up the sounds of many horses galloping toward them.

They're coming!

Yes, Reno answered. *I think there are six of them.* He could feel the ground shaking beneath his paws. *Let's get off the trail. Maybe we can surprise them?* And he told her of a plan that might stop the guards from going after their riderless horses and tracking them back to the cave.

The mercs were riding hell-bent for leather down a straight stretch of the muddy trail. The horses were snorting, the guards intent, rifles raised and ready to fire.

Calen waited just inside the jungle next to the trail. Reno was hidden on the other side. His plan was a clever one, and she smiled to herself. Horses feared jaguars for good reason.

Now! Reno shouted mentally.

Instantly, Calen leaped out onto the trail. She whirled toward the galloping lead horse, not more than a hundred yards away. She felt more than saw Reno leap out from his side. He hurtled swiftly past her, their shoulders grazing. In a heartbeat, Calen moved to his side. Now two jaguars, shoulder to shoulder, charged up the trail toward the six riders.

The horses could see in the dark, but not like jaguars could. The guards would never see them coming at all. Under a jaguar moon, with jungle hugging the sides of the narrow track, the darkness was complete.

Calen felt joy bubbling up through her as they raced

up the trail. For the first time in her life, she was not alone. She had a partner. And what a partner Reno was! His power as a jaguar was like a beacon of light chasing away the night.

The lead horse spotted them, grunted in surprise and tried to stop. The guard atop him yelled a warning when he finally saw the charging cats. An instant later, as his mount dug in its hind quarters, the man was thrown over the gelding's head. The scent of jaguars reached the rest of the horses as they scrambled to a stop. Sliding, rearing animals careened into one another. Two more sentries were torn from their saddles and sent flying through the air.

Chaos exploded on the narrow trail. Another horse's eyes went white and rolled as he saw the jaguars closing in on him. His rider sailed off over his head, landing with a thud in front of the terrified mount. Whinnying plaintively, the bay gelding trampled the screaming man in an effort to escape the charging cats. The alarmed mustang crashed into another startled horse who was struggling to stop, instantly causing a melee of scrambling legs, flailing hooves and shouting, cursing men.

Reno could clearly see the chaotic scene. The guards didn't realize until too late why the horses were in a wild panic to turn around. Six animals on a narrow trail would not allow any of them to run away easily. The thousand-pound bodies of the frightened mounts were covered in mud, foam and sweat. The guards tried to shield their heads from the sharp hooves of the surging, terror-stricken animals.

The first guard, his head bleeding badly from a flesh wound, tried to escape the chaos. The man's eyes widened enormously as he saw both jaguars within arm's reach of where he lay in the mud. The guard uttered a shriek, rolled over and scrabbled desperately for his rifle. But the clay of the trail was thick and wet. The trampling hooves of the wild-eyed horses had buried his weapon.

Let's go, Reno signaled Calen. *It worked. Those horses are going to get out of here as soon as they can turn around. These guards aren't going to follow us now. They'll have a long walk back to their base tonight.*

Right. Good work, Calen replied. Launching herself into a spin, she took off down the trail. Moments later, Reno was at her side, his breathing even and harsh.

Within minutes, the quiet darkness descended upon them once more. She loved the feel of her paws sinking into the cool mud, her claws extended to give her purchase as they raced along. The night was now tinged with gray as dawn approached, and Calen heard monkeys screaming in alarm far above them, warning others that jaguars were on the hunt.

The fragrance of orchids hanging in the trees was strong and like an aphrodisiac. The scent of spices, of vanilla, filled her lungs. All the different sights, sounds and odors were magnified in her a hundred times more clearly than if she were in human form.

And most of all, Calen felt the soaring, joyous chemistry of primal magnetism with Reno, who ran smoothly and quietly at her side. Calen knew that jaguars mated for life. They had only one partner and were true to their mate until death. That was how she felt toward Reno.

There was something so freeing about working together on this night. She had so much to share with him once they reached the safety of the cave. So much…

Chapter 15

"**W**e're safe." Calen's words came out a whisper as
they stood inside the tunnel. Her back pressed against
the rough rock wall, the dizziness from morphing back
into human form passing, she stared across the space
at Reno. His face was sweaty, and tense, his eyes
blazing. This was the warrior, the hunter, Calen
realized with gratitude. If not for his involvement, she
might be dead.

"Helluva night, wasn't it?" Reno said, grinning.

Calen eased away from the wall. "Yes, it was. I
never expected to see you at the villa. How did you
know I was going to get into trouble?"

Relief sheeted through him. Reno came to her side

and slipped his hand into hers. For a moment, her eyes widened beautifully over his simple act of caring. "I can't lie to you, Calen. I've been falling in love with you from the moment you appeared in my precog. And then, when I saw you ride up to my medical shack, and I remembered you from the dream, my heart opened up for the first time since the death of Ilona and Sarah." Squeezing her hand, Reno added tentatively, "Maybe you don't feel the same about me as I do you. But I've got to believe that that kiss we shared meant something to you, as well." Reno swallowed hard after such a confession.

Her face shone with perspiration, her tangled hair gleamed. Everything about Calen charmed him. But did she love him the same way he loved her? That was something Reno didn't know. Being a shape-shifter didn't mean a person knew the thoughts of another, or the future, either. They lived with unknowns, just as any other human did.

Deeply moved, Calen looked up into Reno's searching gaze. The energy around him was one of protectiveness. And more. Her pulse accelerated because of how he was gazing at her. Reno was so close, so incredibly male and powerful. Her senses were acute, and every particle of her being yearned for him as never before. "I—I feel the same, Reno," she confessed, clasping his hand. "Come on, we've got to let Godfredo know we're okay. We have to make sure the horses came back to the cave."

"Fair enough," Reno murmured. Like rain on a hot afternoon in the desert, happiness swept through him, making him feel as if he were walking on air.

As they entered the cave, Calen eased her hand from Reno's and waved to the worried Godfredo. He had the horses in individual stalls, munching on hay. The animals had been unsaddled, washed and then brushed down until their coats shone in the low light. Storm nickered a greeting to her.

"You're okay?" Godfredo demanded, giving them both anxious looks.

"We are," Reno assured the manager.

Calen patted Godfredo's shoulder. "It was a good thing Reno came dressed in the El Espanto costume. Cruz must have hit a buzzer or tripped some kind of warning to his guards before I got out of the villa. If Reno hadn't been at the only other exit from the compound, I'd be dead or captured right now." Calen gave Reno a look of sincere gratitude. "I was never so glad as when I saw you at the gate."

"My gut told me you might get into trouble," Reno told her. "I didn't know how, but I knew I wanted to shadow you and make sure things stayed in your favor."

"You were right, Senor Reno," Godfredo said, seeming relieved as he walked back to the stall area with them. "You said you had a bad feeling about this." After mopping his brow, the man stuffed his handkerchief into his back pocket. "Everything is done here, *patrona*. Why don't you go home and rest?"

"A good prescription, Godfredo. I think I've had enough excitement for one night." Her watch read 1:00 a.m.

"Did you get to Cruz?" Godfredo asked as he walked them toward the tunnel that led to the villa.

Nodding, Calen said, "I saw him and the CIA spook. I delivered the message that I'd killed Reno. I think they bought it. They were sufficiently rattled."

"So," Godfredo said, halting at the tunnel, "how do you think this will affect Cruz? He already knows he's in for a legal fight over the ownership of the mine. And he knows it's only a matter of time until the courts award it to the Santiago family."

Calen leaned against the rock wall and studied her loyal manager. "I'm hoping it will scare him back to the mouth of the Esmeralda River where he came from. I also hope he'll realize that he's no longer safe from El Espanto."

"That could hurry Cruz and his people out of here sooner rather than later," Reno conjectured.

"Correct," Calen said. She patted Godfredo's shoulder once more. "Rest easy, my friend. We're fine. And I'm not visiting Cruz again. He got Reno's hair, and I showed him the sniper rifle. Plus, I dropped Reno's identification papers into James's lap, so I'm sure they think their hired sniper is dead."

"Thank goodness," Godfredo whispered. "You are a free man, Senor Reno. Congratulations."

"I will be free, in time," Reno agreed. "We need to

see what happens next. I think when Cruz finds out there is more than one El Espanto, or at least that the ghostly rider has jaguar help, he's going to go ballistic. He'll realize that he's fighting more than just one person, and that should blow him away."

"And hurry his exit from Ibarra," Calen said grimly. She gave her manager a smile. "We'll see you tomorrow for breakfast with Eliana, *compadre*. Good night...."

Reno was in Calen's large, airy bedroom. He stood uncertainly at the open door. And then she turned.

"Come on in," she invited softly, gesturing for him to enter.

"I wasn't sure," Reno told her, quietly closing the massive mahogany door.

Calen felt her pulse skip as she fearlessly approached him. Following her heart, she lifted her arms and placed them around his strong shoulders. Shoulders that could carry heavy loads without breaking. She moved her mouth close to his ear and whispered, "I'm more scared now than when I was trapped back there at Cruz's villa, Reno. But I have such strong, overwhelming feelings for you that I have to explore them with you, if you want." She moved her lips and captured the hard line of his mouth.

His world shifted. Reno's arms automatically went around her. He liked the fact that she was strong and brave and willing to see what they might have together. He returned her heated kiss, cherishing her mouth. And when he finally released her, he looked down into her glimmering green eyes. "Life isn't for cowards, *mi corazón,* my heart. I'm scared, too. I never thought I could love another woman. I thought when Ilona was murdered, my life was over." His throat closed up with emotions.

Calen threaded her fingers through his hair. Now, with his locks shorn, he looked less the wild outdoorsman and more the wild urban male—though still unpredictable and dangerous. "And I'd given up hope of ever finding a man who would know me and all my secrets. Who would accept me as what and who I am."

Just the gliding movement of her fingertips across his scalp sent heated tingles and scalding reactions through Reno's aching body. "We're the same. We've come home to one another, Calen. What we have is so rare. We deserve to have the time to explore and know one another." He closed his eyes for a moment, savoring her womanly strength against him. There was no way Reno could stop his body from speaking to her in the raw, natural language of need, desire, love. The fact that she pressed herself against him told Reno she wanted him. All of him.

"I agree," she whispered unsteadily. Feeling wrapped in a golden cocoon filled with his powerful love, she reluctantly moved out of his embrace and caught his hand. "Come on. I've got a huge, tiled shower that's large enough for both of us."

The invitation wasn't lost on Reno. Jaguars were

water cats more than any other species, save for their cousins the tigers. Jaguars loved water, and were often found lying in a shallow stream to cool down during the heat of the day. They were strong swimmers and often fed on fish and other water creatures.

"I like showers," he said, grinning down at her. Calen's cheeks were stained pink, which only enhanced her primal beauty. When she released her hair, the black strands falling deliciously around her shoulders, a surge of yearning shot through him.

"Let's get wet together," Calen suggested, heading for the tiled room. She turned on the two brass showerheads in the frosted glass stall. The floor was of white, blue and violet tile laid out in the vesica piscis design. Water spurted from above and fell like raindrops upon the double circles emblazoned there. Calen watched for his reaction.

"The Eye," he said, pointing to the area where the circles overlapped. "You had it put in there. Why?" He watched Calen climb out of her black spandex outfit, revealing gorgeous golden skin beneath. He was unable to stop looking at her even though she seemed somewhat shy about undressing before him. Reno loved her even more because she was painfully human in such a vulnerable, sweet way.

After getting rid of her socks, boots and spandex, Calen chose a magenta washcloth from the towel rack. She sat down on a small mahogany stool. "When I come back from my rides on the mountain, I'm totally stressed out," she confided in a low voice. "Scared, anxious, relieved—you name it." Steam curled up and out of the glass-enclosed shower. The hiss of water sounded like the tropical rainstorms that roved daily across the jungle. "I knew as a child that the center of the linked circles was a place of healing, a place where I could get back into balance and harmony. And trust me, those rides on the slopes really unbalanced me. I was nothing but a ball of nerves when I returned, and not at all in harmony with myself. Godfredo's idea to help me after the rides was to create this mosaic in my shower. It was perfect. I would come up here after a ride, strip out of my costume and stand in the shower for fifteen or twenty minutes. In that double circle I would literally feel all my anxiety, my worry, my stress just melt away because of the power and energy there."

Reno began to remove his own clothing, letting each article drop to the tiled floor. "That was a very smart thing to do. My parents always had me carry a pouch with two sixteen-foot pieces of string in it. They showed me how to lay out the circles, no matter where I was, if I needed to get back into harmony with myself. It didn't matter whether I was outside or indoors. All I had to do was make the circles and step into the Eye in order to get back into balance. I like the idea of us going in that shower and standing in the Eye. Are you ready, *mi corazón?*"

He stood fully naked before her and saw Calen's eyes widen with appreciation. There was no hiding his reaction to the fact that he wanted her. If she was frightened of him, it didn't show in her face. A look of primal desire glowed within the depths of her spring-green gaze, and he felt powerful in a way he'd thought he never would again.

"It's time," Calen agreed softly as she eased off the stool. "Let's get clean together and stand in the Eye. I want to see how that feels, Reno, with you." She brought a bar of milled jasmine soap into the shower with her.

Reno closed the frosted glass door behind him and felt the warm, pummeling water strike the flesh of his neck and shoulders. Steam curled like a lover's hands around them. Everything was perfect, more perfect than he could ever have imagined. Calen soaked her hair, the black strands shining like ebony around her flushed face and making her eyes even more arresting with their slight tilt. Cat eyes. Jaguar eyes. His jaguar woman.

He smiled down at Calen while she lathered the washcloth. The scent of jasmine slowly filled the humid, cloudy space. It was as if they were standing out in the jungle with rain falling around them.

Calen began to gently wash his shoulders and chest with her own cloth. Beneath his feet, Reno could feel the gentle swaying motion that was always found within the Eye. All his tension, the stress of worrying for her safety, of possibly losing Calen out there tonight, dissolved like the drops of warm water streaming down the planes of his body. Reno savored the healing energy as never before.

As Calen's cloth moved with enticing and delicious slowness across his chest, washing away the dirt and sweat, Reno gripped her shoulders and closed his eyes. There was such tantalizing fire in her simple, innocent action. The friction of the cloth made tingles leap wherever she slid the nubby fabric across his appreciative flesh. The soothing rivulets only heightened her graceful movements. As she guided the cloth down, down, down, washing every square inch of the front of his body, Reno felt as if he'd died and gone to the other side, where nothing but beauty, love and peace dwelled.

She suggestively slid the soapy cloth down his narrow hips and caressed his hardened shaft. A deep growl emitted from Reno's throat, and his hands tightened on Calen's shoulders. He heard her laugh softly while she moved the cloth in slow, circular motions. The woman knew how to torture him in the sweetest of ways. And when Reno could stand no more, he opened his eyes, looked down into that face filled with rapture and love, and he pulled the washcloth from her hand.

"My turn now," he rasped, his lips drawing away from his teeth. Once he'd soaped the cloth, Reno moved it from Calen's slender neck across her capable shoulders and then encircled each of her full, lush breasts. The nipples were pink, and hardened in response to his slow exploration of her. Reno heard her moan and watched her eyes flutter shut. He kept his hand upon her, palm pressed against her back to keep her from

losing her balance. She swayed in reaction to his de-
liberate, dulcet assault until she could stand it no longer.

Easing her forward, Reno allowed the thick, warm
streams of water to sluice away the soap from her body.
Then he leaned down and placed his lips around one
of those hard, pink nipples. The moment he teethed it
gently, Calen's knees buckled.

Reno caught and held her so he could continue to
lavish her hard, responsive nipples. With exquisite
slowness, he made each of them captive to his exploring mouth, to his tongue as he encircled and then
suckled. Soon Calen was moaning, her breathing
shallow and swift. She reminded Reno of summer
leaves caught up by the wind of a storm, bending and
flexing with trembling anticipation. She moved against
him, silently asking for more of his heated attention.
Reno recognized her needs, her fingers digging insistently into his chest as he continued to explore and
caress her lovely breasts.

The steam was so thick Reno felt as if they were no
longer on earth. Rather, they were lost in a mist where
humidity, heat and burning sunlight all conjoined in a
magical act of nature to create the clouds in Father Sky.
The power of the Eye had sharpened each of his senses,
and every time he laved his tongue across one of her
nipples, the sensation was tenfold for her. And when
Calen turned her body fully to his, lifting her leg sinuously
around his thigh, pressing her belly suggestively against
his hardness, Reno knew what she wanted.

Calen breathed raggedly as she felt Reno's large, scarred hands come to rest beneath her buttocks. He was going to lift her upward. Water trailed across her face, soaking into her hair and running down across her sensitized breasts. Hooking her arms around his neck, Calen closed her eyes, uttered his name like the prayer it had become to her heart. He lifted her as if she were a mere wisp of a feather. Feeling his face buried between her breasts, she hugged him even more tightly to her.

And as he slowly lowered her aching body down, down, down upon his awaiting hardness, Calen's breath became suspended. Oh! How long had she waited for this beautiful moment spun out of time and place? All her life she'd dreamed of a man who would love her, cherish her and accept her for all that she was. And now Reno held her, an answer to her dreams. As she sheathed him slowly, like heated, wet silk, her body reacting with white-hot ripples of pleasure, Calen moaned softly, her brow resting heavily against his dark, wet hair.

The sensation of moving into oneness was unlike anything she had ever experienced before. In those molten moments as they joined together, she realized so many things. Then her mind was mush, and all she could do was feel the shimmering, sparkling layers that surrounded and flowed through her like crashing waves from the ocean onto the shore. Finally, she had met her mate. Jaguars were monogamous. And there was no question Reno was her equal. As he moved her with a steady, rhythmic slowness up and down, up and down, each thrust sent volcanic eruptions of pleasure through her tense, hungry body. Never had Calen felt so loved as now, with his mouth suckling her breast, his large arms holding her and keeping her safe within his embrace.

The sinuous steam, the gurgle of water from the shower, the heat curling around them made Calen feel as if she'd left the earth far behind. Her lover's body was her sun, her stars, her galaxy. Life, hot and spiraling, filled her belly and flowed up in tidal waves of such intense pleasure that all Calen could do was hold on to Reno, gasp, moan and absorb him—the man she loved more intensely than life itself. She understood on some deep, unspoken level that by coming together, joining with Reno, so much more would occur—a result of their primal mating. Their loving one another was more than just flesh coming together. It was about hearts entwining. The meeting of thirsty souls thinking they were alone, but finding, in truth, they were not. Calen understood, finally, her parents telling her how on her twenty-eighth birthday her life and mission would begin.

The heat centered in her belly, bright and glowing. As she lifted her face, eyes closed, and feeling lost within the fierce fire of Reno's heart, body and soul, Calen sensed that their union was so much more than just physical. And when her body constricted around him and an incredible scalding heat exploded deep within her, he released his masculine seed into her at the exact same time.

A new life would be created from this joining, she knew. Calen savored the fiery bands of pleasure radiating throughout her tense, sleek body, pressed against Reno. Her heart opened completely and embraced him. They were jaguar mates. Joined for life. Living their lives together in a oneness that could never be severed, not even by death. As her lashes fluttered beneath the joyful onslaught of pleasure that Reno was prolonging for her, a series of colorful pictures, like frames from a movie, moved through Calen's mind.

She saw Reno and herself in Egypt as a priest and priestess. In another frame, she was a Roman soldier and Reno her warrior partner. A third frame showed them as man and woman in a Neolithic stone circle performing a solemn ceremony to the sun. A fourth frame flashed in front of her closed eyes. Calen recognized Stonehenge in England. She saw herself standing in the center of it, clothed in heavy white woolen robes, her hands uplifted. And at the entrance to the mighty stone circle, she saw Reno as a Druidic priest coming toward her, with a blue ceramic cup he passed to her. The moment that dark blue goblet touched her outstretched hands and they connected, Calen felt her body radiate with such powerful currents that she nearly lost consciousness. If not for Reno holding her, keeping her pressed against him as she swooned, Calen might have fallen to the ground. Instead, as if in tune with her visions, he sensed the power of what she'd seen and felt, and held her to him, keeping her safe, steady, so that she could perform the winter solstice ceremony for their people.

A raw cry emitted from Calen's open mouth as she sagged weakly against Reno. The past lives dissolved and flowed effortlessly back into the present. The water sprinkling warmly on her hair slowly revived her and brought her back to the here and now. She felt Reno gently lift her off him and hold her against his hard, unyielding body. The tiles warmed her feet once more. Calen leaned bonelessly against him, her arms around his waist.

Inside, she felt her belly glowing like a hot wood stove filled to the brim with fuel. It was a peaceful, joyful sensation, as if Reno's seed had been the power of the sun joining the cool sweetness of the moon within her body. And Calen knew that she was pregnant. This incredibly beautiful, loving connection with Reno had created a child of pure love between them. The knowing filled Calen with awe, with humility, and she experienced the ripeness of being a woman as never before.

"I love you, *mi corazón,*" Reno whispered against her wet hair. Easing his hand across her trembling shoulders, he held Calen tightly against him. "You are my life. And I'll love you with every breath I take."

His rumbled words filled her like a vessel that had been empty for so long. Calen felt sated on every possible level. The water sluiced softly down her face, neck and breasts. Her lips parted and she smiled up at Reno, his face open and accessible to her. "We are one, my beloved. Now and forever. I've waited all my life for you to walk into it. And here you are." Calen reached up and slid her hand against his high, scarred cheekbone. "We've suffered so much, lost so much, but now the Great Mother Goddess is giving it all back to us in another way. Giving us so much. One another." Her whispered words joined the music of the water splashing joyfully around them.

Calen saw such happiness in his burning cinnamon eyes. She felt the last remnants of grief for his wife and child dissolve. *Finally.* And she saw him surrender the last of his hatred and revenge toward the general who had taken their lives. Standing in the vesica piscis together, as one, had healed Reno. A new awareness, a forgiveness, came over his features, like a cooling river of light. To be able to stand with him, hold him as his wound was tended, brought Calen to tears. Tears of joy for Reno.

Swallowing hard, Reno lifted his hand and caressed Calen's cheek. "*Mi corazón,* you are healing me in places and ways I never thought possible. Thank you…."

The humid clouds were so thick she could barely see his face. It was his eyes, flooded with tears of relief, that brought out a fierce tenderness in her. A man crying in the arms of his woman was the ultimate gift of trust, a sign that Reno trusted her with his rawest, most vulnerable emotions.

Calen kissed him, her wet mouth clinging to his. She wanted to restore him with this kiss. And as Reno returned it, she felt her own world being rebuilt.

The emerald sphere had helped Reno not only realize that he needed to forgive, but also to release the past. She knew he would keep good memories within his heart. And in doing so, he now walked into the present with her. They not only had a present together, but a future as well.

"Come," Calen whispered against his mouth. "Let's go to bed and hold one another."

Chapter 16

Two months later

"**I**f you'd told me two months ago I'd be in love, that Cruz and the Guild would be gone and that the Santiago family would be taking over the emerald mine operation, I'd have said you were loco," Calen confided to Reno. She relaxed in his arms as he stood behind her. From the sundeck of her villa, they gazed at the mighty volcanic mountain that bore the riches of emeralds within its mantle.

Moving his palm tenderly across her belly, Reno rested his chin against her newly washed hair. The clove and nutmeg scents were provocative and he inhaled her fragrance. "What's the saying? Change is the only thing we can count on with any assurance?" A flock of blue-and-yellow macaws flew in a squadron formation toward a group of rubber trees beyond the villa grounds.

Morning was Reno's favorite time. Waking up with Calen in his arms, sharing her bed, sharing a love that she gave without reserve, had transformed his entire life. "Change has been good for me." Reno pressed a kiss to her damp hair. "How about for you?"

Calen turned and smiled lazily at him. She was more than happy to rest her back against his strong, steady body. She wore a filmy white nightgown that fell to her knees. His long, scarred fingers gently caressed her belly. Did he know? When should she tell him? Settling her hands over his, she whispered, "More than good. An answer to all my dreams. I always thought I was so different that no man could ever love me for who I really was. And I never thought I'd meet one of my own kind, much less fall in love with him."

"We are different." Reno closed his eyes and absorbed her softness, her incredible womanly strength. "Ilona wasn't one of us, but she loved me anyway."

"I'm sure many of our kind intermarry with normal human beings." Calen tipped her head upward and held his hooded gaze. "Did your daughter, Sarah, have the birthmark?"

"Yes, she did. I passed it on to her. I was going to

start training her when I got back from my last tour in Afghanistan." His mouth flexed.

"Did Ilona know you were a shape-shifter?"

"No. I was going to share the rest of my secrets with her when I came home. I wanted Ilona to support my teaching Sarah what had been handed down through the generations of my family. She had to know if I was going to do that."

"I'll bet she did know, Reno. Ilona loved you. You can't hide parts of yourself from someone when you love openly and fully like that."

Giving her a tender smile, Reno said, "Ilona probably did. She just didn't say anything about it." But he wanted to move from the past and into the present. He turned Calen around in his arms, resting his hands on her shoulders. "And speaking of love, I have something for you. Come back to the bed with me."

Calen grinned. "A surprise?" She was more than ready to love Reno all over again. Their sessions were long, lingeringly sweet and beautiful. She felt as if she were an exquisite flower opening beneath Reno's experienced hands, his passionate kisses and tenderness. It was more than she had ever dreamed of having.

He led her inside and sat her on the edge of the bed, then went to the nightstand. He opened the small drawer and withdrew a dark green velvet box. Sitting down next to Calen, he slid his arm around her shoulders and placed the small parcel in the palm of her hand. "This is for you, for us," he told her, his voice suddenly thick with emotion.

"Oh…" Calen's voice dissolved in wonder as she inspected the small, rectangular box. Her heart began an uneven beat. "Reno…"

"Just open it, *mi corazón*." He held his breath. Would Calen like the ring set? Was she ready to marry him? Reno didn't know. But something pushed him to ask her anyway. In some ways, their two months together seemed like long, dreamlike years. And in other ways, mere moments he selfishly wanted a lot more of.

Calen gave him a shy look and sprung the latch on the case. Her lips parted and she gasped. "Reno!"

He watched proudly as she gazed at the gold-and-emerald engagement ring and the simple gold wedding band nestled next to it. "They're for you, Calen. I love you." His arm tightened around her shoulders. "I'm not very good at asking you to marry me. I want you for my wife, my best friend, my lover, the mother of any children we create between us." His voice faltered as he gazed deeply into Calen's spring-green eyes. Tears beaded on her thick, long lashes. How exotic, mysterious and nurturing she looked in that moment.

"You knew. I figured you would find out. I wasn't sure, but I know as a shape-shifter, you have a strong sixth sense and intuition." Calen touched her belly.

Reno frowned. "Knew what? That I wanted to marry you?"

Laughing softly, Calen eased the rings from the box and placed the engagement ring on her left hand. The emeralds were channel cut, the surface of the gems level with the gold metal. "No, not that." Calen turned and held up her hand. "It's beautiful, Reno. Thank you. The emeralds are spectacular."

"I went to the Santiago family a month ago. I told them I wanted to marry you and buy some clear emeralds for your engagement ring. I tried to pay them, but they wouldn't hear of it. They love you, too, Calen. They said you'd done so much for their family, for old Phelan, that they gifted the stones to you for me. Isn't that something? Generosity in place of Cruz's greed. And with your announcement that you're building a hospital for the *esmeraldos,* they wanted to do something special for you in return."

Touched, Calen moved her fingertips across the rectangular emeralds, which gleamed with the morning light. "Yes, this was more than generous, Reno. These emeralds are just gorgeous." Calen moved her hand up so that the light refracted through the stones. Indeed, they were top quality. Since the Santiago family had taken over the mine, everything had changed. If *esmeraldos* wanted to mine on the Santa Maria property, they could. They kept fifty percent of the profit of the emeralds they found, and the Santiago family received the other half. This agreement was more than fair. Calen had seen a poor, desperate community change to one of teamwork and a fair distribution of wealth. Everyone was making decent money. Poverty and starvation were already beginning to become a thing of the past. There was no longer a need for El Espanto, thank goodness.

Lifting her chin, Calen caught and held Reno's anxious gaze. She slid her left hand across his unshaven cheek and said, "Yes, I'll marry you, heart of my heart. I want to be your wife, your partner, your equal in every way."

Just the caress of those long, slender fingers made a shiver of longing course through Reno. He closed his eyes and pressed his hand against hers. A need to touch her more intimately blazed inside him, so he leaned down and brushed her smiling lips, tasting the salt of her tears. Finally, their breathing ragged and uneven, Reno eased his lips from Calen's. She was smiling through her tears and he smiled with her. "I never thought I'd have a life again, Calen. In some ways, I feel like I'm in some kind of grand dream, and I don't ever want it to end."

"Dreams become reality," she reminded him, her voice husky with feeling. Caressing his brow and cheek, she whispered, "But there's more that you need to know, Reno."

"What?"

"You can't guess?"

"Guess what?" he asked playfully.

Calen grinned, then took his hand and placed it against her abdomen. "I'm pregnant. Two months along. The first day we made love, I knew. And the doctor over in Ibarra just confirmed it for me last week. We're going to have a baby, Reno. A little girl, my intuition tells me." His face blurred as more tears filled Calen's eyes. So much happiness… "I know you lost your darling Sarah, and my heart bled and bled for you. I can't imagine losing a child. You lost your little girl."

She could see the grief in his face. But then he came alive with hope, and with love for her. Calen felt it to her core. "I know the universe takes away, Reno. But it also gives back, when people deserve a second chance. And now we have our chance, my darling. And I'm carrying your baby daughter for you—for us."

His world tilted and spun crazily. Reno didn't quite believe his ears, and yet he knew it was the truth. He would be a father again. He had seen a change in Calen, but hadn't realized exactly what it was. Now, he understood it all: she was having his child. Their child. Their little girl. Reno gripped Calen and crushed her against him, his head pressed against her hair. "I love you so much," he murmured, his voice cracking. Hot tears drifted down his cheeks.

Calen felt him trembling. Reno, of all people! A warrior among warriors. Whispering his name, she held him and rocked him as he wept. Reno had had so much taken away from him. *So much.* She would love him back to health. The baby she carried would assuage the terrible wounds left in his heart from his losses.

His family could never be replaced—Calen realized that. And she wasn't Ilona. But her life with Reno was an incredible new adventure that was quickly taking shape. She was grateful that he was going to be her partner, that they would create the Vesica Piscis Foundation and try to help bring peace to a shattered, violent world.

She didn't know how long they stayed there, holding each other, loving each other. In her dizzying bliss, Calen lost track of time as the white fog hanging above the jungle canopy dissipated beneath the warming rays of the rising sun. Reno's sobs finally abated, his breathing hoarse and ragged as he continued to grip her. Right now, she knew she could be strong for Reno. That was the way a good relationship worked: each partner could lean on the other when necessary.

Gently wiping his damp cheeks with her trembling fingers, Calen said brokenly, "I love you so much, Reno. I know I can never replace what you lost. The baby we carry is ours. Our present, our future…and we have so much to look forward to, my darling. So much."

Reno kissed her fingers. "I don't see you or our child as a replacement, *mi corazón*. Not ever. Since holding that emerald sphere in the cave, my rage, my revenge, my desire to kill the man who took my family has dissolved. You are filling that poisonous place in my heart with goodness. I received a healing from that emerald sphere. Now I have hope, a new love, and I'm looking at the world through the lens of gratitude, not revenge."

"We're a team, my darling. A strong one. I know that the Great Mother Goddess has a mission for us. We were born to do this. Now I understand as never before what my parents meant when they said my life would begin when I turned twenty-eight." Calen gave a soft, giddy laugh. "A new husband. A baby. I now have a family, where before I was alone. Or so I thought." Calen shared a secret smile with him.

He slid his thumb across her lower lip. "Marry me, Calen Hernandez...."

"Is next week soon enough?" Her lip tingled beneath his unexpected caress.

"A week is a long time," he teased, a glimmer of humor coming into his eyes.

"I need to contact Father Pio in Quito," Calen said. "He was the priest who ran the Ibarra orphanage when I wandered in that day off the slopes, after my family had been murdered. He was very kind and consoling to me. I'd like him to marry us, Reno."

"Anything you want," Reno murmured. Brushing a strand of hair from Calen's sparkling eyes, he cupped her face. "All I want to do is make you and our baby happy. I will never need anything more than that."

"Me, either," Calen whispered, kissing his hand. Then she sighed. "I hate to say this, but we have that professor from Northern Quito University showing up here this afternoon. Remember? She's going to look at photos of the emerald sphere and try to decipher the language that's engraved on it."

Reno roused himself and looked at the clock on the nightstand. It was nearly ten o'clock. Time had flown by. But then, he loved Calen so much that time ceased to exist between them. "I'd forgotten." He gave her a grin. "Want to take a quick shower with me? We'll get dressed, grab some coffee, breakfast, and be right on time to speak with her."

"A quick shower with you? You're a dangerous man in that shower stall, Senor Manchahi."

Reno pressed a kiss to her shoulder. "I'll be very quick, but very thorough, *mi corazón*. How's that?"

She laughed. "As long as you're thorough…"

Chapter 17

"This is an exciting discovery and a very ancient artifact, Senorita Hernandez." Professor Maria Castillo sat in the large living room, looking at several digital photos of the emerald sphere. Opposite her, on the creamy, soft leather sofa, Calen and Reno listened with rapt attention. The professor was the foremost South American expert regarding ancient objects. In her fifties, her hair long and streaked with gray, she had a definite air of authority. She wore a simple and professional beige linen suit.

"We thought you might find it of interest, Professor Castillo," Calen said.

Dr. Castillo traced her finger across a photograph of

the sphere. "Your explanation of where you found this emerald raises many more questions for me."

Reno leaned forward, elbows on his jean-clad thighs. "Do you recognize the language that's engraved on the sphere, Professor?"

"I believe it is Sanskrit, one of our oldest languages. We have a number of ancient languages, however, and Sanskrit is but one of them." She frowned and tapped her receding chin. "If I'm not mistaken, I believe this means 'forgiveness.'"

Reno traded a quick look with Calen. She smiled back at him. "You're sure?"

Sighing, Dr. Castillo set the photo aside and picked up her tea. "Not entirely, *señor*. Here's what I'd suggest. Send an e-mail to Dr. Kendra Johnson, who is an archeologist with Harvard University, as well as to Professor Nolan Galloway, a noted historian tenured at Princeton. Tell them what you found, where you found it and my preliminary analysis. I've had the pleasure of working with them on a number of digs around the world. They would be able to tell you more than I can. They are world experts on very ancient artifacts."

Dr. Castillo smiled. "I think they will be fascinated by this huge emerald sphere. I mean—" she shook her head, awe in her alto voice "—to discover one of this magnitude and caliber is just unheard of."

"I know," Calen agreed. "Most emeralds have many, many inclusions, and few are clear like this one. I've seen many emeralds, and most look like they have an overgrown garden within them."

"Quite so," the professor agreed. "I once saw a necklace of emeralds with gold spacers between them, at the Gold Museum in Lima, Peru. The spheres, however, were half an inch in diameter, nowhere near as large as this one."

"What else can you tell us about this? Anything?" Calen didn't want the professor to know about the Emerald Key, because it was secret, ceremonial knowledge carefully passed down through certain families. But she was curious about the professor's expertise. Archeologists were the detectives of the ancient world, and would sometimes accidentally stumble upon secret information from another source. To Calen's knowledge, however, the Emerald Key was never mentioned in writing. Instead, knowledge of it was always verbally transmitted to the next generation.

"A certain myth comes to mind from the Inca traditions. I was at a dig at Machu Picchu, doing research regarding Emperor Pachacuti, about ten years ago," Maria told them, sipping her tea. "He was the last great king of the Inca empire before the Spaniards came and destroyed it all. A stone tablet with text was found at the Condor Temple there. It has never been publicized outside the archeological elite."

She sighed softly, her eyes gleaming as she recalled that special event. "I discovered the tablet on the west side of the beautifully sculpted condor. Carved into the rock, the condor lies flat on the temple floor. While I was carefully digging around it, my trowel struck a stone. It ended up being ten small, rectangular stone tablets lined up and following the curve of the condor's body. These tablets speak of the Seven Virtues of Peace. The stone engravings say there is a necklace composed of seven emeralds that, by order of the Inca Emperor Pachacuti, were hidden around the world."

Calen's eyes widened. She knew nothing of the stone tablet discovery. "That's fascinating information, Professor."

"Yes, isn't it? Each one of the emerald spheres symbolizes what humanity must do in order for peace to reign on earth. And then the Fifth World can emerge." Dr. Castillo placed her cup and saucer on the mahogany coffee table.

"I'm not familiar with this Fifth World, Professor," Reno admitted. "What is it?"

"The Fifth World of the Incas is predicted to occur in the twenty-first century, according to astronomical information we've already recovered. It is the world of the heart, of compassion, kindness toward all. Supposedly it guarantees a thousand years of peace once it manifests upon our planet."

Opening her hands, Calen asked, "Does that have anything to do with this necklace?"

"Yes, they are connected. The emerald necklace was created by Pachacuti's best artisans. Then he had it disassembled and scattered throughout the world. Each of the seven spheres is inscribed with one of the virtues needed to bring peace. I would venture a guess that what you have found in that cave is one of these spheres talked about in the condor stone tablets. Surely, forgiveness is a tenant of creating peace in our world. If we forgive one another, how can there be revenge? The belief in an 'eye for an eye' would disappear forever. That would be lovely, wouldn't it?"

"Yes, it would," Calen said. She recalled her parents telling her about the Emerald Key. The professor knew about it only as an emerald necklace that had been pulled apart and the pieces scattered around the globe. Often, archeologists would stumble upon something but not truly realize the full importance of their discovery or the story surrounding it. Dr. Castillo had found the stone text that Calen was sure referred to the Emerald Key. Only this Inca legend referred to it as the Seven Virtues of Peace. Many labels, same necklace, as far as she was concerned. Other cultures with their oral traditions of imparting information might have used a different name. An archeologist might find a tablet or scroll with another name, but they were all talking about the *same* object or idea. Calen and Reno knew the necklace as the Emerald Key. The professor knew it as the Seven Virtues of Peace. "What else, Professor?"

Dr. Castillo sat back in thought. "The text said that when the seven emerald spheres of the necklace were found and strung back together, it would then be worn by a special pregnant woman. A girl would be born at

a time when Planet Earth was being destroyed, shortly
before the Fifth World was to arise. She was predes-
tined and chosen by the Inca sun god, and his empress,
the moon goddess. If this woman wore the necklace,
then peace would reign on earth and the Fifth World
would emerge and manifest into reality."

Dr. Castillo pointed to the photos. "This reminds me
of one of the spheres from that necklace, because it is
inscribed with 'forgiveness,' which is one of the seven
virtues listed on the tablets."

"What are the other virtues, Professor?" Reno inquired.

Holding up her hand, the woman counted them off
on her fingers. "The tablets listed forgiveness,
courage, trust, honesty, faith, hope and love. The
Incas saw these positive, light-energy qualities as re-
quisites of peace. If people lived these virtues daily,
then peace would follow, and wars and destruction
would cease."

"And if they did not embody these virtues?" Calen
wondered.

"You can obviously see the shape our world is in
presently. How many people do you know who live by
all these virtues on a daily basis? Much less *one* of
them? Look at all the wars around our globe right now.
The fight between major religions and belief systems.
Global warming. Extremism is everywhere now. There
are many more narcissistic and selfish people nowadays, not to mention a lack of general sensitivity and

awareness of others. Rudeness and disrespect are common, unfortunately."

Dr. Castillo picked up her tea and took a sip. "And truth has been replaced with 'truthiness,' a lie in and of itself. Now, people think it perfectly okay to tell half a truth or some part of the truth, but not all of it. This is a sign of the darkness that has infected our world."

"That's not always the case," Reno said, in defense of many people he knew who upheld truth. And who had given their lives in the process.

Dr. Castillo nodded. "That's correct, not everyone is guilty of all of these dark traits. But enough are now that the world is in a downhill slide. We are reflecting the worst of human qualities."

Calen frowned and sat up, placing her own cup on the coffee table. "So, from your perspective, Professor, the world is not improving. Instead, we are regressing."

"Correct."

"So, where does that leave this necklace and the seven virtues that can bring peace to our world? Maybe it exists to encourage people to live virtuous, caring lives and refuse to accept what is going on right now," Reno suggested.

"The stone tablets from the Condor Temple," Maria said, "Speak of an ultimate battle between dark and light forces. In the Incan language, Quechua, the dark forces are referred to as *Tupay*. There are many subtleties to Quechua and this word means conflict, confrontations between people, villages or nations. People who respond to *Tupay* are said to carry 'heavy energy.' The Incas did not see the world in terms of good or evil. Instead, they saw it as heavy energy or light energy."

"And heavy energy means what?" Reno asked, trying to grasp the Incan mind-set.

"*Tupay* is about men and women who thrive on or choose to express negative human traits. For example, they believe war is justified, they support insurrection, applaud terrorism and support the fabric of chaos. *Tupay* live in negative or heavy energy that is expressed as jealousy, envy, rage, arrogance, powermongering, selfishness, lies, cheating, stealing, rape, revenge."

"But we all have these emotions in us. That's only human," he interjected.

"Ah," Dr. Castillo said, smiling, "there is the key to this, eh? A human has a *choice* as to whether to take the high road on something or sink to the lowest common denominator. *Tupay* do not fight or try to do the right thing, *señor*. Without fail, they choose the easy way out, the heavy-energy expression."

"Failing to try and better yourself, regardless of the circumstances you come from, is a sign of a *Tupay?*" Reno asked.

Dr. Castillo nodded. "The Inca believe that heavy energy holds us down and doesn't allow us to evolve or become better human beings." She smiled. "I've studied the Inca religion for many years, and I can tell you that we all carry heavy energy within us. The Incas understood we are all flawed, but they also saw that if we were willing to work to get rid of, let's say, our jealousy, that we could lighten up our energy and the heaviness energy would dissolve. By working through things and not allowing negative emotions to rule or run us, we would become lighter, or what the Incas called *Taqe*."

"And *Taqe* is good?" Reno asked, frowning.

"*Taqe* is Quechua for 'joiner of energy fields.' We all have an aura around us, a sphere of electromagnetic energy. *Taqe* is the ability to join our fields together or to integrate our diverse fields of living energy. Our aura can integrate only if we release the heavy energy we carry. As we release it, we become lighter and lighter, and therefore *Taqe* in our existence. The Seven Virtues of Peace are recognized as light energy. Living these virtues will dissolve your heavy energy—the best choice that any human being could make, according to the Incas."

"To what purpose?" Calen asked.

"A *Taqe* person is working to rise to the heart level of compassion and love for all beings," Dr. Castillo said. "According to Incan texts, when humans move into their hearts, the Fifth World will emerge and integrate with this present one, lifting everyone out of whatever is left of their heavy energy. To help us achieve this, according to the tablets, there is a race of beings known as Warriors for the Light, who try to help this come about on earth. Pachacuti referred to them as jaguar warriors, but from what I understand of the translation, Warriors for the Light are one and the same. They will fight the *Tupay.*"

"Interesting stuff," Reno murmured, rubbing his brow. "So the dark side is *Tupay?*"

"Yes. It's all a matter of semantics. Incas would say that if you call them the dark side, that is judging them. And Incas really dislike judging anyone. They would rather say, simply, that the *Tupay* carry heavy energy by choice."

"And *Taqe* is the good side," Calen confirmed. "The Warriors for the Light have these higher, more positive human qualities and traits?"

"Yes, Warriors for the Light personify the tenants of light energy. To keep this philosophy simple, you could say they are the 'good guys and gals.' One other tenant of *Taqe* is the vesica piscis symbol, which was engraved on the sphere, as well. This sign was also found on the last stone tablet I discovered. It said it had a parallel to the *Qollo Qoyllur,* the pure white star. This is a reference to the Pleiades constellation in our skies."

Dr. Castillo pointed toward the cathedral ceiling of the living room. "I have read many old texts by the Incas that say their 'real home' is this seven-star system we know as the Pleiades. Thanks to astronomers, another fascinating find of late is the discovery of the Hourglass Nebula. Go online and check it out. The nebula looks exactly like the vesica piscis symbol."

Dr. Castillo shook her head in amazement. "Makes

you wonder if it's possible that the Incas, or some ancient race before them, knew of the Hourglass Nebula. That the vesica piscis might have originated from that. Or could there be some connection between this nebula and the Pleiades? So many questions and so few answers," she said, chuckling.

"So, the Incas say they come from the stars?" Reno asked.

"Yes, that is their belief. Whether from the Hourglass Nebula or the Pleiades, I really don't know. Archeologists are now fascinated with this most recent astronomical discovery, but we can't find artifact evidence to link them—yet. I am hoping more stone tablets will be discovered during our continuing digs at Machu Picchu."

Calen traded a look with her future husband. She wondered if the birthmark they shared was a genetic marker of an alien race. Had people from another star system spliced their genes into human beings thousands of years ago? On purpose? As an experiment? Deciding not to pursue these questions with the professor, Calen asked, "Does the stone text from the Condor Temple say who will win this battle here on earth?"

Dr. Castillo shrugged. "No, it does not say who will win. It *does* say that the Warriors for the Light, the elite trained to bring peace to the planet, will try to find the necklace first before the *Tupay* forces do. And whoever finds it, well…" Maria raised her arched brows and said, "One thing the text does point out is that when the first sphere is rediscovered, shortly before the possibility of the Fifth World rising, the ultimate battle between dark and light forces will begin. The fate of this planet will hang in the balance and be decided once and for all. Presently, we live in what is known as the Fourth World. The Incan text, as well, speaks about twelve years of chaos where a final war is fought, between the dark and light forces, for control of the earth and its people."

Reno shifted uncomfortably. "And if the *Tupay* get to the necklace pieces first?"

"Then the world will continue to spiral down into more and more chaos, and even more base and awful heavy-energy qualities will take over. And finally, if this happens, the Incan sun god will destroy the planet, because it has become so evil it can no longer be saved."

Calen cleared her throat. "Do *you* think we have discovered the first sphere of this necklace you refer to as the Seven Virtues of Peace?"

"I don't know for sure. I'm not the expert. The other two educators I've mentioned are. They could tell you, for sure, which is why I would contact them immediately. This is a very exciting find. I hope you have this sphere in a safe place."

"Of course," Calen said. In fact, the emerald was in the villa's well-hidden vault.

Dr. Castillo's eyes brightened. "I always thought it was a myth. But this suggests it could be real." She sighed and smiled. "Wouldn't it be wonderful if it was?

That if the spheres of this necklace are found and worn by this special woman, we could have peace instead of war? *That* would be a miracle."

"Many myths and legends are true," Reno told the professor. "It's just that educated people like yourself tend to see them as nothing more than a fanciful story, when in truth they are as real as you or me. Many cultures have a sacred and secret tradition that they hand down to each new generation orally instead of through writing."

Looking at the digital photo, Dr. Castillo said softly, "I'm not going to argue that at all. I agree historians and archeologists do not give verbal generational knowledge as much importance or respect as they do something written on a stone or on parchment. As I look at this photo, at this sphere, I feel hope. Real hope. I don't know any of my friends or family who don't pray for peace. This world of ours has really gotten awful the last fifty years. Your discovery is so incredible."

Calen wouldn't disagree. The finding of the sphere was exciting, along with Dr. Castillo's information, but now she knew war had been joined to the equation. "Is there anything you can add from your knowledge about this sphere? Was anything else written on the tablets found at the Condor Temple at Machu Picchu?"

"Yes, that each sphere possessed a powerful spirit within it, as alive as you or me. And if you touched it, the spirit within the emerald could heal you using the virtue inscribed upon the surface."

Reno traded a telling glance with Calen. They both had been healed of wounds that dealt with forgiveness. Thanks to them holding the sphere, much baggage from their past had dissolved, and only memories composed of light energy or happiness remained within their hearts.

"That's amazing," Calen murmured to the professor. "I wonder, did the stone texts say anything more about this heavy energy?"

"The Incans say that people who choose to hold heavy energy are not bad." She lifted her index finger for emphasis. "What creates a *Tupay* person is the conscious will to practice black sorcery against others. These sorcerers, male or female, are the real culprits. They can practice the black arts here or in what is known as the other side—the dimensions all around us that we cannot see. Those who are sensitive or psychic interface with them all the time, but most people are closed down and truly unaware of them, seeing only the third dimensional things in front of our eyes and noses."

Dr. Castillo smiled, then again grew serious. "These sorcerers want the world to stay in chaos, because then they can rule world populations through power and fear. Our world has become a place filled with fear. Look at what terrorism has done in the last few years. The media hypes nothing but negative stories. If it bleeds, it leads. What kind of newspeople do we have that look only at the worst of our human traits?

Wouldn't it be better to report positive, uplifting and hopeful stories of humans doing kind and loving and compassionate acts toward one another? What do you think, Senorita Hernandez?"

"At one time our media, particularly our newspapers, reported *all* news. It gave the public information on which to base educated decisions," Calen remarked.

"Do the *Tupay* have a leader? Are they unified?" Reno pressed.

Dr. Castillo nodded and leaned forward to elaborate further. "The stone text referred to the Lord of Darkness. It was said he would spawn a daughter, and together they would rule the world through fear. He had the ability to bring all powerful sorcerers into a team. Even though they usually work alone, he will bring them together. For in this final war, they will join and become one powerful paranormal army. This lord had sorcerers of all kinds not only here on earth, but also working for him on the other side."

"Does he have a name?" Calen asked.

The professor shook her head. "There was no name given on the stone tablets. However, there is a birthmark you will find on anyone who works with the Lord of Darkness." Dr. Castillo took out her pad and pen and drew a circle with a dot in the middle. "This is a physical symbol that will be found on the back of a person's neck that shows they work with heavy energy."

After studying the symbol, Calen exchanged a glance with Reno. The professor didn't know they each had the vesica piscis birthmark. And Calen wasn't going to tell her. "This is interesting," she stated, handing back the notepad.

"Do you know of any distinguishing marks for the Warriors for the Light?" Reno asked. He must have read Calen's mind, for she had wanted to pose the same question.

"Oh yes," the professor said. "The Warriors for the Light also carry a birthmark on the back of the neck." She sketched the vesica piscis and showed it to them. "According to the Incas, this was how you could tell the peaceful *Taqe* from the warring *Tupay*."

Calen tucked one leg beneath her on the sofa and asked, "Professor, is there a leader to the *Taqe* mentioned by the stone text?"

"Yes, they refer to her as the Empress of the Fifth World. The Incas say the queen of the coming world is a human being. It is she who will stand up to the Lord of Darkness and his army. She would have others to help her, of course. She will have her own army of light energy workers who will fight under her banner, the vesica piscis symbol, for peace."

"Man against woman," Calen said wryly.

The comment was obviously not lost on Dr. Castillo. "Isn't that the way it is now? Male domination in the world is real, with women continuing to be relegated to second-class citizenship."

"Exactly," Calen agreed, her voice grim.

"But if peace comes through this legendary woman," Reno said, "that will mean equality between the genders."

"And isn't that a peace in itself?" Calen asked. "No more fighting between the sexes. Men not trying to rule me, disempower me, rather, respect me for who and what I am and what I contribute."

"Precisely," Dr. Castillo affirmed. "In my opinion, the stone tablets I discovered at the Condor Temple mirror another great book, the Bible. Only in the Bible, in Revelations, it speaks of a great war between God and the devil. Each belief system has its labels and players. Interestingly enough, Revelations also speaks of a thousand years of peace, just as the Incan text does. Add to that the Hopi prophecy, which says just about the same thing. And the Mayan prophecy corroborates this. You have four different nations and belief systems agreeing that we're entering the most turbulent, dangerous and potentially destructive time in our history." Dr. Castillo shook her head. "And if the *Tupay* win, then we will be plunged into a final spiral of involution or destruction. If the Warriors for the Light win, we'll be granted a thousand years of peace." She pointed to the photo on the coffee table. "I can't help but think that with the discovery of this sphere, *if* it is from that emerald necklace spoken about in the Incan tablets, now is the crucial time...."

Calen shivered inwardly over the monumental information the woman had shared with them. "You have been most helpful, Professor Castillo. I'll have my driver, Godfredo, take you back to our airstrip and my pilot will fly you back to Quito. Thank you so much for coming." Calen rose and extended her hand.

Reno also stood. "You've given us a lot of good info, Dr. Castillo. If you can leave us contact information for Dr. Johnson and Professor Galloway, we'll see what else we can find out about our discovery."

Rising, the professor shook Calen's hand and then wrote down some information on her notepad. "Of course, *señor.* Kendra and Nolan are fine people with good hearts. You will be in excellent hands with them." She passed Reno the addresses of her colleagues.

"What do you think?" Reno asked Calen later as they sat out on the sundeck, iced tea in hand. The humid afternoon air stirred sluggishly around them. Thunderstorms were once again building over the jungle. "You look lost in thought."

She grinned and moved her foot beneath the aluminum table, touching Reno's bare feet with her toes. "Just digesting everything Professor Castillo said. Some of what she told me is new. The Lord of Darkness, for one. That bothers me. I'd sure like to know who he is. My parents talked about a dark one, but they died too soon to pass on more information."

"My folks said it was a man who had nothing but darkness in place of his heart. They called him the 'heartless one.' And where is he? Where does he live? What continent?" Reno asked before sipping the tangy iced tea. He gave Calen a measured look. "Sorcery is practiced in all realms and dimensions, not just this one. And as a matter of fact, the most dangerous sorcerers are ones who have died and transited over to the other side. My parents taught me that when a dead sorcerer teacher reconnects in spirit with students still on earth, it's the ultimate combination of power. And Dr. Castillo was right, Calen—fear is their method of control. A sorcerer will reflect our fears back to us in order to weaken, control and disempower us."

"I know…. They are a father and daughter team, too. That's news to me. My parents never mentioned a sorcerer family would be running this campaign. If we've discovered the first sphere of the Emerald Key, Reno, that means it's all beginning. We need to locate the whereabouts of that Lord of Darkness."

"We will."

"It's tragic how the loss of honesty, faith, hope, trust, courage, love and forgiveness has spread everywhere." Calen felt depressed over the enormity of it all. "But to be fair, we also have some of the most generous and giving people in the world right now. We live by extremes."

After squeezing in a slice of lemon, Reno stirred his tea. "This is the final battle, Calen. Our job now is to attract others like us to our foundation. We need to gather our army of light, so to speak. 'Build it and they will come,'" he said, referring to the remark from the movie *Field of Dreams*. He grinned over at her.

"You're right," Calen replied softly, watching a dark, churning thunderhead rapidly developing miles away above the green treetops. "We'll need a lot of help, Reno. And we need it fast. Once we find these people, we'll have to determine if they're ready to take on missions against the dark forces."

"I've thought along those lines, too, *mi corazón*. Financially, we won't have a problem getting a school up and running. I can help you organize it. We have to have faith in the Great Spirit that the people will come. That's a start. And that, as I see it, is our responsibility in this coming battle."

Calen licked her lips and finished off the tart iced tea, setting the glass aside. Thunder finally rolled across the jungle. Parrots screeched and monkeys screamed in response. "My faith is solid, Reno. I know if we build the foundation, the right people will show up. And it looks like we will have to balance family with our work and our vision." She placed her hand gently across her belly. "I know we can do that. It means moving back to Quito and building the foundation near a major airport. You said there was a three-hundred-acre parcel of land for sale outside the city limits?"

"We should go look at it," he agreed. Calen's cheeks were flushed, her expression tender as she unconsciously moved her palm across where their child lay. Her hair fell in soft disarray around her oval face, emphasizing those large, intelligent eyes of hers. Getting up, Reno held his hand out to her. "I don't know about you, but I feel like, after holding that sphere, my life was given back to me. I was able to forgive and let go of the past." His fingers curled around hers as he helped her to her feet.

"But first things first. Let's get married," Reno said, pulling her into his arms and cradling her tenderly against him. He nuzzled her hair and inhaled its spicy fragrance. "I love you, Calen Hernandez. Together, you and I are going to start our own dynasty—little Warriors for the Light, who will grow up in our love. And if the Great Spirit has a bigger mission for us, to help bring peace to this poor old battered world of ours, I'm more than willing to do my part, because you are beside me as my equal. My mate for life, my beloved..."

Closing her eyes, Calen pressed her cheek against his shoulder. His arms felt cherishing and protective. "I never thought I'd have a partner," she admitted softly. "But here you are. And suddenly, our lives are much more than just us."

Reno gave her a quick squeeze. "Sometimes more is asked of a person than they ever thought possible, *mi corazón*. Sometimes a person will symbolize something for many others. That's what we're being asked to do—to be architects for peace."

She met his loving gaze. "And I can't think of a more honorable calling. Can you? To help bring harmony instead of war to our planet? To bring forgiveness instead of revenge? To bring love, to remove hate?" Sliding her hand across his cheek, Calen whispered, "More than anything, we are doing it out of love not only for one another, but for our daughter. We want her to grow up in a world filled with peace, not chaos."

Reno pressed a kiss to Calen's parted lips. "Love transcends everything," he promised. "And I'm going to love you forever."

* * * * *

Don't miss Lindsay McKenna's newest MORGAN'S MERCENARIES *story,* BEYOND THE LIMIT, *available from HQN December 2006.*
You'll love it!